Chaos of the Witch

Crypt Witch cozy paranormal mystery series - book 16

K.E. O'Connor

K.E. O'Connor Books

CHAOS OF THE WITCH

Copyright © 2022 by K.E. O'Connor

ISBN: 978-1-915378-14-9

Written by: K.E. O'Connor

Chapter 1

I shook out my fingers as sweat beaded on my brow. I flicked the cleaning spell across the floor of my bar, Cloven Hoof. It didn't work, and this was the fifth time I'd tried casting magic. I could usually do this spell in my sleep.

"Is this your doing, Frank?" I marched across the sticky dance floor, where dozens of drinks had been spilled following last night's revelry. "Don't think you'll get away with messing with my magic."

Frank, my resident demon, barely stirred as I continued to hiss out threats. He'd been like that for months. There was a time, not so long ago, when I'd been worried I was losing control of him, but things had changed, and I had no clue why. He'd barely troubled me for months. But recently, I'd been having difficulty getting my magic to work. It had to be because of Frank's meddling.

I stood on the opposite side of the dance floor. Maybe this blip was because we were close to celebrating an important anniversary for the demon prison. We held an anniversary party every year, but this felt different because we had a thousand years of demon trapping to commemorate.

That could be the problem. The demons were grumpy, and their negative vibes were upsetting my magic.

After three more failed attempts at the cleaning spell, I let out a huff and stomped to the bar. No, this had to be Frank's doing. And he was only giving me the silent treatment because it bugged me. I didn't like him butting in on my life, but I got worried when he was too quiet. It meant he was plotting something. And when a demon plots, you know it's never going to be about candy floss and unicorns.

Merrie Noble strolled along the other side of the bar and set a mug of hot chocolate in front of me. "Still no luck with the cleaning spell?"

"Nope. I can't get it to take. I must be having an off day." Although it had been more like an off few weeks.

"We all get them. I sometimes find my magic plays up around the full moon."

"Have you got werewolf in your family tree?"

She wrinkled her nose. "I don't think so. And I never get furry and start howling, but the lunar cycle unsettles my powers. I make sure I don't plan any complicated spells around that time."

"The moon has never troubled me. It must be something else."

"I'll deal with the cleaning." Merrie nudged my mug closer. "You enjoy your hot chocolate."

I could always rely on her to ensure the club ran smoothly. She was the best bar manager a witch could want.

Ten minutes later, and after a delicious mug of hot chocolate, the place was spotless thanks to Merrie's magic, and I felt less grumpy.

"I love that look on you." She went back behind the bar and began stacking glasses.

I glanced down at my usual outfit of jeans and a long-sleeved T-shirt. "You've seen these jeans about a thousand times."

"Your hair. The blonde stripe."

I grabbed a handful of my long, dark hair and pulled it in front of me. Sure enough, there was a blonde stripe running down one side. "Huh! How did that get there?"

Merrie walked over and studied my new color. "I figured you did it to yourself. It looks good."

I conjured a color change spell and swiped it down the blonde. It didn't budge. I tried several more times, but the color remained.

"You really are having trouble with your magic. Do you want me to have a go?"

"Sure. I don't think I can pull off the blonde look, so this needs to go."

"I like it. Are you sure you want it gone?"

"Yep. Do it."

Merrie stroked a hand over the stripe in my hair. She tilted her head. "That's weird. It didn't work. It must be a strong spell."

I pulled my hair off my face and tied it in a messy bun out of the way. "I'll figure it out later. We've got too much on our plate right now for me to waste time altering my hair."

The door leading to the kitchen was shoved open, and Wiggles, my adorably smelly hellhound, trotted out chewing on something.

"What have you stolen from the kitchen?" I said.

He swallowed and blinked his red eyes at me. "Nothing. Chef was making samples for the party and needed someone to try them out."

"Sure he did. But you've hardly got a discerning palate. Your nose is always stuck in the trash."

"My palate is very refined." Wiggles belched. "And the party food is excellent. I loved the rare beef canapes with mustard relish."

"Do you like Tempest's new hair color?" Merrie said. "Did you sneak in the stripe when she was sleeping?"

Wiggles cocked his head and looked me over. "I don't see any difference."

"Forget about it." I glanced at the main doors of the club. "There's still no sign of the decorations for the party. I'm sure Mom said she was having them delivered here today."

"Oh! I got a message from a delivery driver. He's stuck at the border. You know what our magic is like with vehicles. I sent out a repair crew to make sure he could get here without breaking down again."

There were many benefits to living in a magic community, but if you loved anything electrical, you'd always have problems. "Great. Thanks for doing that. Mom and Granny Dottie have been stressing every day to make sure the celebration is perfect. They spent about a month picking the ideal fairy lights, balloons, and streamers."

"I don't blame them for being stressed. A thousand years of having a demon prison in Willow Tree Falls is something to celebrate. I can't imagine what life would be like if there was nowhere to imprison all those demons."

"And the Crypt witches started it all," Wiggles said. "I'm proud to be a part of the family."

I grinned at him. "Me, too. And once everyone stops stressing over the preparations, we'll have a great time."

As if I'd magicked them to the club, my mom and Granny Dottie marched through the main doors.

"We're here for cocktail ideas." Granny Dottie petted Wiggles and snuck him a meaty chew from out of her huge purse. "Your mom thinks my explosive cocktail mix won't suit all tastes. I don't know what she's talking about. Who doesn't love tequila and magic mixed together?"

I raised a hand.

Granny Dottie tutted at me. "You're a lightweight. What do you suggest we serve at the party?"

"You're the expert when it comes to alcoholic mixes." Mom kissed my cheek and settled on a stool, gratefully accepting a mug of hot chocolate from Merrie.

"Take a look at the menu. I can do anything you like for the party," I said.

They studied the menu for several minutes, pointing out several things they wanted to sample.

"And what about the music?" Granny Dottie said. "Everyone will want a boogie over the demons."

"It's all sorted. The extra drinks are ordered, the decorations are almost here, and the music won't be a problem. Everyone will have a great time," I said.

Mom set down the menu. "I'm sure they will, but it's more than just having fun. We need to remember the Crypt witches who lost their lives defending everyone against the demons. We haven't had a death in the family for years, but we must never forget the fallen."

"We'll have time for the solemn stuff," Granny Dottie said. "I have a list of one hundred and five names I plan to read out."

"You're reading out all those names in the middle of a party?" I said.

"Why not? The least I can do is mention them since they can't be there in person."

"We could do something more discreet. This is a celebration, after all."

"We must respect those who sacrificed their lives so we might live." Granny Dottie thumped me over the head with a cocktail menu.

I ducked and backed away. "Sure. But how about we put up a memorial board? People could drop by and pay their respects and leave offerings to the fallen. Standing there and reading out one hundred and five names of dead witches will kill the mood. It's the opposite of what you want to achieve."

Her lips pursed. "It's not a bad idea. There'll be people coming from other magic communities who knew the deceased. We could ask them to bring photos to put up. How about you—"

"No! Not me. Don't put another thing on my list of party stuff to do," I said. "I still have this place to run and all the party food, drink, and music to finalize."

Mom tweaked the blonde hair out of my bun. "This is cute. When did you do that?"

"Err... maybe this morning. It wasn't there when I got out of bed, though. It must have appeared during the day."

"You changed the color of your hair and didn't realize what you were doing?" Mom's eyes narrowed a fraction.

"Looks like it. Hopefully, it'll fade as quickly as it arrived."

"I like it. Although you should have tried silver. Or green. I once dyed my hair green with yellow tips. Your grandpa said I looked like a beautiful blonde pineapple." Granny Dottie chuckled. "While we're here, let's try some of these cocktails. I've got a thirst on me, and hot chocolate won't quench it."

I grinned at Merrie, who lifted a cocktail maker and shook it. "Sure. We've got a couple of hours before the after-work crowd turns up. What will it be?"

We spent the next hour sampling cocktails, most of them explosively alcoholic under Granny Dottie's orders, and we were all soon laughing and joking and more than a little tipsy.

"We should invite that group of angels to join us." Granny Dottie hiccupped as she slopped her drink on her hand. "They looked tense loitering around outside the front of Angel Force."

I jerked up in my seat, checked the time, and groaned. "No! I'm late."

"For what?" Mom said.

"Dazielle asked me to help. Conan Nox is being brought here to be tried for Violet Oakley's murder."

"Violet Oakley? I know that name." Granny Dottie's forehead wrinkled.

"She was married to Elman." I was already grabbing my jacket and keys.

"The visiting shaman?"

"Yep. And Dazielle needs magical muscle as backup. Conan is a seriously bad guy. He loves using dark magic and curses."

"Oh! I heard about him in the bakery," Granny Dottie said. "What's he doing coming to Willow Tree Falls to be tried for murder?"

I was yanking on my jacket and running to the door. "Don't ask me. I need to go. Wiggles!"

He bounded after me as I ran out the door. "What's the hurry? The angels can handle one guy."

"This is one dark, evil warlock. But I'm not worried about him. Dazielle will be raging because I'm late. And when she gets mad, she gets mean."

"Meaner than usual?"

"Exactly. This won't put me on her good side, and I've got enough to think about without having to dodge an angry angel." I jogged to the brilliant white Angel Force building in the village.

Dazielle stood outside, her foot tapping the ground, her arms crossed, and her wings spread out as far as they'd go. Her brilliant blue gaze latched onto me, and her scowl deepened.

"I know. I'm sorry. I got distracted by Mom and Granny Dottie." I stopped in front of her. "I'm not too late, am I? Conan's not here, is he?"

"You smell like a brewery." Dazielle flipped her long blonde hair over one shoulder and stepped back. "Are you drunk?"

"Mildly tipsy. And it was for research purposes. We were testing cocktails for the party." I grinned at her. Maybe I was tipsier than I realized. "I hope you're coming."

Her scowl didn't improve. "I got my invitation. All the angels did."

"It would be good to see you there." I glanced at the main doors leading into Angel Force. "Granny Dottie saw a group of angels hanging about. Were they waiting for Conan? Am I really too late?"

"Fortunately for you, no. Conan got delayed during processing. He fought an angel, and there were problems with his paperwork. He won't be long."

"So everything is fine." A small hiccup escaped before I could stop it. "Why are you still so grumpy?"

Dazielle jabbed a finger at me. "This is a simple job. Keep an eye on the criminal and make sure he doesn't try anything funny. My angels can be too soft, and you need a firm hand with types like Conan Nox or they'll take advantage."

"You don't need to worry about me being soft on this warlock. After everything I've heard about him, I won't let him out of my sight."

"Make sure you don't until he's in his cell and has nowhere to go. This must go smoothly. Don't let me down."

I splayed my hands. "Have I ever let you down?"

She growled at me. "More times than I care to remember. Let's get inside. Reporters have been hovering, and we don't want them snapping pictures of us looking anxious."

"You're the only one with the anxious face. We're cool as cucumbers."

Wiggles trotted in ahead of us. "And smooth is my middle name."

Dazielle shook her head. "I always thought it was podgy."

Chapter 2

Dominic, my cute but dim angel friend, paced in front of me as we waited for Conan's arrival in the main office of Angel Force. His hands were clasped, and his wings shivered every time he moved.

"Hey, settle down. You're making me nervous," I said.

He glanced at me, anxiety shining in his blue eyes. "This is the baddest warlock I've ever met. I was reading through his list of crimes yesterday. Do you know what he's done?"

"I know he killed Violet Oakley with a dark curse. Isn't that enough?"

"She was such a sweet lady, and he killed her in cold blood." Dominic continued his pacing, only slowing when he almost tripped over Wiggles, who was mooching about. "Conan has twelve counts of robbery using malicious spells to his name. He's caused grievous bodily harm to twenty people using dark magic. And, although it was never proven, it's alleged he used the paralyzing curse on someone and left them to starve. Dark magic runs through his black veins."

"Conan's been caught now. His dark curse days are over."

"He won't get away with this." Dominic gave a determined nod but kept pacing.

"We'll make sure he doesn't. We've got all the evidence to put him away forever."

Dominic glanced at me. "Have you got any room in the demon prison? He'd fit right in."

"And they'd probably welcome him with open arms, even though he isn't a demon. We can always squeeze one more in if we need to."

Dominic's wing almost whacked me in the face as he strode back and forth. "I always try to see the good in people, even if they're mean to me, but I can't see anything decent about Conan."

"You must constantly have to do that when you're around Dazielle," Wiggles said.

I snorted a laugh. "And she's definitely not in the mood for fun this evening."

Dominic shrugged. "It can be a struggle. But since our divorce, she's been less mean to me."

"I thought you handled the whole awkward marriage situation maturely," I said. "She strong-armed you into that, and you could have made life difficult for her and paid her back for all the times she wasn't nice."

"I'd never do that. And she's even given me a couple of cases to work on. After all these years, I'm finally gaining her trust."

"And it only took getting married and divorced to do that," Wiggles said.

I chuckled. "That's great news. What are the cases?"

"They're cold cases, but I've been in the evidence room a few times and looked over the clues left behind. I'm getting loads of experience." Dominic finally stopped pacing and sat in the chair next to me. "I like your hair. Aurora's got a stripe in her hair too, but it's black."

"She didn't have a black stripe when I saw her the other day. How long's it been like that?"

"I dropped by her store first thing this morning. She looked at me like I was crazy when I mentioned the stripe. It must be fun when you dye your hair together. I wish I had a sibling to share things like that with."

"Would you dye each other's hair?" Wiggle said. "What color would you be if you weren't a natural blond?"

I nudged him with my foot. "Maybe Aurora's been messing with color change magic. She could have mixed up hair samples, so the magic got spliced. You said her stripe was black?"

"Yup. Maybe that's what happened. You got some of her blonde, and she got some of your black."

"I reckon so. I'll have to remind her not to change my hair without checking with me first."

"It suits you. Maybe you should go all blonde," Dominic said.

My nose wrinkled. "Blonde isn't my thing."

Dominic looked crestfallen as he slouched in his seat. He wasn't great at hiding that he had a crush on me, even though I was in a long-standing, sometimes messy, relationship with Rhett Blackthorn.

Dominic lifted his head. "What does Rhett think of your new color?"

"He hasn't seen it. But he doesn't have a say in what I do with my appearance. Just like I don't get a say about his. Although I wouldn't love it if he grew a full beard."

"Oh, sure. I didn't mean that." Dominic sat up straight. "And I'd never grow a full beard since I know you hate them."

"That's good to know."

"Beards are useful for catching food," Wiggles said. "You always find a treat if you hunt around in the hair. I'd love a beard. Then I wouldn't miss anything tasty I dropped."

Dominic stood, paced the room, and then sat down again. "Are things good between you and Rhett?"

"Things are great. We're happy." It hadn't been so long ago that Rhett and I had gone through a sticky patch. We'd argued, and he'd left the village but had come back full of remorse, and we were making a go of things. He'd even left the biker gang, and his business as a metal sculptor had exploded. He was so busy, he sometimes didn't have time to see me. I didn't love that. He always had time for me when he'd been in the biker gang. But I shouldn't complain. Rhett was happy, and our relationship was blossoming.

"All this talk of food is making me hungry," Wiggles said.

"When were we talking about food?" I said.

"Beard food! All those delicious crumbs and bits of meat stuck in the hair." He swiped his tongue across his nose. "Do any angels in here have beards?"

Dominic thought about it for a moment. "No beards. Although I could try growing a mustache for you, Tempest. You might like it on me. I can pull off almost any look with my bone structure."

I patted his knee. "How about we find you someone at the party? You could find your perfect woman among the tombstones."

"I guess so." He didn't sound enthusiastic.

"You are coming?"

"Oh, yes. I got my invitation. I'm looking forward to it. You'll be there, right?"

"Yes, but I'll be busy. Although I'll add finding you a date to my list of things to do if you'd like."

"Nah. I don't mind going solo. All the other angels are coming, too, so I'll have plenty of company."

Dominic was such a sweet guy, and I felt a touch guilty he still had a crush on me, but there was nothing I could do about it. And he was too nice to be mean to and chase away.

An angel led Elman Oakley into the main office. He radiated calmness and composure in his plain red ankle-length smock and gray sweater.

Elman traveled around the local villages using his shamanic ability to provide healing and cleansing to those who were troubled.

He was led over to us and nodded a greeting when he arrived.

"How are you doing?" Dominic said. "This must be a difficult time for you."

"I'm sorry for your loss. I liked Violet. She was always so smiley and friendly to everyone when she visited the village," I said.

Elman lowered his head for a few seconds, as if in contemplation. "She was the light of my life. We had twenty blissful years of marriage. She brought me so much joy."

Dominic stepped forward and wrapped his wings around Elman. "We'll make sure Conan pays for his crime."

Elman embraced him. "My heart is full of sadness, but I'm pleased justice is about to be done. You've done excellent work in making this happen so quickly."

Dominic stepped back and nodded. "Of course. And our higher angels have taken an interest in your case. A wonderful woman such as Violet deserves only the very best."

"And I'm certain she'll get it." Elman looked around. "Is Conan still pleading guilty to her murder?"

"He is," Dominic said. "Conan had no choice, given that the dark curse he used on your wife was found in his home."

"His arrogance got him caught," I said. "Conan's been getting away with serious crimes for too long."

"That ends today," Elman said. "I'll be forever grateful for that. It is a fitting memory to my wife that Conan will go away for the rest of his life. He'll never be able to hurt another person again."

"I can look after myself! Keep those dumb wings away from me or I'll sue you for sexual harassment." An angry female voice reached us.

I turned to see Tatiana Monroe being escorted into the office.

"You don't have to watch me. I'm not a criminal." She strutted ahead of a worried looking angel. Tatiana wore perilously high black shiny heels, her long auburn hair floating around her heart-shaped face. Her gaze locked onto us, and she headed our way.

"We should go to another room." Dominic caught hold of Elman's elbow.

"If Tatiana wishes to speak to me, I'll listen. She's suffering because she's about to lose a loved one," Elman said. "Conan and Tatiana won't have much of a relationship once he's behind bars."

"That's decent of you to say," I said. "But from the look on Tatiana's face, she doesn't want to play nice."

Tatiana was Conan's girlfriend. She'd visited Angel Force several times to complain about not being kept informed about his trial. Every encounter had grown tenser, and the last time she'd visited, she'd been thrown out for attacking an angel and yanking out some of her wing feathers.

"I would like to speak to her," Elman said. "I sense the tension radiating from her. She isn't at peace."

I looked at Dominic and shrugged and then followed Elman as he walked over to meet Tatiana. He held out his hands to her as they got near.

She stared at him. "What do you want?"

"I hope you can find peace during these troubling times."

"I'll find peace when Conan is let out of jail. He made a simple mistake. We all do." Her fingers were flexed, as if she wanted to rake her shiny pink nails across Elman's face.

I stepped up to his side, ready to drop Tatiana if she got difficult. "Your boyfriend's mistake was murder. He didn't have to do that."

She glared at me. "Were you there? Did you see Conan do it?"

"He's confessed. And the evidence against him is overwhelming."

Elman lifted a hand, and a wave of warmth drifted from him, instantly slowing my racing heart. "I wish you well in your future journey, Tatiana. All of us have a limited time on this beautiful planet, and we must spend it wisely. Sometimes, we fall off the righteous path and allow darkness to take over. I hope that—"

"There's nothing dark about me." Tatiana whacked Elman's hand down as he reached for her. "And there's nothing dark about my man. It's not my fault your stupid wife got in his way. She probably provoked him."

I glanced at Elman, but he didn't flinch under the harsh words. He was a better person than me. I was already tempted to slug Tatiana.

"I wish you the best for the future," Elman said. "If you ever want cleansing or restorative magic, feel free to visit me. No charge. I always help those who are most troubled for free."

"You can stick it, you self-important oaf. I want nothing to do with your magic. Your wife ruined my life." Tatiana turned and stamped out of the office, heading back to the reception area.

Elman shook his head. "It's so sad when you see all that potential lost to darkness and destruction."

I shrugged. All I saw was attitude and anger. "Tatiana must love a bad guy."

"It hasn't made her happy," Dominic said.

"Tatiana has had a tough life. And her choices have made her sad. She's entrenched in bitter emotions." Elman smacked his lips together as if tasting the air. "I hope one day she'll see there is light at the end of her tunnel. That's all people want, to find a path to happiness. Anything else leads to misery and destruction." He turned away and dabbed his eyes.

"Let me get you a coffee," Dominic said.

"Thank you. I'd prefer green tea if you have it. It's very calming."

"I can sort that." Dominic led Elman away.

"That was intense," Wiggles muttered. "It almost put me off the tuna and meatball sandwich I found sitting on someone's desk."

"Stop stealing the angels' food. They get mean when you pinch their provisions."

"Is it ever my fault if they leave food unattended? I'm a hellhound. I have needs. High calorie food is a must at all times, especially when there's a bitchy witch wanting to rip off someone's head. I need to be fueled and ready for danger."

Dazielle strode out of her office and over to me. "Sorath is almost here. And just a reminder, the higher angels are watching this case. They want Conan behind bars for good."

"I don't see any problem with that happening. Dominic was telling me his long list of misdeeds.

And with the evidence against him for Violet's murder, he's not getting away with this."

"This needs to be watertight. Conan's wriggled out of crimes before on technicalities. This criminal is clever. Watch him like a hawk."

"You've already said. I know what I need to do."

"Let's go outside to meet Sorath. He'll be landing in a few minutes." Dazielle looked around. "Where's Dominic? He's never here when I need him."

"He's calming Elman. He had an encounter with Tatiana, and things got tense."

"Is she here already? I'd hoped to avoid her." Dazielle stroked a wing. "She tried to bend one of my wings when we met. And she said I'd put on weight."

I stifled a smile. "She's gone outside. Let's try to keep out of her way." I tweaked a loose feather from the edge of Dazielle's right wing and got whacked on the back for my trouble.

We walked through the office, out to the reception area, and through the main doors.

It was a warm, pleasant evening as we waited for Sorath's arrival. A breeze stirred my hair, and I looked up to see an enormous white shape flying toward us. It was Sorath. He looked like he had a parachute strapped around him, but when he got closer, I realized the parachute was Conan.

"You strapped the prisoner to Sorath?" I said to Dazielle.

"It's the safest way to transport him. Conan wouldn't dare unstrap mid-flight. He'd crash to the ground and die."

"Did you secretly hope that would happen?"

"I never hope for someone's death." She slid a glare my way. "Well, almost never."

"You love me really."

We backed up as Sorath rocketed to the ground, his wings spread out. He made the perfect landing, running along as he slowed. He spun in an elegant pirouette, and his wings folded behind him.

You could always guarantee any angel would be easy on the eye, but this angel, well, he was something else. He was tall, broad, had surfer style hair messed up by the wind, and when he smiled, my heart did all kinds of strange things. But it was just angel magic messing with my head.

Sorath walked toward us, that perfect smile popping his dimples. "Dazielle, it's been too long. How are you?" He leaned forward and kissed her cheek.

Dazielle was blushing as she stepped back. "It has. And I'm well. It's good you could make the journey."

"I'm always happy to help stop the bad guys." He looked down at me. "And you must be Tempest Crypt. I've heard a lot about you."

"From Dazielle?" It wouldn't be good if the information came from her.

"Partly from Dazielle, but your reputation precedes you in many places. I've been looking forward to getting to know you." He reached out a hand.

I shook it. "Thanks, I guess. How's the passenger?"

"I have motion sickness." A miserable sounding voice came from behind Sorath.

Sorath punched the safety strap release on his chest, and Conan was dumped in the dirt.

Dazielle gestured me to follow her as she caught hold of Conan's arms.

I stepped around Sorath and discovered a wiry middle-aged guy with jet black hair and eyes sparking with anger. He had a broad nose, full lips, and a jagged scar running down the side of his face.

"On your feet," Dazielle said.

"Give me a minute. I might puke," Conan said. "That idiot was doing aerobatics on the way here. I'm sure that's against the rules."

"There was turbulence." Sorath spread his arms wide. "I had to take evasive maneuvers to avoid disruption to the flight. And we were running late because Conan questioned the paperwork."

"I had every right. If you fill in the paperwork wrong, I get to go free. I know all the rules." Conan remained on the ground.

"The paperwork is pristine." Dazielle hauled Conan to his feet. "You're not getting away with this murder. You killed an innocent woman."

"Allegedly," Conan grumbled.

"Your confession suggests otherwise." I caught hold of his other arm.

His cold stare leveled on me. "Who are you?"

"Someone you don't want to mess with," Dazielle said, "unless you want to be introduced to the demons in the Crypt witch prison."

Conan's gaze flickered over me. "You'd definitely be breaking the rules if you put me in there. I'd file a complaint and sue you."

"You'd have to find a way out of the prison to do that," I said. "And we don't put up signposts to the nearest exit."

He grunted. "I'd be able to get out."

"I reckon you'd stumble around in there for a few months before giving up. That's if you weren't eaten by a demon or had your insides pulled out and worn as a hat by the other inmates. They'd do that for fun."

"I'm not going in a demon prison." Conan glared at me.

"Providing you play nice, you won't have to. We're reasonable. We can find you a comfy cell in a high security prison where you can spend the rest of your days," Dazielle said with a hint of pleasure in her voice.

"Just don't send me off with this witch." Conan's forehead wrinkled as he tried to shake me loose. "She's giving off a weird vibe."

"That's why we use her," Dazielle said.

I glanced at her. "It is?"

She waved a hand at me. "Let's take him inside."

We escorted Conan through the reception and into the small cell block. Sorath followed close behind, calling out greetings and nodding hello to everyone he met. He was a popular angel, and I noticed several of the female angels stopping to take a second look.

Dazielle secured Conan in a cell and then turned to us. "It won't be long until the trial starts."

"There might be another delay," Sorath said. "Isda will be attending."

Dazielle blinked rapidly, and her mouth opened and closed. "I didn't know about this. Why is she coming here?"

"The higher angels want this warlock off the streets. They need to make sure that happens."

"Of course, but Isda doesn't need to be at the trial. I'll send a full report as soon as it's over and Conan is behind bars." Dazielle's hands fluttered against her chest.

Sorath squeezed her shoulder. "This is an open and shut case. We've got the bad guy, a confession, and I'm sure the witnesses will show up. There's nothing to worry about. Isda is here to observe only."

"Oh, yes!" Dazielle's wings continued to quiver. "And we have Conan's confession."

"Then we should relax and wait for Isda to arrive," Sorath said. "Conan's not going anywhere but jail."

Dazielle let out a sigh. "You're right. I'm worrying about nothing. Of course, the higher angels want to make sure this goes smoothly. Just as we do."

"Exactly." Sorath rolled his broad shoulders. "I wouldn't mind a break after all that flying."

"Of course! I didn't think to offer you a drink. Let's get refreshments and you can catch me up on everything happening in West Oak." Dazielle walked away with Sorath beside her.

I remained by the cell with Wiggles, checking the magic. The wards were stable and the door secure.

Dazielle looked back at me. "What are you doing?"

"You told me not to let Conan out of my sight."

She tutted. "Until he's behind bars. He's not getting out of there."

"I don't mind staying here until the trial begins." And I wasn't sure I wanted to hear all the angel gossip. They'd probably talk about feather whitener and haloes.

"We could miss out on cookies if we stay here." Wiggles was following Dazielle. He'd go with anyone as long as there was a free meal attached to it.

I glanced back at Conan. He was surprisingly calm for someone about to go down for murder. Maybe he'd made peace with his future behind bars.

"Tempest, let's move." Dazielle gestured at me.

Conan sneered and shook his head. "You'd better obey your angel boss."

"I will, especially since it means I won't have to look at you anymore." I walked away from the cell, shut the door, and followed the angels.

Chapter 3

Dazielle, Sorath, and Wiggles entered the break room in front of me, Wiggles barging through first to get any food on offer.

Dominic caught up with me just before I walked into the room. "Did everything go okay with Conan? He didn't cause you problems, did he?"

"One prisoner safely delivered to the cells," I said. "How's Elman?"

"He's on edge, but I made him a drink and suggested he have a walk around." Dominic followed me into the room and greeted Sorath, who was already settled in a seat. "It won't be long until we get Conan behind bars for good. I'll be happy to get back to checking reports of knocked over trash cans and noisy cats mating."

Sorath chuckled. "It sounds like they keep you on your toes around here."

Dominic nodded. "They do. It's always busy. I love my job."

I patted his shoulder. "And you do a great job of dealing with those trash cans."

Sorath leaned forward in his seat. "I've brought a surprise for everyone. I figured we deserved it after bringing such a hardened criminal to justice."

"What is it?" Dazielle said.

He reached under his wings and pulled out a flat-looking box. His smile slipped. "Ah! We have a problem." He opened the box to reveal six squashed cream cakes.

Dazielle leaned away from the box. "I'm sure they were nice when you bought them."

"They must have gotten damaged during the flight. I kept telling Conan to stop wriggling around, but he said he wasn't comfortable." Sorath flipped the lid shut. "These are no good."

"I'll eat them," Wiggles said.

Sorath stared at the box. "I wanted to show my thanks because you're hosting this trial."

"There was no need for that," Dazielle said. "It's our pleasure to take on this case. Violet didn't live here, but we all knew her through Elman."

"I appreciate that. And the higher angels wanted the best on this," Sorath said.

"Why suggest coming to this Angel Force if they wanted the best?" Wiggles said.

I hid my laughter behind a cough.

"Oh, it wasn't this place they were interested in, but you, Tempest." Sorath's gaze lifted to the angel mark on my forehead. "They speak so highly of you. The Crypt witches are such a powerful branch of magic users, and it's an honor to work with you."

I didn't miss the annoyance in Dazielle's eyes. "Dealing with bad guys is what we've always done. And if you can stick around for the rest of the week, you can come to our anniversary party at the demon prison. Then you'll see the Crypt witches in action."

"You have a party for demons?" Sorath shook his leg as Wiggles attempted to clamber up and get the cream cakes.

"Not in the prison, but on top of it. Everyone in the village is invited, and all the angels are coming."

"I might make an appearance early on," Dazielle said. "It gets too rowdy when Dottie mixes her cocktails."

"I love a party. I'd be thrilled to join you." Sorath bowed, almost putting the box of cakes within Wiggles' reach. He lifted the box at the last second. "I should throw these out."

"Don't toss good food." Wiggles pawed at Sorath's leg. "And I'll only eat them out of the trash if you do that."

Sorath glanced down at him. "Are you sure you should eat all of these?"

"He's a hellhound, so he burns off calories easily, but maybe don't eat them all in one go, Wiggles," I said. "Too much cream isn't good for your digestion."

"He's not going to get gassy, is he?" Dazielle pinched her nose. "If he does, he'll have to go outside."

"I never get gassy! And Sorath brought those cakes all the way here. It's a shame for them to go to waste."

"You can have one," I said.

Wiggles leaped as Sorath lowered the box, head-butting the bottom and making the cakes jump on the floor.

"Wiggles! That's not polite," Dazielle said. "Sorath is our guest. You shouldn't barge him like that."

"I'm being helpful," Wiggles said around a mouthful of cake. "You're all missing out. Floor cake is amazing. Tempest, try one."

I shook my head. "I'm good, thanks."

Wiggles went back to munching on the cake, his tail thumping from side to side, having achieved his victory.

"I have a solution to this problem," Sorath said. "On my way in, I saw some delicious cookies on a plate in the reception area. One of your angels must have put them there. She might give us some to share."

Dazielle shifted in her seat. "Those cookies belong to Cassiel."

I snorted a laugh. "And she never shares."

"Cassiel shares with me," Wiggles mumbled, his words just about understandable since he had two cakes wedged in his mouth.

"You steal from her lunch pail. There's a difference." Dazielle shooed Wiggles away from the cakes, but he growled and kept eating.

"I'm sure Cassiel won't mind offering her food," Sorath said. "And I'll replace them. I can bring her fresh cookies later. Do you have a bakery here?"

"We do. And it's great, but it's probably shut," I said. "There's no harm in trying, though. But don't be surprised if Cassiel snaps your head off and tells you to get lost."

"I'll be right back with cookies." Sorath grinned and left the room.

I admired his optimism. But he clearly hadn't spent any time with Cassiel, or he'd know this was an impossible mission.

As we waited, the only sounds in the room were munching and the occasional burp from Wiggles.

Dominic politely pretended not to hear the noises. Dazielle, on the other hand, was glaring at Wiggles and sighing repeatedly.

"Is something bothering you?" I said.

She pointed at Wiggles. "Does he have to be so repulsive?"

"Wiggles' table manners aren't great, but he's an enthusiastic eater. I don't like to tell him off," I said. "He might get disordered eating."

"And there's nothing wrong with enjoying your food." A slobbery piece of cake flew out of Wiggles' mouth and landed on Dazielle's shoe.

She flicked it away. "You'll make yourself sick. And you deserve to be. You've had three cakes."

An earsplitting alarm had me jumping out of my seat. "Is that the fire alarm?"

Dominic leaped up, his smile gone. "No!"

Sorath rushed into the room a second later. "That's your cell alarm, isn't it?"

Dazielle was already up and racing past Sorath. "No. It's the general intruder alert. Something must have triggered it. All of you follow me. We need to check on Conan."

Even Wiggles abandoned the cakes to see what was happening as Dazielle led us through the office and into the cells.

When we arrived, Conan was on the floor. He wasn't moving, and there was blood on his shirt.

She unlocked the door and opened it. Sorath rushed in and crouched over Conan, pressing his fingers against the pulse in his neck.

"Is that a bullet wound?" Dazielle said.

Sorath stared at the red splashed across Conan's chest. "No. I think he's been stabbed."

"Is there a pulse?" I said.

Sorath's fingers remained on Conan's throat. "We're too late. He's already dead."

I stared at the body and then at Dazielle and Dominic in disbelief. "How could this have happened?"

Dazielle shook herself. "I have no idea, but the killer must be close by. This only happened a minute or two ago. We need to seal the building and find them."

I looked along the corridor. "There's only one way in and out of the cells and we've just come through it. How did the killer get past us and all the angels in the office?"

"We'll find that out as soon as we catch them." Dazielle was striding away. "Sorath, stay with the body. We'll do a sweep of the building."

He nodded, his face pale as he remained kneeling beside Conan.

I raced out behind Dazielle and Dominic, Wiggles by my heel.

"Everybody, I need your attention," Dazielle said. All the angels in the office shot to attention and hurried closer. "Conan Nox has been stabbed."

There were several gasps and low murmurs.

"This has only just happened. Did any of you see anyone entering or leaving the cells in the last few minutes?"

No one raised a hand or made a comment as they looked around for a solution.

"We must do an immediate search of the building. The killer is still here," Dazielle said. "Be careful. This person was desperate enough to commit such a heinous crime in an Angel Force building. They could still have the knife on them." She directed groups of angels to different parts of the building to start a search.

"I'll go to the reception area and see if Cassiel saw anything." I hurried off with Wiggles.

Cassiel glanced at me as I raced in. "Was it you who set off that annoying intruder alarm?"

"No. Did someone come through here a few minutes ago?"

"Why do you want to know?"

"Because they could have murdered Conan Nox."

Cassiel's mouth dropped open. "He's dead?"

"Yes! Did you see anyone? This is important. We have to stop them from getting away." I'd have shaken her, but she was much bigger and meaner than me.

"No one's come through here. If they had, I'd have insisted they sign out."

"Are you certain? You didn't have your back turned or go to the washroom in the last five minutes?"

"No! I know how to do my job. What happened to Conan?"

"We think he's been stabbed." I hurried to the main reception doors and peered out. My heart raced as I spotted someone running away from the building.

I flung open the doors and raced after them. "Hey! Stop. I want to talk to you."

Whoever it was kept running. They were solid looking, dressed in black, and had a hat pulled down so low, I couldn't get a look at their face, but I was pretty certain it was a guy.

I flung out a restraining spell. The magic bounced off my fingers, whirled in the air, and splatted on the ground with an unimpressive fizzle.

"What was that?" Wiggles said.

I flicked out my fingers a few times to get the magic working and tried again. The restraining spell got closer to whoever was running, but it failed and flopped on the ground, fading to nothing.

"Do you want me to charge him? I can take him out at the knees?" Wiggles said.

"Yes! Wiggles, go get him."

He trotted forward and then looked back at me. "I'm too full after all that cake."

"Move your furry butt. Go get the guy who stabbed Conan."

He trotted a little further and then flopped on his side. "I have a stitch."

I marched up to him. "You're the worst hellhound ever. No more cream cakes for you."

"I agree. I think I'm lactose intolerant." The burp that rattled out of him had me backing away.

I shook my head and glared at my hands. Why did my magic have to fail me now? "This is your fault,

Frank. It's another one of your tricks to mess with me and make my life difficult."

As was the norm, Frank didn't respond, but I felt him lurking in the background. He was most likely chuckling, thrilled he'd helped a killer get away.

"Maybe that wasn't Conan's murderer." Wiggles was still on his side.

I tipped back my head and stared at the sky. "Why else would he be running? If he had nothing to hide, he'd have talked to me."

"Maybe not. You're scary when you yell. I sometimes run off when you raise your voice."

"I never raise my voice to you."

"You just did when you ordered me to chase the bad guy." He weakly waved his stubby legs in the air. "Carry me inside. I need a peppermint tea and a belly rub to calm my stomach."

"If Dazielle hears about this, she'll be furious with us." I picked him up and placed him over my shoulder, keeping his nose pointed away from me in case the cream cakes came back up.

"If you say nothing about me getting a stitch, I won't say anything about your spell going wrong."

"Deal. But my magic almost worked."

"And I almost ran fast and caught the killer. We were both half successful. Join the halves together, and we have a win."

"I like your thinking, but I doubt Dazielle will see it like that." I petted his back as we headed inside. "Let's go to the cells and see if we can make sense of what just happened."

So much for this being an easy job.

Chapter 4

I returned to the cell to find Sorath still inside. Dazielle was examining the body, and Dominic stood by the open door.

"Did you find anyone in the building?" I said.

Dominic shook his head.

"They must have gotten inside, somehow." I paced along the corridor, uncertain what I was expecting to find. There was only one way into the cells, and I'd just walked through it.

"I don't know how they got in." Dazielle emerged from the cell. "Conan is definitely dead. It was a single stab wound to the heart. It would have killed him instantly."

I looked back at the entrance. "The killer must have come through that door. Unless..." I glanced at Dazielle. "I'm going in the cell. I won't disturb the body."

"Be careful. We haven't swept for evidence."

I crept around Conan, more than happy not to pay his corpse too much attention, and headed to the barred window. I checked it carefully. "It's not damaged. I wondered if someone created a gap to throw the knife through."

"If they'd done that, the knife would still be lodged in Conan's heart," Dazielle said.

I nodded. "So the killer still has the murder weapon. But how did they get in? Especially with all those angels out there."

"An invisibility spell?" Dominic said. "Someone could have crept into the building, snuck through the cell door when no one was looking, and stabbed Conan when he got close enough."

"No spell of that power would work around these cells," Dazielle said. "Even if someone tried, the magic wards would have weakened them. They'd have been revealed and triggered the alarm."

"And the alarm we heard wasn't linked to a disturbance in the magic around the cell?" I said.

"No. We have three alarms. The fire alarm, an intruder alarm that alerts us to someone damaging the building or getting in without authorization, and a cell alarm for when a prisoner tries to break out."

"And we heard…"

"The intruder alarm. Someone must have triggered a magic ward around the building," Dazielle said.

"It could have been the killer," I said.

"It's possible," Dazielle said. "But they wouldn't have been able to get out unnoticed. And they were holding a bloody knife."

"Occasionally, your angels aren't the quickest off the draw," I said.

She arched an eyebrow at me. "They'd have noticed that."

"You're going to hate me for suggesting this, but could it be one of the angels out there?" I said.

"Conan wasn't popular, and he killed someone who was highly thought of. Maybe an angel decided to give him payback. They didn't think he deserved to stand trial. He was better off dead."

She shook her head. "None of my angels are involved. They uphold the law, even with unpleasant criminals such as Conan Nox."

"It's worth speaking to them. We can rule out anyone who wasn't in the main office and who wasn't working alone, but we need to cover all the bases."

Dazielle's scowl showed her displeasure, but she nodded. "I'll check. But I can guarantee it wasn't an angel."

The main door to the cells slammed open, and Cassiel stomped in. "You've given me even more work to do." She glared at me.

"Me! The killer walked past you, and I didn't see you tackling them to the floor."

"What's this?" Dazielle said. "You saw the killer, Cassiel?"

"No, I didn't. Tempest has gotten it into her head that I let a crazed killer saunter past me. It didn't happen. I didn't leave my post, and no one came out of the office." Cassiel's stare turned evil. "But I did see Tempest chasing someone."

"Who was it?" Dazielle turned to me.

I glared at Cassiel, not thankful she'd dropped me in it. "I don't know if they had anything to do with this, but when I went out the front doors, someone was running away."

"What did they look like?"

"I've no idea."

"You must have seen a glimpse of their face."

"Nope. They were dressed head to toe in black and had a hat pulled down low. From their build, they were most likely a guy, but I don't like to make assumptions."

"You should have used magic to bring them down," Dazielle said.

I glanced at Wiggles. "They were moving too fast, and I didn't want to risk hitting innocent bystanders."

Cassiel snorted, as if she didn't believe me.

I remained quiet. The angels didn't need to know about my glitching magic. It would only put Dazielle's nose even more out of joint that I'd let a potential suspect get away because I stuffed up a spell.

"As certain as I am my angels had nothing to do with this, I'll speak to them," Dazielle said. "Cassiel, process Conan's body. Get it moved and begin the autopsy as soon as you can."

"Sure thing, boss."

"If you like, I can interview the angels with you," I said.

"No, you wait with Sorath and Dominic. They're my angels, and this needs to be handled sensitively." Dazielle stalked away, slamming the door behind her.

Cassiel was grumbling under her breath as she assessed Conan's body.

"Let's go wait in the break room," I whispered to Sorath and Dominic.

We all hurried out and left Cassiel to her work.

"I'll make coffee. Then find those cookies, shall I?" Dominic said.

"Good idea. We've all had a shock." I was left in the room with Sorath and Wiggles.

Sorath shook his head. "I feel terrible. Maybe we shouldn't have left Conan in the cell, but I was certain it was secure. He was such an unpopular guy and hurt so many people. We gave someone a chance to murder him."

"I'm not disagreeing with you, but how did the killer get to him?"

"I've no idea. When the alarm sounded, I was coming back from the reception area after unsuccessfully pleading with Cassiel for cookies. I didn't see anyone rushing out of the cells. Dominic could be onto something with this invisibility theory."

"Not according to Dazielle. And the magic around the cells is powerful. When I've been inside one, my powers get weak."

He tilted his head. "Dazielle has arrested you?"

I chuckled. "Yes. It's a long story, but our relationship hasn't always been friendly. She used to think I was guilty of all kinds of heinous crimes. She's mellowed as she's gotten to know me, though. We both have."

"You're not a criminal. And you have an angel mark. The higher angels don't bestow those on just anyone."

"I'm not so certain I should have it."

Dominic returned with a plate of cookies and coffee for us all, and we sat around, waiting for Dazielle to return from quizzing the other angels.

It took about half an hour before she came into the room.

She slumped into a seat and shook her head. "As I suspected, the angels in the office were working together or nowhere near the cell area. None of them did it."

"That leaves us with the people who knew the victim and had a reason for wanting him dead," I said.

"You're not suggesting Elman Oakley?" Dazielle said. "He's a man of peace. It's what he teaches everyone."

"He teaches it, but Conan murdered Violet. Maybe Elman's teachings have gotten dark since then."

"There's also Conan's girlfriend, Tatiana, to consider," Dominic said. "I'm not sure where she was when the alarm went off."

I glanced at Sorath. "And I'm sorry to say, we need to consider you. After all, you made a point of leaving the room to get cookies."

Dazielle hissed at me. "Tempest! That's ridiculous."

Sorath's eyes widened, and he gulped. "That's all that I went to do. Cassiel will vouch for me. I walked straight through the office into the reception area and then came back. I didn't go into the cells."

I nodded. I'd check with Cassiel, but it sounded impossible for Sorath to be involved.

"I'll find Elman and Tatiana." Dazielle stood and headed to the door. "I'll bring them in here. I won't be a minute."

My gaze settled on Sorath. "Sorry for putting you on the suspect list. But I don't know you, and you weren't in the room with us. I had to make sure you couldn't have done it."

"I understand. You did the right thing. But it made me feel guilty." His smile was cautious. "I see now why the higher angels like you so much. You're very thorough."

Dazielle returned a moment later with a perplexed looking Elman and a scowling Tatiana. "Please, take a seat. We've got some unfortunate news to share with you."

Elman nodded and settled in a chair, crossing his legs and resting his hands on his knees. "Does it have something to do with that alarm? It made me jump when it went off."

"What's going on?" Tatiana said. "The trial should have started ten minutes ago. I want to see Conan."

Dazielle cleared her throat. "While Conan was in his cell, someone got in. I'm sorry to tell you this, but he's dead."

Elman's mouth fell open.

Tatiana squeaked as her hand flew to her mouth. She lowered it and jabbed a finger at Dazielle. "What are you talking about? He can't be dead."

"We haven't completed our investigation, but Conan was found in his cell with a stab wound to the chest."

"This is crazy. One of you lot did it." Tatiana's voice was so high-pitched, every hellhound within a five-mile radius would have heard her. "He should have been protected in here."

"We secured the cell once he was inside. There should have been no way for anyone to get to him," Dazielle said.

"My man is dead because of you." Tatiana bared her teeth at Dazielle.

"We need to check your alibis," I said. "Both of you knew Conan, and you were close by at the time of his death."

"I wouldn't kill my boyfriend, you moron," Tatiana said. "Besides, I was outside. I didn't like all the angel stink getting up my nose. I heard the alarm go off when I was out there."

"You were on your own?" I said.

She nodded. "I wouldn't be hanging out with any of you, would I?"

"And Elman, where were you?" I said.

"After Dominic made me a green tea, I also stepped out for some air. I tried to speak to Tatiana, but she wasn't receptive."

"You were being preachy again. I didn't appreciate it," Tatiana said. "I wanted to be on my own. I had thinking to do about my future and didn't want you healing me, or cleansing me, or whatever it is you do."

"You were together when you heard the alarm?" I said.

"No. I was walking back to the building when I heard it," Elman said.

"Did either of you see anyone running away from the building?" I said. "Or anyone who came out of the building just after the alarm went off?"

Elman shook his head. "No, and I'd have seen them because I was looking at the front doors. There was nobody."

"I didn't see anyone," Tatiana said. "Who do you think it was?"

"We're not sure," I said. "They could be connected to what happened to Conan."

"Then you find them," Tatiana said. "And why are you talking to me like I had something to do with this? You get a team out there to hunt this person. My future has been wiped out because of your incompetence."

"There'll be an explanation for this," Dazielle said.

"Yeah, and I know what that explanation will be. None of you liked Conan. You wanted to see him dead, so saved yourself time and money by getting rid of him. I know your game." Tatiana's pink nails flashed in the air.

"None of my angels are involved in this murder," Dazielle said.

"What about the witch? Or that thing shuffling about by her feet?" Tatiana said.

"Neither me nor Wiggles wanted Conan dead," I said. "Conan was about to be put away for the rest of his life. That was punishment enough as far as I was concerned."

"And for me, too," Elman said quietly. "Of course, I was angry with Conan, but I was here to see justice done. Sometimes, people end up on the wrong path and need help if they're ever to recover their footing."

"Don't preach that garbage to me," Tatiana said. "If someone had given you a gun and left you in the cell with Conan for five minutes, you'd have pulled the trigger with a smile on that smug face."

Elman lowered his head. "I never condone violence. Conan knew in his heart he'd done a terrible thing to Violet, and he was ready to pay. That was enough for me."

"What about you, Tatiana?" I said.

Her head whipped my way. "What about me?"

"Any problems in your relationship?"

She twirled an auburn curl around one finger. "We had our ups and downs, just like all relationships. But I didn't want him dead."

"Because you loved him?"

"Sure. He looked after me. Now he's gone, and I'm on my own. And it's all your fault." Her glare shot around the room, spearing all of us.

A thudding came from somewhere in the building.

"That's the front door," Dominic said.

"I had it locked so no one could get in or out," Dazielle said.

"I'll go see who it is." I needed a break from the death stares shooting my way from Tatiana.

As I entered the reception area, I was surprised to see Aurora outside with a huge pale blonde angel beside her.

She waved at me and gestured at the door.

I hurried over and unlocked it. "Hey. What brings you here?"

"I found Isda wandering the village. She'd gotten lost and couldn't find the Angel Force building, so I said I'd bring her here."

The angel, Isda, nodded. "I always find it confusing when I come to this plane of existence. All the smells, sounds, and colors are so vibrant I find myself distracted. And this is my first visit to this particular Angel Force building."

"I figured all Angel Force buildings would look the same," I said.

Her laugh was like a dozen tiny tinkling bells. "Yes, they do. But this wonderful witch came out of her odd smelling store and asked if I needed help."

"Aurora is good like that," I said.

"Isda!" Dazielle's voice was so high-pitched I leaped in the air and had to step to one side to avoid her barging into me.

"Greetings, Dazielle. I'm looking forward to experiencing the trial and ensuring there's a happy resolution." Isda's blonde hair shimmered around her head in a halo, and her skin had a glittering shimmer to it. Higher angels were so beautiful, it hurt my eyes if I looked at them for more than a few seconds.

"You'd better come in," Dazielle said. "There's been a... complication."

"Oh, I never like complications. I would like cake, though. This sweet little witch gave me something called a pear drop. It was delicious. Do you have anything like that?" She patted Aurora on the head.

"Sure. We can get you a whole bag of pear drops. Let's talk first." Dazielle flapped around Isda as she hurried her inside, while I resisted the urge to roll my eyes.

Aurora grabbed my arm. "Nice hair. Is that blonde stripe new?"

I nodded as I tugged the black stripe in her hair. "I heard you've been experimenting. Did you do this to us?"

"No. I figured it was you." She yanked on the black lock of hair and frowned before glancing around. "Is your magic okay?"

My eyebrows rose slowly. "Nope. It hasn't been right for a while. What about you?"

"My magic has been terrible. Every time I cast a spell, it doesn't do what I need it to do. I'm almost too afraid to mix up anything and sell it in case it blows up in a customer's face." She huffed out a breath. "And it's not just us. I saw Zandra a couple of days ago, and she's also having issues."

"She's got problems with her magic too?"

Aurora nodded. "And wait till you see her hair. She's tried everything to change it."

"What does it look like?"

She bit her lip. "Promise you won't laugh when I tell you."

"I'll do my best. I'm guessing she's got a stripe like us?"

"She's got stripes. Lots of them. Zandra looks like an angry badger."

I pressed my lips together, doing my absolute best not to laugh. "Nothing works to get it to change back?"

"No! Every spell I've done doesn't touch this." She pulled on her hair again.

"It looks like we're stuck with these new stripes." I shoved my hair off my face. If I couldn't see it, the blonde stripe didn't bother me. "I thought it was just me having a few off days or Frank messing around.

But it can't be Frank if you and Zandra are also being influenced."

"We need to figure out what the stripes mean and why our magic is being affected."

"I supposed this could be a side effect of a spell we're under."

Aurora looked startled. "Who'd want to cast a spell over us?"

"I can think of a few people who'd want to mess with me. Not you, though."

She worried her bottom lip with her teeth. "Can you come to the store so we can figure this out? I want to get things back to normal."

I looked over my shoulder. "I wish I could, but someone's just been murdered on my watch. I can't say too much, but they were in a cell on their own when they got stabbed. It's a puzzle we need to figure out fast. Especially with a higher angel lurking about."

Aurora took a step back. "Oh! That's terrible. I suppose it trumps color changing hair and misfiring spells. This can wait, but not for long. I sold a beauty enhancing spell to a customer and turned her green. I was so embarrassed. I gave her a refund and promised her a free potion of whatever she wanted, but she ran out of the store crying."

"I'm sure she'll recover. Maybe she'll get used to being green," I said. "I'll stop by this evening. Get Zandra there, too."

"I will. I'm sure we can work it out, but I wish I knew what was causing it."

"We'll fix this. I'll catch up with you later." I hurried back into the building.

Our problems would have to wait. I needed to figure out how a killer snuck past me and a dozen angels, stabbed Conan, and got away with it.

Chapter 5

After several hours of going over the same information with Elman, Sorath, and Tatiana, we were no closer to figuring out who murdered Conan.

"We can't hold Elman and Tatiana for much longer," Dominic whispered as we stood around the coffee table, taking a break from the unhelpful questioning.

Dazielle tapped her foot on the floor. "It wasn't any of my angels. And it wasn't Sorath. It must be Elman or Tatiana. But how did they do it?"

"How about we let them go so they can think about it overnight?" I said. "The killer could get nervous and make a mistake."

"Or make a run for it," Dominic said. "That would prove their guilt."

"I can't see Elman running," Dazielle said. "His whole life is based around these villages. Most of his customers come from here and the surrounding area. And he doesn't have the resources to start a new life anywhere else."

"Which leaves us with the grumpy girlfriend," I said. "But Tatiana was outside the building when Conan was stabbed."

Dazielle's wings fluttered, and several white feathers floated around us. One settled in my mug of coffee. I hooked it out with a finger and flipped it into the trash.

"Tatiana looks about ready to chew someone's head off," Dominic said. "Unless we arrest her, we have to let her go, along with Elman."

I nodded. "We need more proof before anyone can be charged."

"Very well. Tell them to go," Dazielle said. "But make sure they know not to leave Willow Tree Falls."

"You want me to do it?" Dominic said.

"Of course. You're not scared of a small angry witch and a peaceful shaman, are you?"

"Of course he is," I said. "And Tatiana is terrifying. She snaps at anyone who asks her a question."

Dazielle pursed her lips. "That's because she has something to hide. I'm sure of it."

"Or because she's a mean person," Wiggles said. "Tempest, I'm bored. The trash is empty of food, and the angels are hiding treats from me. I even tried begging Jophiel for a cracker."

"We'll be out of here soon," I said. "I'll get you pizza."

"Good. Because I'm also starving. I'm going to look for any last-minute hidden snacks. I'll look around for clues while I'm at it."

Unless those clues were hidden in the trash or someone's lunch pail, he wouldn't have much success.

"Go tell Elman and Tatiana they can leave," Dazielle said to Dominic. "Then we'll take another look around the cell. Maybe this break from the crime scene will have given us a fresh perspective."

Dominic looked like he wanted to protest, but instead he nodded and hurried to the interview rooms where Elman and Tatiana were being held.

"I see you're still being horrible to Dominic," I said. "Surely he's proven himself by now. He's your most loyal angel."

Dazielle shrugged. "I have no problems with Dominic."

"I guess, since you two were married, there'll always be that affectionate bond, even though things didn't work out."

She growled at me. "Don't push it. And I'm still not happy with you for letting our prime suspect run off."

I wasn't all that proud of myself for that, or my misfiring magic, so I stayed quiet.

Sorath walked over, yawning loudly. "Is there anything else I can do to help?"

I shook my head and glanced at Dazielle. Sorath was working the case with us after I'd checked his alibi.

"You can go if you want to," Dazielle said.

"Thanks. I wouldn't mind getting my head down. And I want to check in with Isda. She didn't know where she was staying tonight when she left."

"She should. I told her the directions to the hotel five times," Dazielle said. "You don't think she's gotten lost, do you?"

"How can an all-powerful, all-seeing super angel get lost when the hotel is a five-minute walk from here?" I said. "And why does she even need to stay in the village? Can't she poof herself back to her usual plane of existence and poof back in the morning?"

"Isda wants the full experience." Dazielle grimaced. "I decided not to ask what that meant. I think it involves lots of shopping and wandering around."

"And the plane the higher angels operate on isn't as straightforward as turning left or right to get to a destination," Dominic said. "It's easy for them to get confused when they visit here."

"Their home territory is weird. I wouldn't want to hang out there for long. Maybe that's why Isda is staying. She wants a vacation from her odd life," I said.

"I expect she finds this space unsettling and wants to get home," Dazielle said. "Which is why we need to solve this case quickly. If Isda notices we're struggling, she'll report back on our work less favorably."

"I'll take good care of her," Sorath said. "I'll make sure she's gotten to the hotel and see if she needs anything. I can even take her out for dinner if that would be helpful."

"Yes. That's a great idea. Ensure she wants for nothing."

"I will. And it's no trouble. I'm staying at the hotel, too." Sorath ducked his head. "I'm just sorry this murder happened on my watch. Conan's victim deserved justice. She sounded like a good woman."

"I guess a kind of justice has been served," I said. "He won't be able to commit more crimes now."

"But we never condone murder," Dazielle said, "no matter how bad the criminal is."

I looked up as Elman and Tatiana came out of the interview rooms, led by Dominic. Tatiana stomped away without a glance at us. Elman raised his hand and nodded as he passed by before heading into the reception area.

"I'll get out of your way and check on Isda." Sorath headed out, leaving me with an angry looking Dazielle.

"This looks terrible for all of us," she said.

"Not me. I'm just the hired muscle. You pointed out where I needed to go, and I followed your orders."

"We're all involved in this mess. You might even lose your higher angel mark if the angels consider you incompetent."

I shrugged. "I'm not bothered if I do. It freaks me out how the angels stare at my forehead."

Dominic walked back from the reception area after seeing off Elman and Tatiana.

"Let's go back to the scene of the crime. I want to take one more look around." Dazielle led us to the cells. None were occupied, and there was an eerie quiet along the corridor as we stood outside the cell Conan had been in.

"Only angels can unlock these cells, is that right?" I said. "But no angel was seen coming in here at the time of Conan's murder."

"That's right. And I have accounted for everyone on shift," Dazielle said. "It would take someone with serious power to break through the magic, and brute strength would be needed to break open the cell door without a key."

I inspected the door. It hadn't been forced. "You had to unlock this door when we arrived and found Conan. It didn't feel odd when you put the key in the lock?"

Dazielle shook her head. "The key turned with no problem. Nothing was out of place."

"We need to see if anyone could have magically transported into the cell," I said. "Maybe they found a way around your wards."

"Do you want to try getting in and out of a cell using your magic?"

"Sure. Why not?"

Dazielle waved a hand at the cell. "The wards are in place. Try getting in. I guarantee you'll fail."

"I love that you have so much faith in my abilities."

"Don't say I didn't warn you." Dazielle nudged Dominic back.

I focused on creating a transportation spell to take me inside the cell. There was an instant pushback from the magic wards, giving me a warning they didn't like what I was doing. I kept imagining myself on the other side of the bars as I pulsed the spell through my body.

"You're doing it!" Dominic said.

I was doing something, but it felt wrong. The floor beneath my feet seemed to move.

"Give up," Dazielle said.

There was a whooshing in my ears, and I found myself in the cell.

Dominic hurried over and stood on the other side of the bars. "Wow! You've got some power to be able to do that."

I bent over and dry heaved in the corner before sinking to my hands and knees. I felt like I'd been whacked over the head by a troll's hammer.

"Now try to get out, genius," Dazielle said. "That's the point of the magic wards. You might be able to sneak in, but once you're in their clutches, there's no way out."

I raised a hand as I calmed my somersaulting stomach. "Give me a minute. I've got this."

"If the killer used this method to get to Conan, they wouldn't have had a minute. We can already hear the cell alarm blasting in the office. It's letting every angel know there's a problem," Dazielle said.

I'd barely noticed the noise. I was so focused on ensuring I didn't lose the contents of my stomach.

A few seconds later, the door leading to the cells slammed open and several angels charged in, their wings spread wide.

"It's okay," Dazielle said. "We're running an experiment. Tempest has a point to prove, despite how bad it's making her feel."

I forced myself to stand on shaking knees and swiped a hand across my sweaty brow. "I concede to you. It's not that easy to get in and out of here without being noticed."

"As I keep telling you. Will someone shut off that alarm?" Dazielle snapped.

The angels who'd arrived swiftly backed away and shut the door behind them. A few seconds later, the alarm stopped.

"I can do this. I need to calm my magic, get used to the feel of your creepy angel wards, and I'll be on the other side of these bars in no time," I said. "Maybe whoever did this practiced, so they got used to the weird sensations."

"You'll only end up hunched in the corner about to puke again if you keep going," Dazielle said.

I lifted my hands, and a blast of sickly green light shot from my palms and slammed into the wall an inch above Dazielle's head.

She shrieked and dropped down.

Dominic remained frozen in place, his eyes wide. He turned his head and looked at the scorch marks on the wall.

I lowered my hands and clenched my fists. "Oops! Maybe you're right. These wards are messing with my power."

Dazielle scrambled to her feet. "Enough experiments. Get out of the cell. We've proved no one transported in." Her gaze cut to the scorched wall, and she scowled.

I didn't object as she unlocked the cell door to let me out. "How about we check the window again?"

We spent a few minutes double-checking the window, but it was as secure as it had been the last time we looked. No one used that to get to Conan.

"Whoever stabbed Conan needed to be close to him." Dominic made a stabbing motion at my chest.

"Could they have thrown a projectile from the doorway?" I said. "It would have been a tight angle. Can you see this cell from the door?" I strode to the door, turned, and inspected the cell.

"I'm not so sure that would work," Dazielle said.

"Go inside the cell and let me throw things at you."

Her eyebrows rose. "Will you be using more rogue magic blasts?"

"Of course not. That was just your wards making me malfunction." At least, I hoped it was the wards and not my magic going off the rails again.

"Dominic, you go in the cell. Stand there and pretend to be Conan," Dazielle said.

Dominic scurried inside and turned to face me. "Like this?"

"That's perfect. Give me a minute to get my weapons of choice." I ducked into the office, grabbed a handful of pens, and returned to the doorway. "If the killer threw the knife, they wouldn't have stood here with the door wide open. That would have been too obvious. So, they must have cracked it open. I'm trying that." I lobbed several pens at Dominic. They all missed. Two pens didn't even make it through the cell bars, ricocheting off the metal and hitting the floor.

It took a dozen throws before I hit my target.

"This is getting us nowhere," Dazielle said. "If the killer inched open the door and lobbed a blade through, they had no chance of hitting Conan. And he'd have needed to be facing the door and waiting for the killer blow to strike. That's not how it happened."

"Hey! Less snappy and more support. I'm trying out theories to solve your murder. This is helping you." I gathered the pens and opened the cell door to let Dominic out.

"This is helpful," he said. "We've ruled out someone magically transporting into the cell, and a ninja knife thrower creeping in and hurling a blade into Conan's chest."

"I keep coming back to that running man. It must have been the person seen fleeing the scene," Dazielle said. Her glare cut to me. "The individual Tempest failed to stop."

"You're not going to let me forget that, are you?"

"You let a vital clue run away. If you'd prevented them from leaving, we could have had this case wrapped up. Isda would report back to the higher angels that we're doing our jobs effectively." Dazielle's wings fluttered around her. "The longer we don't find the killer, the more concerned she'll become."

"And the more stressed you'll get," I said. "And we all know what you're like when you get stressed."

"You get shouty," Dominic said. "And you stop saying please and thank you."

"And manners cost nothing," I said.

Dazielle tutted at us.

"Even if the person who ran off is our killer, we still haven't worked out how they got in the cell," I said.

"Could they have used a disguise?" Dominic said. "Someone came in disguised as an angel. Then when everyone's attention was away from the cells, they snuck in and killed Conan."

"That's unlikely," Dazielle said.

"And Cassiel was on the reception desk," I said. "She insists on everyone signing in."

"She wouldn't have let an unknown angel come in without informing me. We can rule out a disguise," Dazielle said.

"So magic wasn't used and not a disguise. And the killer didn't come in through the window." Dominic looked around. "Could they have dug a tunnel under the cells?"

"The floors are solid," Dazielle said. "Besides, the magic wards prevent that from happening."

"Which means, we're missing something, but I don't know what it is," I said.

"Tempest Crypt! Where are you?"

I flinched at the anger in Cassiel's voice. "Do I have time to run?"

The cell door slammed open, and Cassiel marched in. She held Wiggles out at arm's length. "This thing was licking our victim."

Chapter 6

"What have you done to him?" Wiggles' head was slumped forward, and his paws hung limply. I hurried over and grabbed him away from Cassiel.

"The only thing I did was prevent him from further contaminating evidence. He snuck into the examination room, and I found him on the victim's chest." Cassiel made a show of wiping her hands with a tissue. "He shouldn't be allowed to roam about loose. He's out of control."

I was paying her no attention, more concerned about why Wiggles was out cold. "You must have done something to him. He won't wake up."

"That's not my fault. I heard a slurping noise and turned to see what it was. I was about to yell at him when he collapsed on Conan's body. I caught him as he rolled off the examination table."

"Are you sure you didn't put an angel hex on him? I've never seen him like this." I checked his gums and they were a healthy pink, but his breathing was labored, and he wouldn't stir.

"You're missing the point," Cassiel said. "A crucial piece of evidence has been contaminated. Wiggles was jumping on Conan and licking him."

"The body is hardly contaminated. Take a spit swab and fur sample from Wiggles and eliminate them when you're running tests on Conan's body." My attention remained on Wiggles. "I don't see what the big deal is."

"Tempest! He was licking the stab wound."

"Oh. Well, that's gross. I mean, Wiggles likes his steak rare, but he's never done that with a dead body before. He's respectful." I stroked Wiggles' back.

Cassiel crouched, her wings extending, and her lethal gaze focused on me. "He's a menace. Just like you."

"Perhaps we've all had enough for today." Dazielle stepped in between us. "This is a stressful event, and none of us could have anticipated what would happen to Conan. It's been a shock, but we need to keep control of our emotions."

"Didn't you hear me say that filthy hellhound contaminated the body?" Cassiel said. "How am I supposed to give you the information you need now it's covered in drool?"

"Calm yourself, Cassiel. I understand your frustration." Dazielle glanced at me. "Tempest, it's time you left."

"I'm going." I glared at Cassiel. "If you've hurt Wiggles, I'll make you pay."

"You bring Wiggles near me again, and I'll make him regret ever stamping on my corpse and slurping at the victim's wound like it was a piece of pie."

"That's enough," Dazielle said. "Tempest, take Wiggles home. Cassiel, get a chamomile tea and take a ten-minute break."

She snorted her disbelief. "You're siding with the gross hellhound?"

"Go!" Dazielle said. "You too, Tempest."

I stomped past Cassiel and marched out of the reception area and into the chilly evening air. Wiggles weighed a ton, but I had no choice other than to carry him. "What has that awful angel done to you?"

He grumbled something, but I couldn't make out what it was. I adjusted his weight, moving him so his front paws were over my shoulder. I cupped the back of his head with one hand and tucked his butt in the crook of my arm, making sure he was secure.

Rather than going to my apartment, I headed to Aurora's store. She had restorative spells and potions that helped with most problems. I was certain she'd have something to get Wiggles out of the stupor that evil Cassiel had put him in.

Although it wasn't far to Aurora's store, my muscles ached by the time I reached the door. I peered through the glass front of the store and gave a snort of surprise. The place was a mess. Aurora prided herself on having a pristine store, but there were things scattered on the floor, the counter was littered with boxes, and my sister stood with her back to the counter and her head down.

I shoved open the door with one hip and hurried inside. "What happened? Have you been burgled?"

She spun around, and I saw she'd been crying. "I thought I'd locked the door. I can't even get that right."

"Aurora, what's the matter? Is someone sick?" I hurried over to her.

She wiped her face with the back of her hand. "No, but everything is going wrong. I've had three customers today complaining about my products. I can't get the simplest spell right. Everything I touch explodes, sparks, or turns the wrong color. Just like my dreadful hair."

"It can't be that bad." I eased Wiggles out of my arms and settled him on the counter after clearing a couple of boxes out of the way.

"She's not the only one having trouble." Zandra emerged from the back room. She carried a tray with mugs on and a plate of cookies. She set them down. "I didn't know you were coming over."

"I said to Aurora I'd drop by. Nice hat."

Zandra tugged the black woolen hat lower over her ears. "You'd wear one too if you had hair like mine."

Aurora sniffed back more tears. "I think your hair is adorable. You look like a cute stripy badger."

"I look like an idiot. What's up with Wiggles?" Zandra prodded him in the side.

"He's been zapped by an angel. Cassiel caught him snooping around a body. I can't get him to wake up."

"I don't see any injuries on him." Zandra inspected Wiggles' paws before looking inside his mouth. "What did this angel do?"

"Not a clue. She was acting like it was all his fault. I should have whacked her with a spell."

"What's Wiggles saying?" Aurora tilted her head so her ear was by his muzzle.

"He was muttering on our way over here, but I couldn't make out any words."

"He's saying something about cake or sugar. Maybe it's sweet. I think that's what he's saying." Aurora raised her gaze to meet mine. "Does he want something to eat?"

"When doesn't Wiggles want something to eat?" Zandra said. "Shove a cookie under his nose. That might wake him up."

I took a cookie from the plate and sat it by Wiggles' mouth. He didn't stir.

"I'll go get more options from the kitchen. Maybe he just needs something to entice him awake." Aurora already seemed brighter now she had something else to focus on.

"It could be a sleep spell," Zandra said. "Although I don't think angels have that kind of magic."

"They don't. They're more brute force, the occasional miracle, and showing off their wings. I can't figure out what Cassiel's done to him."

"See if these help." Aurora returned and set out different sweet treats to see if Wiggles would respond. She tried a chocolate brownie, a pecan caramel muffin, a meringue slice with cream, and a cherry tart.

He wriggled around a bit when each treat was put next to him but still wouldn't wake. Not even when Zandra balanced a cookie on his nose.

She took it off, wiped it on her shirt, and took a bite. "He's out for the count."

"Maybe it's only temporary," Aurora said. "But keep an eye on him overnight. If he's no better, demand Cassiel release him from whatever she's done."

"Don't worry, I will." I yanked off Zandra's hat. "Wow! You do look like a fluffy badger."

She jammed the hat back on her head. "You're not much better."

"I've only got one blonde stripe."

"You've got two. One is at the back."

"Are you kidding me?" I grabbed a handful of my hair but couldn't see more stripes.

"It's there," Aurora said. "And I got another stripe at the back of mine, too. It showed up a couple of hours ago."

"What is going on with our hair?" Zandra said.

"It's not just the hair, though," Aurora said. "It's the magic. I feel powerless. My magic doesn't seem to be my own anymore."

"How long has it been like this?" I said.

"It's been a while. It was only small things at first. A potion didn't turn out right a few weeks ago, and I had to redo some spells because they weren't effective. I figured it was the stone circle pulsing out the wrong vibes and making the magic wonky."

"Same here," Zandra said. "Although I figured it was a control issue with me. I'm still learning how to use this Crypt witch power, but everything I did felt off. I can't remember when it started, but it's gotten worse over the last few weeks. How bad is yours?"

"I almost blasted Dazielle's head off her shoulders when my magic misfired," I said.

"Are you sure that was an accident?" Zandra snorted a laugh.

"It was this time. I was thinking about a spell, but it was shooting straight at Dazielle's head before I could control it. And she's already unimpressed with me because I let a possible suspect in this murder investigation run off."

"Who's dead?" Zandra said.

"Have you heard of Conan Nox?"

She tilted her head from side to side. "Vaguely. Someone was talking about him in the bakery the other day. Didn't he kill someone?"

"More than one person, but this is the first murder the angels have had enough evidence to charge him with. Conan's got a long criminal history and is overdue spending the rest of his life behind bars. It was arranged he'd come to Willow Tree Falls for his trial and sentencing. Dazielle was in charge and asked me to back her up if Conan got difficult to handle."

"Someone killed him when you were looking after him?" Aurora said.

"They stabbed him when he was inside his cell, and we can't figure out how the killer got in and out with no one noticing."

"And you think it was this person you saw running away?" Zandra said.

"Maybe, but I have no clue who they were. We're looking into other suspects, but there aren't many to choose from."

"Should you be involved in this investigation? It'll be harder to solve if your magic isn't working," Aurora said.

"I want to be involved. There has to be a way to get in that cell, stab Conan, and get out without anyone seeing." I stroked Wiggles. "Although I'm not here to talk murder. I was hoping you could do some healing spells on this fuzz ball."

Aurora sucked in a breath, a worried look crossing her face. "I could try something simple, but any intense magic I do backfires, and I don't want to hurt him."

Wiggles was still muttering in his sleep, one paw occasionally flicking up. "Sweet," he grumbled.

"Is he waking up?" Aurora said.

"Wiggles, can you hear me? Tell me what you need," I said.

"Sweet," he repeated.

"He's talking in his sleep," Zandra said. "Wiggles is still obsessed with food, even though he's unconscious."

"I wish I could help you with the healing magic," Aurora said. "But I don't want to make him any worse."

"No, you're okay. I'll take him home and make sure he's comfortable overnight." I hated not having my smart talking sidekick to hang out with. And Wiggles never got ill. He was someone I could rely on, so long as there wasn't a full trash can of discarded treats nearby.

"We have to make sure our magic works properly," Aurora said. "We've got the cemetery celebration in a week's time. We can't embarrass the family by turning up and blasting out the wrong spells."

"Maybe they're having problems too," Zandra said.

"Mom and Granny Dottie came into the club," I said. "Neither of them commented on their magic being strange. They seemed fine. I think this is a problem only affecting the three of us."

"Who would want our magic to go wrong?" Aurora said. "Everyone likes me."

"Not everyone," Zandra muttered. "I used to think you were a giant pain in my butt."

"Likewise. But we're over that now, aren't we?"

Zandra took a few seconds to think about it. "You still have your moments when you're so sickening I want to stick my fingers down my throat. But you're less grating than you used to be."

"There's sisterly love for you," I said. "It's good to see you two getting on so well."

Aurora grumbled under her breath and wouldn't look at Zandra.

Zandra nudged her with her hip. "Relax. You're not a terrible half-sister."

"I wish I could say the same about you," Aurora said.

"No bickering, you two. We've got more important things to think about. And you're right, with the celebration coming up, we need to make sure our magic is flowing smoothly. We don't want to be known as the three misfiring witches messing things up. And if the demons get wind some of us are malfunctioning, they'll cause trouble and spoil things for everyone else."

"Maybe our magic will sort itself out," Zandra said. "These problems showed up without warning. Maybe they'll go away again."

"I wouldn't be so sure about that," Aurora said. "I have a bad feeling in my stomach. It's even putting me off these cookies, and I made them myself, so I know they're delicious."

I ate a cookie, leaning against the counter and gently stroking Wiggles. Everything felt weird and out of sorts, from the impossible murder at Angel Force, to my unconscious hellhound. Something was wrong in Willow Tree Falls.

After eating my cookie, I hefted Wiggles back into my arms. "I'll leave you two to it. Maybe fix up the store before tomorrow, or you'll scare away customers."

"I might not even open if my magic is still messing about," Aurora said. "I hope Wiggles feels better. Sorry I couldn't be any help." She walked me to the door, kissed Wiggles on the head, and then hugged me before we all said good night.

I headed back to my apartment, taking it slowly because of the extra weight I carried.

Once I was up the stairs and inside, I tucked Wiggles in my bed, giving him his own pillow and making sure the covers were snug around him.

He barely stirred, other than occasionally shuffling around, although he was still muttering about cakes and sweet things.

I usually stayed up late to oversee things at the club, but I was tired. After doing a quick check with Merrie to make sure everything was fine for the evening, I decided to have an early night. I got into my most comfy pajamas and snuggled next to Wiggles in the bed.

Hopefully, by the morning, everything would have fixed itself.

Chapter 7

I rolled over, and my nose bumped into a pungent, hairy belly. Wiggles was on his back, his legs in the air.

My hand rested on his belly, and I ruffled his fur. "Are you ready to wake up?"

He didn't respond, other than shifting around.

"No more excuses. We've got a killer to catch."

Wiggles stayed silent.

"Well, it looks like it's just me and the angels catching the bad guy." After making sure he was comfortable and tucking the covers back around him, I headed into the bathroom.

My hair still had its odd blonde stripes, and no spell I did shifted them. After a shower and a change of clothes, I headed into the kitchen and made coffee.

I took out Wiggles' dog kibble and made lots of noise as I tipped it into his bowl, filling it to the brim. "Extra rations this morning, since you didn't have supper."

He didn't come bounding out of the bedroom to scarf down his food.

"I'll even rustle up some bacon if you hustle your furry behind out here."

Wiggles would do a lot for a slice of sizzling bacon but not this morning.

I drank my coffee, ate an almost in-date cereal bar I found at the back of the cupboard, and then pulled on my jacket and boots. I grabbed my keys and turned back to the bedroom. It felt wrong leaving Wiggles here. What if he got sicker and needed help?

Technically, he was an immortal hellhound, so dying wasn't possible, but it didn't feel right leaving him behind. And if I lugged him around over my shoulder, I'd put my back out.

I returned to my bedroom and stood at the bottom of the bed, looking at him. "I need to figure out how to carry you around."

A harness like Sorath used to transport Conan would do. It needed to be sturdy and comfortable, and I needed a way for Wiggles' legs to stick out. A backpack wouldn't cut it.

I hunted through my closet and pulled out belts, long scarves, and a thin blanket. After ten minutes of tying things together, I had the makings of a papoose. I shunted it on my shoulders and adjusted the straps until they were comfortable.

"Are you ready to give this a go?"

There were no objections from my slumbering hellhound, so I lifted Wiggles and took a moment to get his butt settled, then I adjusted his legs, so his back was pressed against my chest and his paws stuck out in front of him. I tugged his tail out to make sure it didn't get squashed and moved to stand in front of a full-length mirror. We looked ridiculous, but he was easier to carry this way, and it meant I got to keep my hands free.

"It's like having my very own fat smelly furry baby." I shook my head, grabbed my purse, and left the apartment. I walked down the stairs, through the empty club, and out the main doors.

The atmosphere crackled as I headed through the doors of Angel Force as angels bustled around, looking busy.

Dominic hurried over the second he saw me and grabbed my elbow. "I need to give you a heads up. Dazielle's been here all night. She's not slept, and she's had six mugs of coffee."

"Dazielle rarely drinks coffee." I glanced at her office. "Should I leave before she sees me?"

"Maybe you should. I wish I could. She's yelling at everyone. I'm too scared to move in case I go in the wrong direction, but then she yells at me because it looks like I'm doing nothing."

I looked over my shoulder. It was so tempting to run, but Dazielle would only find me. "I'm staying. You sound like you need backup."

"Thanks." Dominic looked at Wiggles. "How's he doing?"

"Still acting like Snow White after eating the poisoned apple. I haven't been able to get him to wake."

"You don't think he's in pain, do you?"

"Wiggles seems comfortable. He just won't open his eyes. I'm keeping an eye on him today. If Cassiel didn't do this to him, he could have stumbled into magic he wasn't supposed to touch and got in trouble."

"Cassiel can be blunt, but she's not cruel. I don't think she did this to him."

"You think better of her than I do." I sighed. "But you're right. I don't think she harmed him. She was just angry about the whole licking the body thing."

"I can babysit him if you like. Or would that be dog sit?" Dominic petted Wiggles. "And at least none of us have to worry about him stealing food while he's like this."

"There's always a silver lining." I followed Dominic to the coffee stand, and he made us both coffees before handing me one.

"Any information from the autopsy yet?" I asked.

"Cassiel's still working on it, but it was definitely a single stab wound straight through the heart with a thin blade."

"Some kind of rapier, perhaps? That's the only thin bladed weapon I can think of."

"Maybe. I'm not a blade expert."

"Is there any sign of the weapon?"

"Tempest, at last! I was thinking you'd forgotten about this investigation." Dazielle stomped over to us, her wings fluttering.

"I'm hardly going to forget a murder. I was just getting an update from Dominic."

"It's good to see him doing something useful." She grabbed the coffee mug out of Dominic's hand.

I grabbed it back and set it on the table. "You've had enough caffeine. When was the last time you ate?"

"I'm too tense to eat. And I need something to keep me going."

"Not Dominic's coffee. Go get some food and have a walk around the block. It'll clear your head."

"There's no time for that. We have to solve this murder. Isda's been sending me messages on the snow globe, and I can't rest until we find the killer."

"Have any new clues shown up?" I said. "I've just been hearing about the autopsy results."

"No. And there's still no sign of the murder weapon. We did an outside area sweep and a cell sweep. There's not a single clue to lead us in the right direction."

"What if the killer hid the weapon inside Angel Force?" I said.

Dazielle's forehead crinkled. "I don't know where they'd hide it. Would they have had enough time to conceal a knife?"

My gaze shifted around the open-plan office. "Are we still thinking it was Tatiana or Elman who stabbed Conan?"

"Unless we're dealing with the invisible man or woman, that's logical to assume," Dazielle said.

"However they got to the cell and stabbed Conan, they wouldn't have had a chance to take the murder weapon outside and dispose of it. It must be here somewhere. Have you searched the place?"

Dazielle's lips thinned, and tiny red dots flared on her cheeks. "We looked for the killer in here yesterday."

"But not the murder weapon? You didn't look in here for the knife?"

"I... I've had a lot on my mind. I assumed the weapon was disposed of as far away as possible from the crime scene." Dazielle placed a hand on her stomach as if she'd gotten a cramp.

"In an ideal situation, your killer wouldn't want the murder weapon anywhere near the victim. They'd destroy it, bury it, or throw it in the river. But this is an unusual murder, and they only had a moment to kill Conan."

"It could still be that person you saw running away. They would have tossed the murder weapon when they fled the scene," Dazielle said. "It could be outside."

"Your area sweep didn't turn up anything useful, though." I did a slow turn on my heel. "We should look closer to home. Let's search the office."

Dazielle whacked Dominic with her wings. "Why didn't you suggest that to me yesterday?"

He spluttered out words that were lost as Dazielle kept thumping him. "We were told to look for the killer, not the murder weapon."

"We could have been sitting on it all this time." She lifted a wing to take another swipe at Dominic.

I grabbed her wing and squeezed it. "Dazielle, take a breath. Dominic was doing what you were telling him to do. You need to cut your stressed out angels some slack. They all want the killer found as much as you do."

"They don't have to deal with the higher angels asking questions I have no answers for. They're stressful to be around. Isda seems sweet, but she's been difficult."

"Or maybe you're stressing out unnecessarily."

"I have a right to be stressed. The higher angels expected the trial to go smoothly. All that's been achieved is a dead body, escaped suspects, and a missing murder weapon."

"One potential escaped suspect. And we don't know this person had anything to do with the murder. Stop hanging onto that as the solution." I dropped her wing. "We should organize a search of the building to make sure nothing got missed. Then we'll decide what to do next."

Dazielle huffed out a breath. "Dominic, organize an immediate search. Ensure all angels stop what they're doing and make this a priority. Create a search line pattern from the back of the cells to the other end of the building. Make sure to include the reception area."

"I'll get right on that." Dominic shot me a terrified look before dashing away and rounding up the rest of the angels.

There was a swirl of cool air around us, and a second later, Isda drifted through the main doors. She smiled and nodded, her hands clasped in front of her. She was dressed in a long white fitted robe with a gold belt and matching headdress with feathers. She looked like something out of a Greek tragedy.

"Greetings, Tempest and Dazielle. I trust this morning brings welcome news of a resolution to this murder."

"Isda, I said you didn't need to come in today," Dazielle said. "Everything is in hand. And you'll be the first to know when I have an update."

"I can't stay away. This matter must be swiftly resolved. And this is my only priority." Isda looked around as angels scurried about.

"Of course. And we're doing our best." Dazielle sounded squeaky and her wings trembled.

"I'm interested in the victim's background." Isda floated a few steps away. "Would you be so kind as to talk me through his history?"

"No problem." It was time I stepped in before Dazielle popped her cork. "Would you like a coffee, Isda?"

"Thank you, but I've already had a chamomile and licorice tea. It was most calming."

"You should have brought some in for Dazielle."

She stood on my foot and crushed my toes. "This way, Isda. I have the information laid out in an interview room. I can tell you everything you need to know."

I limped along behind her, my toes tingling from where she'd ground them under her heel. We settled around a table covered in paperwork and photographs.

Isda leaned over and went to pet Wiggles, but her nose wrinkled, and she leaned back. "Your dog smells odd."

"He always smells like this." I was so used to Wiggles' unique hellhound odor I barely noticed it unless he'd been roasting himself in the sun.

"What a curious creature you have. He has a tang of the underworld about him. Am I correct in that assumption?" Isda's hand hovered in the air as if uncertain whether to touch Wiggles.

"He should. Wiggles is a fully fledged hellhound. I brought him back from the dead with my sister. I recommend everyone get a hellhound."

"Tempest, not now," Dazielle muttered. "Isda's not interested in getting a pet."

"Wiggles isn't really a pet," I said to Isda. "And everyone needs a sidekick. What sidekick is more loyal than a dog? Especially one with special powers and who can talk. You should look into getting your own. I know some angels have pets. Doves seem popular."

"I don't need a familiar. My powers are perfectly sublime as they are, but a companion would be nice," Isda said. "Perhaps you can assist me with that. Do you know of anyone who is handing out animals?"

"Err... it doesn't work like that. But I could take you to—"

"Perhaps we should focus on this murder," Dazielle said. "You wanted to know about Conan's background."

"Oh, of course. My apologies. There are so many wonderful distractions in this village. It's amazing you get anything done around here," Isda said.

"My team is always focused," Dazielle said. "And I have no doubt—"

"Not focused enough to see Conan get stabbed while in a locked cell." The sweetness in Isda's voice faded, and I saw a flash of the intensity Dazielle had alluded to.

"Perhaps not." Dazielle rifled through papers, keeping her gaze lowered. "Conan Nox was a fifty-year-old warlock who peddled dark magic to anyone desperate enough to use it. He specialized in violent crime, robbery, assault and battery on individuals to gain property or information, trading in illegal spells, and theft."

"It's always a tragedy when people become so misguided," Isda said.

"What about Conan's associates?" I said. "He must have hung out with some shady types. Perhaps one of them figured out how to get in the cells. He must have put noses out of joint over the years."

"Yes! That's an excellent line of thought," Isda said. "Well done."

I grinned at Dazielle as she glowered at me. "I aim to please. Go on, Dazielle."

"I was coming to that. Conan kept his dark magic dealings mainly in the family. He had a few external contacts but worked closely with his younger brother, Grady."

"Where is he?" I said.

"Grady got a long sentence for robbery using illegal magic. He was sent away based on information Conan revealed."

I leaned forward. "Conan snitched on his own brother? Grady went down for a crime Conan was involved in?"

"Conan served some time, but his sentence was a fraction of what it should have been. He laid the blame for the robbery on his brother's shoulders and claimed to be an unwilling participant. He also revealed where the stolen goods were hidden and all their plans."

"Grady must have hated him for that," I said. "It gives him the perfect motive for revenge. Where is this brother?"

Dazielle shook her head. "He can't be involved. He's in prison."

"Are you sure? Maybe he broke out and came after Conan?"

"Yes! That's another excellent question," Isda said.

Dazielle sighed. "I examined Grady's file, and he should still be inside. He has another year left on his sentence."

"You must be so grateful for having Tempest on your team," Isda said. "You might not have thought the brother was involved if she hadn't suggested it."

"I give thanks every day she's in my life," Dazielle growled out.

I stifled a laugh. "Same here. And I'm always happy to give the angels a helping hand."

Isda nodded enthusiastically. "This is so exciting. Tell me more about the crime Conan committed. I know it was a murder, but I didn't have the opportunity to process all the information. I became entranced by a shop full of tiny knitted items for infants. There were so many bright colors. Is there a store I can procure an infant and an animal? I should like to have one so I can dress it in pretty things."

I glanced at Dazielle and saw her biting the inside of her mouth. "You can't get babies from a store. I can show you Fur Baby Emporium, though. All the furry babies you could desire, all under one roof."

Isda clapped her hands together, and a shower of blinding white sparkles shot out. "Wonderful."

"So... the murder. Conan murdered Violet Oakley," Dazielle said. "He was about to meet a contact to sell some illegal magic. Violet was taking an evening walk and wandered in on the deal. Conan threw a deadly curse at her. She died in agony. It was a terrible death."

"And how do you know Conan killed this woman?" Isda said.

"We received an anonymous tip he was the killer. A search of his home in a nearby village revealed a rare cursed scroll. It was a match to the curse used to kill Violet." Dazielle flipped through more paperwork. "And one of his clients revealed where Conan got the cursed scroll. This individual had outstanding warrants against his name, but in exchange for those warrants disappearing, he revealed everything he knew about Conan's business."

Isda whacked her hand on the table. "This is all very interesting, but my colleagues and I are eager for this to be dealt with."

Dazielle gulped. "It is being dealt with. We have our best people on it."

"Why are the higher angels so interested in this case?" I said. "Was Violet someone special?"

Isda's smile was indulgent and a touch condescending. "We're all special. But we're concerned dark powers are gaining a foothold. We have to make sure that doesn't happen."

"There's always been darkness when it comes to magic. It helps balance things out."

She glanced at me. "I'm aware it's not only your dog that has a touch of the underworld about him. I believe you have a demon guest. Are your thoughts becoming troubled with darkness?"

"No more than usual. And my demon is called Frank. I've had him since I was a kid. He used to be a problem, but I barely have trouble with him anymore."

"How fascinating." Isda tilted her head as her gaze shuffled over me. "Do you ever succumb to his darkness?"

"Not often. But he's a demon, so he'll always be a chaos maker. He used to be strong. Sometimes I'd harness that power in dangerous situations. Demon strength is hard to beat."

"You let the demon loose?" Her big blue eyes blinked rapidly. "That must have been dangerous."

"If he ever got out of control, Dazielle stamped on me." I leaned closer to Isda. "She might not always look like she knows what she's doing, but Dazielle gets there in the end."

"Thanks for that ringing endorsement," Dazielle said.

There was a knock on the door, and Dominic walked in. "We've completed the search. There was no sign of any weapon."

"Thanks, Dominic," Dazielle said. She looked at me and lifted her shoulders, a hint of despair in her eyes.

"What's this?" Isda's wings fluttered. "You don't have the murder weapon."

Dazielle sighed. "Let me explain."

"You must. This is most concerning."

I shared Isda's concern about how this investigation was progressing. We had plenty of motives, but no opportunity for anyone to kill Conan, and no sign of the murder weapon.

Where did we go next?

Chapter 8

After a long morning spent with Dazielle and Isda reviewing the case information and everything we knew about Conan, I was overdue a break. And my back was aching. The hellhound papoose had been a brilliant idea, but it still meant I carried a lot of extra weight, and my muscles weren't used to it.

I checked Dazielle was occupied with Isda in her office before sneaking to Dominic's desk. "We deserve a long lunch break."

His stomach growled. "I am starving. I've barely had anything to eat since last night."

"I was thinking Tilly's restaurant. She does the most amazing artisan pizza with olives and fresh basil. I know you love pizza."

Dominic pressed a hand against his stomach. "I'm almost drooling. Are you sure Dazielle won't mind?"

"Positive. And Isda is grilling her. Dazielle's so busy with that, she won't notice us going. Besides, there's not much else we can do. We've searched the office for the murder weapon, we've reviewed Conan's case file, and all the suspects. We need food. Let's get out of here while we can."

Dominic needed no more persuading, and we snuck out of the building. Tilly ran an amazing restaurant, which was handy since she was also my best friend. I loved hanging out there, sampling the menu, and catching up on the gossip.

It wasn't busy when we got inside, and we found a table by the window.

Tilly hurried over, an order pad in her hand. Her warm smile faltered as she spotted Wiggles strapped to my chest. "Tempest, you know the rules. When it's opening hours, Wiggles needs to be outside."

"Normally, I have no problem with that. But he's not feeling himself." I rested a hand on his furry head.

"Which is even worse. I can't have a sick dog on the premises. Health and safety will shut me down."

"He's not sick. At least, I hope he's not. He just won't wake up. I think something magical got him. Possibly mean angel magic."

Tilly's eyes widened. "Awwww. Poor pup. What did he do to make the angels mad?"

"It's best you don't know. It's kind of gross."

She leaned closer. "What's he saying?"

"Wiggles keeps mumbling about sweets. I think he wants something sugary, but everything I offer won't wake him."

"We could try my desserts. I've got an incredible triple berry torte with mint cream frosting."

"You're tempting me with that," Dominic said.

"Bring over a slice with our order," I said. "And I promise, he won't move from my lap. I don't want to leave him outside when he's like this."

Tilly glanced around. "If any of the other customers complain, you'll have to eat outside." She petted Wiggles on the head. "What will it be?"

We ordered the artisan pizza and strawberry vanilla cream milkshakes. Tilly hurried off to get our order ready.

"Do you know how much longer Isda will be here?" I said to Dominic.

"I think she's sticking around until the case is solved." He played with his napkin, settling it and then moving it around on his lap. "Which isn't good for us."

Tilly brought over a tray of nibbles. "These will keep you going until the pizzas arrive."

Dominic snagged a cheese straw. "Thanks. I haven't left the office all night."

"Is Dazielle cracking the whip?"

"She is. Over all of us. Have you heard about the murder?" I said.

"Some gossip filtered through, but it's confusing. I heard someone was killed in a cell, but that can't be right," Tilly said.

"It's one hundred percent right," Dominic said. "Conan Nox was stabbed through the heart."

"Keep your voice down," I said. "Dazielle will tear a strip off you if she learns you've been gossiping."

"Sorry. Of course, but this is Tilly. She'll be discreet."

"I'm the soul of discretion." Tilly grinned. "Tell me everything."

We gave her a rundown on the victim and what we'd learned.

She shook her head as we finished the update. "If I was a betting witch, I'd say the brother is involved. It's got to sting if a family member reports you to the angels in exchange for a lighter sentence."

"It's more than that," Dominic said. "Conan's girlfriend, Tatiana, used to date Grady."

I dropped the olive I was about to pop into my mouth. "How do you know that? Why didn't Dazielle mention it?"

"She must have forgotten. She's tired. Why? Did I say something wrong?" Dominic said.

"No! You said something right. We need to know where Grady is. He has the perfect reasons for killing Conan. He wanted revenge on his snitching brother, and he wanted his woman back."

"I'll investigate." Dominic rose from his seat.

I waved at him, so he stayed where he was. "You're good. But if Dazielle hasn't checked him out thoroughly by the time we get back, we'll contact the prison."

"Your pizzas should almost be ready. I'll go grab them." Tilly hurried away.

"Conan had so many people who wanted him dead, I'm sort of amazed this hasn't happened already. But why kill him in such a difficult place?" I said.

"To make it hard on us," Dominic said. "We're tied up in knots. We've got plenty of motives but no weapons and no opportunity."

"It's possible. But we must be missing something." I chewed on a still warm cheese straw while we waited for our pizzas.

Tilly returned a moment later with two amazing smelling pizzas and set them in front of us.

"Thanks. These look incredible," I said.

Dominic lifted a slice of pizza and sniffed it, a huge smile on his face. "We should have brought Sorath with us. He doesn't know anyone around here. I bet he loves pizza, too."

"Who's this?" Tilly said. "A new recruit to Angel Force?"

"No. Sorath brought Conan over for his trial. He works at the Angel Force branch in West Oak," I said.

"West Oak. Oh, I think I know him. He's tall, ridiculously gorgeous, and makes you hot under the collar when he smiles."

"You're describing most angels," I said. "It could be him. I've never met another Sorath who works at Angel Force."

"Do you think I'm gorgeous?" Dominic said.

I grinned at him. "Don't fish for compliments. You know you are."

He chuckled and then bit into his pizza.

"How do you know Sorath?" I said to Tilly.

"I had a friend who dated him. It was a few years back, but she was really into him. He seemed serious about her, but it turned out Sorath was a ladies' man. She learned she couldn't trust him when she found a note written by another woman." Tilly tucked her pad in her pocket. "Sorath protested his innocence and said it was harmless fun, but my friend didn't want her heart broken by a smooth talking angel. She ditched him."

"We aren't all like that," Dominic said. "Some of us are desperate to settle down with the right woman."

I was careful not to make eye contact with him. "Sorath seems like a nice enough angel now. I didn't get the ladies' man vibe from him."

"It was a while ago. And I heard he settled down as he matured. Maybe he was going through a phase, wanting to sow his wild angel oats. My friend's happy now. She's married, and her first baby is on the way. I remember Sorath being a sensitive angel, though. He must be gutted this case is falling apart."

"We're all confused by it. And the suspects we have aren't lining up perfectly as the killer. Elman Oakley is one of them," I said.

Tilly's head jerked back. "But he's a shaman. He wouldn't hurt anyone."

"It was his wife Conan murdered. He has the strongest motive for killing Conan."

She pursed her lips. "Maybe Violet's death unhinged him. Could Elman have snuck in and stabbed Conan?"

"If he did, we can't figure out how," I said. "But we need to find out something conclusive soon, or Dazielle will chase after us."

"Excuse me, I couldn't help but overhear you say the name Elman Oakley."

I looked up to see Gladys Bovary hovering near the counter. "Hi, Gladys. That's right."

She bustled over. "We've all heard the terrible news about the murder at Angel Force. Was Elman involved?"

I glanced at the others, realizing we hadn't been discreet. "We're not sure. It's being investigated."

Gladys shook her head and clasped her hands under her ample bosom. "It's such a pity. Although everyone would understand why he'd seek justice on such a terrible individual. Elman's wife was a kind woman. People only ever had good things to say about her when she came to the village."

"How well do you know Elman?" I said.

"Better than most people. I've used Elman's cleansing magic for my bad back. And Elman and Violet were regulars at our knit and natter group at the village hall. We have a session tonight. I must check in on Elman and see if he'd like to come. Oh!" Her hand went to her mouth. "Or is he being held for questioning?"

"Elman knitted?" I said.

"Yes. He was enthusiastic but struggled to pick up the skills to produce anything wearable. At least, nothing you'd put on in public." She tittered. "Not that we objected. Our group is about getting together and catching up on local events, while creating beautiful items of clothing. Violet, now, she was an incredible knitter. I remember, she made a stunning rainbow sweater with a ruffled neck. It was almost too good to wear. I miss her knitting. I miss her company." Gladys leaned closer. "If Elman did anything to that bad man, we should give him a medal. We don't want dreadful types like that around Willow Tree Falls."

"Just to be clear, Elman and Violet attended your knit and natter group?" I said.

"They did. And Violet traveled miles to go to different knitting groups. She loved finding other knitters to share her passion with. Elman only came to our group, though. I think he wanted to spend more time with Violet. He was such a loyal husband."

I stared at Dominic, hoping he had the same idea as me. The fact he was ignoring his pizza and staring at Gladys with his mouth open, suggested we were thinking the same thing.

A knitting needle would make the perfect murder weapon.

Chapter 9

"Tilly, we need to take our pizzas to go," I said.

"Sure." Her gaze was full of questions, but she glanced at Gladys and nodded before taking our plates to the kitchen.

Gladys smiled broadly. "If you ever want to take up a new hobby, we have room in our little group. Angels are always welcome." She touched Dominic's arm.

He blushed, but his attention was on me. "Knitting needles?"

I shook my head. We didn't need to fuel Gladys and her gossip wagon any more than we already had. "That's right. You'd get to use knitting needles." I hopped from my seat. "Well, nice to see you, Gladys. We won't hold you up any longer."

Less than two minutes later, we were clutching our bags of food as we dashed out of Tilly's restaurant. Wiggles was still snoozing, bumping against my chest and making little snoring sounds, as we charged along the street.

I couldn't believe what I'd just discovered. Elman had access to the perfect murder weapon.

"I'm in shock," Dominic said. "Have we just figured out who killed Conan while eating lunch?"

"It's too much of a coincidence that he could have gotten his hands on something the same shape as the murder weapon. And it would have been easy to conceal. We weren't looking for a knitting needle but a thin blade. We missed this."

"Would a knitting needle be strong enough to stab someone?"

"I know little about knitting, but I think you can get metal needles. And it would have been simple to slide it up one sleeve and conceal it. None of us thought to check."

"Should we tell Dazielle what we found out?" Dominic said.

"Let's talk to Elman first. We both consider him to be a decent guy. If he did murder Conan, it'll be playing on his conscience. He'll probably be grateful for a chance to confess without Dazielle stamping into his store and accusing him of murder. And I can't wait to find out how he did it without being seen."

Elman rented several stores around the area, so he had a secure, quiet space to run his healing practice. The door to his local store was unlocked as we reached the wonky dull red front, and I headed in first. It smelt strongly of patchouli, and there was a light film of smoke from numerous incense burners dotted around the room. There was also a large feathered dreamcatcher in the window that fluttered in a light breeze.

"I won't be a moment," Elman said from out the back. "Please, take a seat and help yourself to some complimentary green tea."

"Look around for knitting needles," I whispered to Dominic.

"We don't have a search warrant. Anything I find won't be able to be used as evidence."

"Look, but don't touch. We need to know where those knitting needles are in case he tries to use them on us."

"I'll have a hunt around." Dominic poked about the shelves lining the store. They seemed to contain mainly books and positive mantras set in frames.

Elman appeared a moment later and smiled at us. "Tempest and Dominic. I take it you're not here on healing business."

"We're not. Have you got time to talk about Conan?" I said.

"Of course." His gaze settled on Wiggles. "Although is there something else I can help you with?"

"Yes. We also need to talk about your knitting."

His eyebrows flashed up. "Very well. What can I tell you about it?"

"You do knit?"

"I do." Elman gestured to some seats in one corner, and after a second of hesitation, I settled in one. He wasn't behaving aggressively and seemed more curious about why we were here than anything else.

Dominic walked over and stood behind my seat, like he was standing guard over me and Wiggles.

"How long have you been involved in the local knit and natter group?" I said.

"Three or four months."

"Why did you join that group?"

"My dear wife loved to knit. She made me this sweater." Elman plucked the front of his plum colored sweater. "She was talented with her needles."

"But why join the group as well if it was your wife's hobby?"

Elman clasped his hands together. "Violet loved to be sociable. She had commitments most days of the week. She was always out with her social groups or volunteering for a good cause. And she helped with the business too, but she'd often visit people in their homes when they were too weak to come to the store for healing. Sometimes, we barely saw each other, and I missed her company. So, I took up a hobby she enjoyed so we could spend more time together. It's always good when couples share things."

"It's also good when you give each other space."

"Oh! Of course. We didn't get in each other's way. But I liked her company. And she was happy to have me there. Even though I wasn't any good at knitting."

I decided to try a gentle approach, since Elman was being so helpful. I leaned forward in my seat, careful not to squash Wiggles. "Everyone would be sympathetic if you killed Conan. It's understandable you'd want revenge. Taking away such a wonderful woman was cruel. Perhaps, in a moment of weakness, you saw a chance to get Conan and make him pay for his crime."

Elman had been nodding along with my words. "You're right. I had an excellent reason for wanting him dead. And I wanted to see justice done. I'm aware Conan was a career criminal. Violet wasn't the only one who suffered at his hands. Conan deserved to go away for all his crimes."

"You admit you had thoughts about killing him?" I said.

"Many times. And I'm proud of none of them." He leaned forward, matching my position. "I see plenty of troubled people doing this job. I think everyone has found themselves on the wrong path and needed help to recover. Some find it easy to see where they went wrong. Occasionally, there are those who will always stumble along creating chaos and misery."

"Just like Conan. Which is why you killed him?"

A gentle sigh slid from Elman's lips. "Tempest, I practice forgiveness in all areas of my life. I teach it to others and give it to all. Even on the man who murdered my wife. I won't deny I've had dark times when I wished harm on Conan. But he was a troubled soul, and my bitterness would have only made things worse for him. I was relieved when he was arrested. It meant he could harm no one else. It was too late for Violet, but others are protected."

"No one is that decent and forgiving," I said. "You saw a chance for revenge and you took it while Conan was in his cell. How did you do it?"

"I promise you, I didn't. I loved Violet very much, but she's now serving the angels. She's doing good work in another place. And I'll see her again, one day."

I was yet to be convinced. Even the purest of hearts skipped a dark beat now and again. "You didn't take a weapon into Angel Force to use on Conan?"

Elman looked away and lifted the teapot on the table next to us. "Would either of you like green tea?"

"Not for me," Dominic said. "I always find it bitter."

"Perhaps you're not brewing it correctly. Green tea is delicate. If you use boiling water, you scorch the leaves and bring out the bitterness. Boil the kettle and wait for it to cool a moment. Then pour the hot water onto the leaves. It makes for a most refreshing drink." He lifted a cup for me.

I took it but didn't take a sip. "Walk me through your movements when you arrived at Angel Force for Conan's trial."

"Very well. If it'll put your mind at rest. Give me a moment to think." Elman took a sip of his green tea and set the cup down. "I got there ten minutes before the trial was due to start. I'd hoped to be there when Conan arrived."

"So you could figure out a way to kill him?"

"No, but I wanted to look him in the eye and see if there was any remorse. I planned to stand outside and watch as he was brought in."

"But you weren't there when he arrived," I said.

"I missed my opportunity. I was feeling unsettled when I got there, so took a walk around the building."

Most likely looking for a sneaky way into the cells, but I kept that to myself.

"When I came back, I saw you inside the reception area. For a second, I was overcome with anger, but I embraced it and allowed it to pass. Then I came into the building."

"What did you do after that?"

"Tatiana arrived, and I tried to speak to her. Then I went to the washroom before Dominic made me a tea."

I glanced at Dominic. "Were the washrooms checked during the search?"

He nodded. "They were."

"Everywhere?"

"I'll have to ask Dazielle. I didn't check them."

A flash of annoyance crossed Elman's face, but it swiftly disappeared. "I didn't kill Conan."

"Maybe not, but Conan had enemies, and some of them were there to watch his trial and sentencing. You're one of them. I'll be back in a moment." I stood and walked over to the door, taking Dominic with me. "Head back to Angel Force and do a thorough search of the washroom. Check everywhere you could conceal a knitting needle. Pipes, inside the toilet cistern, wherever there is space. Don't leave any area unsearched."

He nodded and dashed out of the store.

I returned to my seat and finally took a sip of the green tea. It was pretty good. All these years, and I'd been making it wrong.

Elman let out another sigh. "I assume your angel companion is off to find my murder weapon."

"This isn't personal, but the angels are looking pretty stupid because a prisoner was killed inside their supposedly secure cells."

"That must be difficult. I wish I could be more helpful."

I set down my cup. "Just between the two of us, how did you get inside the cell without being spotted?"

A small smile crossed his face. "I wouldn't have a clue how to do that. The place was busy with angels, and I was concentrating on remaining centered. I wanted to miss nothing during the trial and make sure I heard Conan's confession and hopefully his expression of regret." His head lowered a fraction. "I miss Violet terribly."

I didn't want to keep pushing Elman, but I felt close to getting an important answer. But there were tears in his eyes, which he'd been holding back since we started this conversation.

"May I give you something?" he said.

My eyebrows shot up at the sudden change in subject. "I've got nothing that needs centering or healing."

"We all need healing now and again. But it's not that. Violet was a prolific knitter. She loved making hats and scarves. I have something that would look perfect on you."

"Oh, there's no need."

"I insist. And I'm sure Violet would, too. I won't be a moment." Elman was up and heading into the back room before I could stop him.

I adjusted Wiggles' weight on my lap and sipped more tea. The store had a calming vibe, and even though I was questioning a murder suspect, I hadn't felt this relaxed in a long time.

Elman returned with a bulging bag of knitting. Over one arm, he had a red hat and scarf. "This color will be perfect with your skin tone. And your hair."

They were beautiful, and if my hair kept changing color, I'd need a way to hide it. "I shouldn't. It's not right to accept gifts when I'm questioning you about Conan's murder. Some people might think I'm taking bribes."

"They're not from me. Violet made them. She was always giving away her knitting as gifts. She said it brought her joy to give things to others and make them happy."

I took the soft woolen scarf and hat and stroked my fingers over them.

"Violet would have brought something to the celebration at the cemetery. We were looking forward to attending. You take these, instead, since she won't be there."

"I remember her coming to a family party a few years back. I think she gave everyone gloves."

"That sounds like my Violet. She always got excited about parties, because she knew she'd be able to chat with people and share her gifts with them. She was a social butterfly."

"Will you be at the cemetery party this year?" I said.

"I will if you don't arrest me for murdering Conan." There was a smile on his face as he spoke.

Elman was making me feel guilty for suggesting he had anything to do with Conan's death. "I sort of hope you didn't do it. I'd have to give back this hat and scarf if you did."

"No, you wouldn't. I was directed by Violet to give you those. They're gifts from her, not me. And I'll say that to anyone who questions it. Perhaps Dominic would like something, too. A royal blue would go well with his coloring."

"You'd better draw the line at giving gifts to angels whilst they're investigating this murder. I'm freelance, so I can get away with it. And definitely offer nothing to Dazielle."

"Heard and understood. No gifts for the angels."

"What about your knitting?" I said. "Do you give any away as gifts?"

He chuckled and patted the bag beside him. "I'm too embarrassed to do that. Violet was a natural with her needles, though. She'd look at a pattern and away she'd go. She could be chatting and only have half an eye on what she was doing, and it would still turn out beautifully. She was so clever."

"You found knitting more of a struggle?"

"I did. Perhaps you'd like to see some of my efforts, since it's just the two of us." He rifled in the bag and pulled out a holey dull green dishcloth. At least, I thought it was a dishcloth.

"Um... that's interesting."

"It was meant to be a sweater, but I kept dropping stitches and then got the wool in a knot." He held up the square and sighed. "I'm fine doing short rows, but if I have to do an angle or anything complicated, my knitting needles fail me."

"Are you going to keep knitting?"

He placed the green square back in the bag. "I'm not sure there's much point. I haven't been to any groups recently. I should find a hobby I'm more suited to."

"We can't be good at everything."

Elman nodded, and his gaze went back to Wiggles. "Is there something I can do for him? He's not usually this quiet."

"Wiggles has been weird for a while. He won't wake up. I tried a couple of spells, but..." I decided not to mention my magic was misbehaving, just in case Elman took advantage.

"He's such a remarkable creature."

"I always think so, but why do you say that?"

"I remember you having him when you were younger. When he was a... more normal creature."

"He's anything but that now."

"Wiggles is an asset to you. It's important to take care of the ones you love."

The door to the store was flung open, and Dominic rushed in. He held up a plastic evidence bag.

I jumped up and hurried over to him. "Did you find something?"

He nodded and passed me the bag. A long steel gray needle was inside. "It was wedged inside a pipe in the washroom. It was right at the back, but when I looked inside, there it was."

I turned to Elman. "Is there something you'd like to tell us?"

His shoulders rounded. "It's not what you think."

"You didn't put this needle in a pipe in the Angel Force washroom?" I returned to my seat with Dominic but didn't sit.

Elman didn't speak for several seconds. When his gaze lifted to meet mine, his eyes were full of regret. "I was angry with Conan. He didn't have to kill Violet. He could have chased her away or frightened her and told her to be quiet."

"Would she have kept quiet if she saw something illegal happening?"

"Most likely not. She hated to see injustice done as much as I do. But to use such a vicious curse on her." His head lowered again. "Violet didn't die peacefully, and that will haunt me forever."

"So you did something about it. You planned your revenge and took this knitting needle into Angel Force."

He nodded, not meeting my gaze. "I'd spent a long time justifying my need to kill. Violet was my best friend, and we shared everything. I don't feel whole without her. When she died, I lost part of myself."

"How did you do it?" Dominic said.

"That's just it. I didn't go through with it. I came to the building with that needle concealed up my sleeve, but I changed my mind. In my heart, I knew it was wrong. I'm not a killer. I'm a man of kindness and acceptance."

"You took a weapon into Angel Force that's a perfect fit for the wound on Conan's body," I said. "You must see that's a huge coincidence."

"I... yes, I do. But when I went to the washroom, I concealed that needle in the pipe without using it. And I was shocked when I heard Conan had been murdered. Although it felt like I had a friend helping me out."

I glanced at Dominic. He looked as confused as I felt. Elman had to be the killer.

"I understand this looks bad for me, but I'm not sorry Conan is dead," Elman said. "And I'd like to thank the person who committed the crime. It's a terrible burden to carry, but I give them my blessing. They did what I was unable to do."

"I'm not so sure about that. Elman, you need to come with us. You have questions to answer, and we need to make this interview official," I said.

His eyes widened, and he shook his head. "I have a full schedule of healing this afternoon. I'm working with a woman who survived a powerful dark spell. She needs me."

"You'll have to rearrange that appointment."

"Please, I have no plans to go anywhere. Allow me to continue my work, and I'll cooperate with you fully." Elman clasped his hands together in a prayer position. "I'm an honorable man. I just want to help others. I won't leave the store if you allow me to remain free."

"We could put an angel outside the store while we run tests on the needle," Dominic said.

"I'd appreciate that," Elman said. "My work is all I have, and there are so many people who need my help. I assure you, that's all I wish to do. You have the needle, and I'll admit to hiding it in the washroom and that I intended to murder Conan, but I didn't go through with it. Your tests will show that."

We had a possible weapon, but that wasn't enough evidence to charge Elman. "We'll arrange for an angel to guard the store. But don't leave Willow Tree Falls. If you make a run for it, we'll know you're guilty."

"I won't do that." He remained in his seat. "Thank you for having faith in me."

I headed to the door with Dominic. We left the store, and I stood outside in silence, mulling over everything Elman had said.

"What do you think?" Dominic said. "Have we found our prime suspect?"

"Yes, I think we have. We need to run those tests, but I reckon we've found our killer."

Chapter 10

We hadn't found our killer. I slumped in a chair in Angel Force and dropped my head in my hands.

Wiggles shifted around, suggesting I was squishing him too tight.

"Sorry I don't have better news." Dominic pushed a carton of carrot cake muffins toward me. "We ran the tests three times. Elman was telling the truth. There was no blood on the knitting needle."

I stifled a yawn as I lifted my head and took a carrot cake muffin. I was up far earlier than normal. After questioning Elman yesterday, I'd worked at the club all night and only gotten a few hours of sleep before I was out of bed again. But I wanted this mystery solved, so sleep sacrifices had to be made.

I munched on the muffin. "Did you find anything on the needle? Maybe Elman wiped it clean before he hid it."

"He didn't. His fingerprints and clothing fibers were on it, but there was nothing from Conan. Not a single hair or a speck of blood. That needle didn't go near him."

"I was so sure we'd found our killer." I finished the muffin and licked cream frosting off my fingers. "Elman has a great motive but still no opportunity. Even with a concealed weapon up his sleeve, he couldn't have gotten to Conan."

"I was as convinced as you. And a knitting needle would have made that hole in Conan's chest. It was metal and barely bent when Cassiel tested it. It could have been used."

"It wasn't." Cassiel strode over to join us. "Come with me. I've been working on something."

I grabbed my coffee and followed Dominic and Cassiel into her office near the back of Angel Force. She had two rooms for her exclusive use. One to examine bodies and an office to write up the reports after she was done with the slicing and dicing.

As I entered her examination room, I stopped in the doorway. There was a variety of fruit lined up on a table, and they all had holes in them. "What's been going on in here?"

"I've been running through my stabbing theories." Cassiel grabbed a metal knitting needle from a pile on her desk. She hurled it at a watermelon.

"This is what you get up to when you're on your own back here?" I grinned at her.

"It's scientific work. And it disproves the theory that the knitting needle was the murder weapon." She grabbed another needle and slung it at a large green melon.

"Can I have a go?" Dominic said. "It looks like fun."

She shooed him away from the needles. "It's my fruit. Hands off."

"Let Dominic stab a melon. It does look like a laugh," I said.

"It's work, not fun." Cassiel hurled another needle. "What all this proves is that this knitting needle didn't murder Conan."

"Which means it definitely wasn't Elman." I sighed. We'd been so close to closing this case, and now we were back to square one. "Could someone else have used the knitting needle? They saw Elman stash it and took advantage?" It felt like I was clutching at straws, or rather, knitting needles.

"There are a number of reasons this knitting needle wasn't used. The hole made in Conan's chest is slightly different to that made by the needle found in the pipe. It's a close match, but there is a two millimeter difference."

"Maybe whoever stabbed Conan wriggled the needle around a bit." I grimaced at the gory thought.

"They wouldn't have had time to jiggle the murder weapon around. They had seconds to stab Conan and flee from the scene."

"What about throwing the knitting needle from a distance?" Dominic said.

"It's not an option. To puncture the chest and get to the heart, whoever did it would have had to be physically close to the victim. And Conan would have needed to be by the bars and stabbed when he wasn't expecting it." She hurled knitting needles at more fruit. "You see. Even this close, my aim isn't accurate. The crosses on each piece of fruit are the hearts. I've missed every time, and I've been doing this for hours."

"What has that fruit ever done to hurt you?" I said.

Cassiel rolled her eyes at me.

"Does this mean we need to keep looking for a different murder weapon?" Dominic looked longingly at the fruit.

"I think so. It also means we have no suspects. Elman planned to murder Conan but changed his mind at the last minute. And Tatiana wasn't anywhere near the cells," I said.

"That we know of," Dominic said. "She could have tricked us."

"I'm not sure how," I said.

"What about the mystery person you saw running away from Angel Force?" Dominic said.

"We don't know if they were inside the building when the killing took place. And if they were, how they got to the cells without anyone noticing."

Dazielle charged into the room. "Isda's here. I need to update her immediately. Tell me you've got evidence off the knitting needle. I've already got angels poised to arrest Elman."

"Um... not exactly," I said. "Although Cassiel has been showing off her fruit stabbing technique. It's impressive work."

"No joking. This is serious." Dazielle swiped a wing over my head. "I was thrilled when Dominic found that needle in the washroom, and I told Isda we'd almost solved the crime. I said we had a prime suspect and the murder weapon, and it was only a matter of hours until we made a formal arrest."

"You maybe got ahead of yourself," I said. "It wasn't Elman, and the knitting needle isn't the murder weapon."

Dazielle's face changed color several times. "Now I look like an idiot."

"Well, it won't be the first time that's happened."

She jabbed a finger at me. "You're not helping."

"I am. We've discounted Elman. An innocent shaman won't go to jail for a crime he didn't commit. That's a win in my book."

Isda flitted through the door, wearing an impressive white toga style dress. She had a small crown on her head, encrusted in glittering gems. "There you are, Dazielle. I'm so looking forward to seeing this criminal charged with murder. When is it happening? Where shall I sit? Should I bring snacks? Ooo! Is that fruit our snack?"

Dazielle pasted a false smile on her face. "There's been a small delay in bringing charges against Elman."

"Oh! How disappointing. And I was planning to spend the rest of my time in Willow Tree Falls sightseeing. Should I postpone my planned walking tour? It starts in two hours. I thought I'd have plenty of time."

"You can still go sightseeing," I said. "Have you tried the thermal spa?"

Her intense blue eyes sparkled like the gems in her crown. "I intend to. I was looking at the sessions you can book. I want to try the mud. It sounds wonderful. It doesn't stick in our wing feathers, does it?"

Dazielle shook her head. "Why don't you go this morning after your walk? I'm sure by this afternoon, everything will be wrapped up."

I frowned at Dazielle. She was making promises we couldn't keep. We had no murder weapon, no suspects, and no way of knowing how Conan was killed. We were exactly nowhere.

She ignored me. "I'll take you to my office, and we can book you in at the thermal spa. Right this way."

Isda hesitated by the door. "You should come with me, Dazielle. I want to talk to you about the modernization plans we have for Angel Force."

"Great. I can't wait." Dazielle shot me a death stare as she hurried Isda out of the room.

"This is bad," Dominic whispered. "Dazielle seems to think it's our fault we haven't solved this murder."

"She's only stressing because Isda's on her case. She just wants someone to blame."

Cassiel picked up a knitting needle and slammed it into a watermelon.

"You can stop doing that," I said. "Your theory has been proven."

"It's a great way of burning off anger." Cassiel grabbed another needle and turned to me. "Although I need a bigger target."

I backed to the door. "I need a break from all this angel anger."

"Wait! You're not giving up on the investigation, are you?" Dominic followed me to the door.

"No, but I need to do something productive. If Dazielle and Isda are off getting mud baths, we've got some breathing room. And I have a huge family party to be involved in."

"When will you be back?" Dominic hurried after me. "Can I come with you?"

I stopped by the main doors. "Relax. I'll be back. I just have other things to do."

He looked over his shoulder. "Promise?"

I patted his arm. "Yes. I'll catch up with you later." I hurried away from Angel Force, clutching Wiggles in his papoose. I was at a dead end with this mystery. Maybe time away would give me a clear head. And what better distraction than planning an enormous party in a cemetery.

***

"The extra drinks order will be here tomorrow. I've double-checked the playlist you've selected for the music, and there are no problems there." Merrie grinned at me from behind the bar. "I can't wait for the party. I even got a new dress."

"It's all looking good." I leaned against the bar in Cloven Hoof. I'd spent all day and most of the evening going over the final plans for the cemetery party. It had been great to not think about the mysterious murder or have Dazielle breathing down my neck. And Isda must have convinced her to go to the thermal spa, because I hadn't heard from her all day. I was hoping it stayed that way.

Merrie slid around the bar and walked over to where Wiggles was fast asleep in a booth. She tickled him under the chin. "He's still not getting up?"

"Nope. Nothing will convince him to open his eyes. I need to get the specialists in. Granny Dottie might know a spell, or I'll take him to Fur Baby Emporium. Abigail will know spells specifically for animals. Between us, we'll figure it out."

"I don't mind trying another healing spell."

"Sure, go for it." I hadn't tried any more healing magic on Wiggles. My power still felt wonky, and I didn't want to blast him with the wrong spell.

Merrie rested her hands on Wiggles' side, and a warm pink glow covered him from nose to tail.

His paws kicked in the air a few times, but his eyes didn't open.

She kept the spell in place for five minutes before drawing it back, a frown on her face. "I'm sure he's not ill. Healing spells aren't having any effect because there's nothing wrong with him, at least, not physically."

"Not waking up is a problem, though. What else could it be?"

"A sleeping hex? You know, like in the fairy tales. What has he been eating?"

"What hasn't he been eating? Maybe he did pick up something he shouldn't. Some rogue magic user left a tainted burger on the ground and Wiggles gobbled it up without me noticing." I shook my head. "This happened after Cassiel dragged him off Conan's body. Maybe Conan had something on him he shouldn't. But he'd have been searched for dangerous magic before going in the cell. It can't be that."

"You need to do some sleuthing into what Wiggles got up to before he slipped into this sleep state," Merrie said. "And he needs to wake up soon, or he'll miss the party. Wiggles loves a good party."

"He does. He'll be mad if he doesn't get a chance to snaffle food from the huge buffet we've got planned."

Merrie headed back to the bar and joined me as I sipped on a lemon drop.

"I should threaten to bathe him," I said. "That would wake him up."

"Awww. You can't do that. Not when he can't fight back. I always love seeing him race down the stairs soaking wet and covered in soap suds every time you give him a wash."

"It's the highlight of my month as well." I chuckled. "We've been at this for hours. Take a break before it gets busy with the evening crowd. Go grab some food."

"I've already eaten. Do you want anything? I can get something from the kitchen if you're hungry."

"No, you're good. Are you sure you don't want a break?"

She shook her head. "I'm happy here. I'll just hang out by the bar until the first customers arrive."

"I'm going to get some fresh air."

Merrie raised her chin at Wiggles. "Do you want to leave him here with me? I'll keep an eye on him."

"My back would love you forever for doing that."

"Put him behind the counter. I'll make him comfortable."

I collected Wiggles and tucked him at the back of the bar so he wouldn't roll off the counter. I grabbed my jacket and headed into the early evening. It was quiet on the streets, most of the stores just shutting for the night. I nodded greetings to several store owners as I headed to the edge of the woods. As soon as I stopped thinking about the upcoming party, my thoughts turned to Conan's murder.

There had to be a solution to this puzzle. I needed to find that mystery person who'd fled the scene. They were the key to all of this. Find them, learn how they crept into Angel Force without being noticed, and charge them with murder. Then this would be dealt with, and I'd have Dazielle off my back.

A flash of movement in the woods made me slow. It wasn't unusual to see supernatural creatures roaming around. And Fallon, the forest guardian, was often out checking on things and setting traps for unwitting people to stumble into.

I peered through the trees. Whoever it was, they were too big to be Fallon. And they were on two legs, so it ruled out a lot of forest creatures. I crept into the woodland a few feet to see what they were up to.

A large black shape continued further into the trees, so I followed. Maybe it was a member of Rhett's former gang up to no good. He'd hooked them up with a new leader, and so far, things were going well, but maybe someone got tempted back into their old ways. The gang sometimes used the seclusion of the woodland to do dodgy deals.

I stopped in front of a small white feather on the ground. I picked it up and turned it over. I'd seen plenty of these feathers over the years.

This belonged to an angel. I kept following the path, keeping a safe distance between me and the stranger in black.

Several more feathers appeared. I was certain I was following an angel, and they were in disguise. All angels wore white. It was their trademark, along with the gorgeous looks and blonde hair. Why would an angel dress in black and skulk about the woods?

I drew closer, ducking behind a tree as the mystery angel reached up and tucked something in between two tree branches. I waited until they'd walked away before hurrying over to see what they'd left behind.

It took a few jumps to reach up high enough, but my fingers closed over something bulky, and I pulled it down. It was an envelope, and when I opened it, it was full of money.

I flipped through the notes. There was no message to say what this money was for or who'd left it. But you didn't leave a huge wedge of cash in a tree if you were doing something legitimate.

There was a gasp, and my head shot up. Sorath stood in front of me, the hood on his black sweatshirt down, revealing his blond hair.

I lifted the envelope. "Did you leave something behind?"

Chapter 11

"This isn't what it looks like." Sorath held his hands up, palms facing me.

"It looks to me like you've made a dodgy money drop in the middle of nowhere. That's hardly normal behavior. What's going on?" I lifted the envelope full of money.

He scrubbed at the back of his neck. "It's complicated."

"These things usually are. How about we head to Angel Force and you tell Dazielle what's going on?"

Sorath glanced around, as if looking for an escape route.

"Don't do anything dumb. You won't get far if you make a run for it." Although I didn't want to test my misfiring magic on a strong angel.

His shoulders rounded, and the nervous energy faded out of him. "I'm so embarrassed. I was trying to make things right by leaving the money here."

"Let's walk back to the office. Dazielle won't believe one of her angels has done anything wrong unless she hears it from you herself."

"Do we have to? Can't I tell you what I did and you pass it on? She's scary when she's cross."

"You haven't seen her when she's really angry." I pointed over my shoulder with my thumb. "Let's move."

Sorath dragged his feet as he walked along, and we headed out of the woods.

I kept a tight hold on the money, but he didn't seem anxious to get his hands on it. "Were you buying something illegal with this?"

"No! I'd never do that."

"So you were paying someone off?"

His wings drooped around him. "It was only supposed to be fun, but things got out of control. I should have known better."

I tucked the money inside my jacket. This story did sound tricky. "You'd better hope Dazielle's had her dinner. She's even meaner when she's hungry."

His expression was one of defeat. "I'm not a bad angel."

"Sure, you aren't. And we all make mistakes. Come on."

We headed into the Angel Force building and through to the main office. Dazielle's office door was closed. She was in there with Isda.

I thought about waiting, but the news would eventually get back to the higher angels about what I'd discovered. I knocked on the door and opened it.

Dazielle glared at me. "We're in a private meeting."

"This can't wait." I gestured Sorath into the office. "Sorath has something to tell you."

"Has there been a development with the case?" Dazielle stood from her seat.

Sorath tugged at the collar of his sweatshirt and spent a long time adjusting his cuffs. "Tempest found me doing something I shouldn't."

I took out the envelope of money and placed it on the desk.

His cheeks flushed. "I got myself in trouble."

"What kind of trouble?" Isda said. "I'm sure it can't be anything serious. We all have little hiccups now and again."

He glanced at me, and I gestured for him to go on. "A friend introduced me to an online gambling site a few months ago. Then we visited a town full of mortals and heard this noise, and there were bright lights everywhere. She said it would be fun. So we went inside, and before I knew it an hour had passed."

"You're talking about a casino?" I said.

"Yes. It was incredible. There were so many fun games to try, and we were served free food and drink. I started small, placing the occasional bet and learning the games and how to win."

"You don't win when you're in a casino," I said.

"I realize that now. But I kept going back. There was this incredible power pulling me to the casino. Before I knew it, I'd burned through my savings. I was broke, but I still wanted to play. Then someone approached me and asked if I wanted more money. She said their rates were reasonable, and I'd have time to pay it back once I was on a winning streak."

I groaned. "And you couldn't resist getting this loan?"

His head hung down. "I was taken advantage of. I feel so stupid. I didn't win the next game, or the ones after that. All the money I borrowed was gone, and I had no way of paying it back."

Dazielle looked like smoke was about to come out of her ears as she listened to Sorath's tale of woe. "Where did you get this money? Is this another loan?" She tapped a finger on the desk.

"No. Someone approached me when I was outside the casino," he said hesitantly.

"And they gave you a stack of cash to pay off your debt?" I said.

"Yes." He gulped loudly. "After I agreed to help them with a small job."

"What did you agree to do?" Dazielle said.

Sorath licked his lips and stared at the ceiling. "I agreed to set off the alarm and cause a distraction when Conan was brought here."

Isda made a funny screeching sound, and Dazielle sucked in a breath.

"You were paid to help the killer get to Conan?" Dazielle said.

"Or maybe you were the killer," I said.

"No! I didn't kill Conan. That would have been impossible. I was simply paid to set off the alarm. I had no idea there was a plan to stab Conan. I'd have never gone through with it if I'd known."

"You must have wondered why they wanted the distraction caused," I said.

"I did, but they said I didn't need to know the whole plan. Just set off the alarm once Conan was behind bars, and they'd do the rest. And I really didn't think they planned to hurt Conan because he knew about it."

"How do you know that?" I said.

"He spoke to me during his pre-trial and said he knew I was having difficulties and had a way to help." Sorath gulped again. "I told him I didn't know what he was talking about, but he said to watch out and someone would be in touch to give me a financial boost. Nothing happened for weeks, and I forgot about it. Then one evening, I was at the casino. Someone slid out of the shadows, dressed head to toe in black. They shoved the money in my hand and told me to set off the alarm once Conan was here."

"You didn't think about protesting? Or tell them to get lost?" I said.

"I should have. I thought about it, but they'd already gone." Sorath's worried gaze went to the door. "And there was a game in the casino I really wanted to win. I didn't spend it all, though. The money in the envelope you found is what's left. I intended to pay off my loan."

"What did this person look like?" Dazielle said. "Maybe it's a suspect we've already spoken to."

"It was dark and late, and they'd hidden their face. It was a man, but I can't say more than that. They weren't that tall."

"That's no help. Everyone looks short when you're an angel," I said.

"I can't tell you anything else about them," Sorath said. "And I changed my mind a dozen times about setting off the alarm on my way here. It's one of the reasons we were late. I took the long route because I couldn't make up my mind about what to do. The money in that envelope would have paid off half of what I owe and given me time to get the rest."

"I don't understand why you were leaving the money in the woods," I said.

"I arranged with the debt collector to meet at a secure drop-off point. I told her I'd gotten some money, and we fixed up a meeting." His sad gaze moved around the room. "That was all I did. I found myself in trouble and was offered a solution. I didn't kill Conan. I was in the reception area with Cassiel and hit the alarm on my way back to you. I didn't have time to get to the cell."

"I'm disappointed in you," Isda said. "Other magic users hold angels in the highest esteem. We can't allow ourselves to become distracted by such simple things as gambling. Although the casino sounds fun. I might have to investigate, purely for research reasons."

"Be careful," I said. "Those places are designed to be addictive."

"We are above such things." Isda shook her head.

"I really regret what I did. But I had no reason to want Conan dead. If the deal had been to kill him, I would never have agreed," Sorath said.

"I'll have to remove you from this case," Dazielle said. "But you're to remain in Willow Tree Falls until we figure out what to do with you. Sorath, you've committed a serious crime."

"But I'm no killer."

She pursed her lips. "I believe you. Other angels saw you when Conan was being killed."

He nodded. "I'll admit to being involved with setting off the alarm, but that's it."

"It's more serious than that," Dazielle said. "Conan was killed because of your distraction. Your actions had serious consequences. You'll lose your job and possibly be charged with a serious criminal offence."

"Please, I just made a mistake."

"I should take this matter to the higher angels, and we'll discuss it," Isda said. "We'll check Sorath's record and determine the sentencing for this unfortunate event."

"This doesn't need to go up the ranks any higher," Dazielle said. "This is a disciplinary matter. I'll liaise with Sorath's superior, and we'll decide what to do with him."

"No." Anger flashed in Isda's eyes. "I'm involved in this case. And I want to make sure things are done properly."

Dazielle looked like she wanted to scream but instead nodded. "As you wish."

"I'll leave you to it." Isda vanished.

"You'd better go too, Sorath," Dazielle said. "Are you staying at the hotel?"

"Yes. I'll be there. And I really am sorry."

We waited until he'd left the room, then I sat in the chair opposite Dazielle. "I never expected that. Sorath is a crooked angel."

She huffed out a breath. "Why were you following him? Did you know about the money?"

"No. I was taking a break from the club when I saw him sneaking about in the woods. He was acting suspiciously, so I watched him. I saw Sorath leave something in a tree and retrieved it. He must have heard me poking about because he came back. And he didn't protest when I brought him here. He knows he's guilty."

"Guilty of being an idiot but not of murder."

"Even so, why don't we check out his story? We go back to the drop-off point and see who shows up. We don't want him to pull the wool over our eyes for a second time. I thought he was an honest angel."

"It's not a terrible idea. And I need a break after being cooped up in here. Isda keeps going over the case file again and again. I promised I'd keep her informed whenever we have new evidence, but this is getting ridiculous. She won't leave me alone."

"I know someone who can be like that. It's annoying, isn't it?"

Dazielle snapped her fingers. "Get up and take that money. Let's go back to the woods." She marched out of Angel Force ahead of me.

I couldn't help but grin as she strode along, her wings fluttering with indignation. I hurried ahead of her and led her back into the trees. "Does Sorath's behavior make you question your other angels?"

"He's not one of my angels. He's from a different division."

"Sure, but over the years we've worked together, you've always said your angels were infallible. They can't be corrupted and are always pure of heart."

"That's true. What's your point?"

"We've proven otherwise more than once. We've met vengeful angels, gambling addicted angels, cheating angels, lying angels. Could it be, angels aren't as pure as they make out they are?"

"Most of us are unaffected by the corruptions of the outside world, but there are always exceptions."

"Would you consider yourself an exception, considering you forced Dominic into marrying you?"

She was silent for several seconds. "That was different. I was under a lot of stress."

"You say that often. Do you think it's an excuse for your bad behavior?"

"I need to find an excuse to make you disappear," she grumbled. "Where's the tree you found the money in?"

"Just up ahead." I stopped by a broad oak tree and pointed at the branch above me. "You can do the last bit. Place the money up there. That's where I found it."

Dazielle snatched the money out of my hand and shoved it in between the tree branches. We retreated behind a nearby birch and waited.

She slid me a glare. "Perhaps I was unfair on Dominic with the whole marriage situation. I'm making amends for that."

"I heard. He told me about the cold cases you've got him working on."

"It keeps him happy. And... perhaps he's a better angel than I realized."

"Don't tell me you've developed a crush on him. That would complicate things, crushing on your ex-husband after a fake relationship."

"Absolutely not. And after my brush with marriage, I'm happy to live the single life for a long time."

"That's what I like to hear. You're a strong, independent angel. But are you sure Dominic hasn't turned your head? He's very sweet."

"Completely sure." She glanced around. "Where's Wiggles?"

"I left him in the bar with Merrie. He's still not waking up."

"It's odd not having him around."

"I thought you'd be happy. You can't stand him."

"I never said that."

"Your actions speak volumes. You're always chasing Wiggles away whenever he gets too near to you."

"That's because he smells funny and is always stealing food. What else am I supposed to do?"

"Tell him he's a good boy and give him a cookie?"

She muttered under her breath. "I don't like to think of him being ill."

"Then make Cassiel tell me what she did to him."

"It wasn't her. I asked her about it. Our power can't harm the innocent." Dazielle shuffled her wings around. "If you keep having trouble with him, I know some contacts in the angel community. They're experts in healing magic. That could be what he needs."

I was taken aback by her show of kindness. "I appreciate that. Although I don't think he's sick. I suppose it could be my magic still messing about. Maybe it's influencing Wiggles, too."

Dazielle stiffened and turned to me. "Your magic is still going wrong?"

"Oh, kind of. I mean, not really."

"Tempest! You should have told me if you can't do your job properly."

"I can do my job perfectly. It's just now and again, my spells don't come out the way they're supposed to."

"You should get that looked at."

"It'll sort itself out. It's a magical glitch. Zandra and Aurora are having the same problem. It's most likely the stone circle kicking out the wrong vibes."

"Make sure that glitch doesn't get any worse, or I'll have no use for you."

"You know I'm indispensable."

"You're incorrigible."

I tilted my head. "Someone's coming."

We crouched as footsteps approached. A moment later, a slim figure wearing a black hat appeared. She looked around then hurried to the tree, hopped up, and grabbed the envelope.

As her feet hit the ground, I emerged from behind the tree with Dazielle. "Hey. Are you out for a spot of late-night birdwatching?"

The woman stumbled back and clutched the money to her chest. "Maybe. What's it to you?" She was in her mid-thirties, with short dark hair peeking out from under her hat.

"What business do you have in Willow Tree Falls?" Dazielle marched over and towered over the woman.

Her eyes widened as she licked her lips. "I'm picking something up. I'll be getting out of your way now."

"Not so fast," I said. "Who told you that money would be here?"

Her fingers tightened around the envelope. "It's mine."

"I'm not saying it isn't, but who left it for you to pick up and why?" I said.

"It's a private matter."

"And we won't gossip. But you need to tell us, unless you want my winged friend here to put you behind bars."

"I'm not doing anything wrong. This is a legitimate pickup."

"So tell us the name of your contact."

She scowled at me. "Sorath the angel. That's all I know. He's tall, eye wateringly gorgeous, and as dumb as they come."

"Where did you meet this beautiful dumb angel?" I said.

"In a casino in Mudlark. He had no clue how to play any of the games, and when he ran out of money, I offered to keep the fun going."

"You gave him a loan?" Dazielle said.

"I did. And now he's paying some of it back, just like he said he would. I figured he'd come good, eventually. Not that it's going to help him. I've seen him in the casino again. The guy doesn't know when to quit."

"So you were right," I said to Dazielle. "Sorath is an idiot, but he's not a killer."

"Wait. What's this about a killing? I'm not involved in that. I just loan the money, then I get it back with interest." The woman backed away.

Dazielle pulled the envelope of money out of her hand. "Not this time, you're not. This money is evidence."

"Evidence of what?"

"Evidence that if you don't get out of here quickly, we'll bring you in for further questioning," I said.

She scowled but turned and walked away. She looked over her shoulder. "Tell Sorath I'll be coming for that money. He's not getting out of paying his debt because he's got powerful friends."

"Did you hear that? She thinks we're powerful," I said.

Dazielle thrust the money at me. "I can't help Sorath, but his story has been confirmed. It still means he'll lose his job. Maybe worse. He helped facilitate a murder."

"And it also means we're running out of suspects," I said. "We have barely anyone left to question."

"We have Tatiana, and the criminal brother, Grady."

"True. Let's find out what the brother's been up to. We can visit him in prison. You have checked he's still there?"

"Not yet, but that's what his file said. I've no reason to doubt it."

"Paperwork isn't always right. Let's go see him."

Dazielle shook her head. "I wish I could, but I have to take Isda to dinner. She's excited about going to Tilly's restaurant and made me promise I'd take her there tonight."

"She prefers stuffing her face to solving crime?" I shrugged. "I can get on board with that."

"I can't put her off. It'll only give her another reason to dislike me." We stopped by the edge of the trees. "And she won't forget I've made the reservation. I get the impression she's more interested in sampling life on this plane than helping with the murder."

"She does seem excited by mud baths and meals out."

"I'll get Dominic to run background checks on Grady tonight. We can get to work on investigating him in the morning," Dazielle said.

"Excellent idea. And I have a club to run and cocktails to sample for the party."

"Don't show up at Angel Force with a hangover tomorrow."

"Would I?"

Dazielle arched an eyebrow at me then turned and stomped away.

I watched her go and laughed. It was the end of another fun evening with my favorite grumpy angel. What entertainment would tomorrow bring?

Chapter 12

"It's another dead end." Dazielle heaved out a sigh as she tapped the paperwork in front of her.

I was seated across from her the next morning, a large coffee in one hand and the other clasping a sleeping Wiggles in his papoose. "What did the background check on Conan's brother show?"

"He's just as shady as Conan. He's the younger brother but also into dark magic." She shoved the file at me.

I flicked through the papers and studied the photos. "Is Grady still serving his sentence?"

Her eyes narrowed. "Grady recently got out early for good behavior. It's only just happened, so the information I had on him was out of date."

"This is good news. If he's on the loose, he could be here. Grady could have snuck into Willow Tree Falls and killed Conan."

"That's not possible. He needs a permit to travel as part of his probation. He has to get permission to leave his village."

"Okay, but permits can be faked. Or he ignored the fact he needed a permit and came here, anyway."

"That's possible on both counts, but he also wears a tracker. That's not moved from his place of residence in over forty-eight hours. You can't fake those so easily."

"But they can be faked?"

"With money and skill. And Grady's been inside for over a decade."

"Gathering shady contacts to help him make a fake tracker?"

Dazielle shrugged. "From his record, he was a model prisoner. He had no time added to his sentence and even took a degree in mythological creatures while he was inside."

"What's he planning to do with that? Become a monster hunter now he's free?"

"What I'm saying is he's a reformed character. No fights, no black marks on his report, and he even volunteered in the prison library twice a week."

"Which is great, but he could still harbor a grudge against his brother. He got away with a serious crime and Grady ended up inside. And we're not forgetting the whole girlfriend stealing thing. Tatiana dated Grady. Then she moved on to Conan. If Conan stole Tatiana from Grady, he won't have forgotten that."

"Grady's at home. No permit has been processed, and the magic tracker is where it should be. He can't be in two places at once," Dazielle said.

"Have you sent any angels to his house to check if he's really there?"

A muscle twitched in her jaw. "I'm not an idiot. I was about to do that."

"After I reminded you?"

"No! It's on my list." She tapped a pad on her desk.

"Great. Then you do that, and I'll look into taking a degree in mythological creatures. It sounds interesting." I petted Wiggles on the head. "What do you reckon?"

There was a knock at the door, and Dominic strolled in.

"What's that half-dead looking thing around your neck?" Dazielle's gaze ran over the hideous lime green and yellow scarf covering his throat.

Dominic grinned. "I've been undercover, gathering information."

"What kind of information? And why do you need to wear an ugly scarf to do that?" I said.

"You don't like it?"

"Maybe it's the clashing colors setting my eyeballs on fire," I said.

He patted the scarf. "I had to take part, or I'd have looked suspicious. I joined the knit and natter group last night. Those ladies are intense. They know everything about Willow Tree Falls and the surrounding villages. They're a fount of knowledge. And they were so welcoming. I told them I was a novice and didn't know the first thing about knitting, but they promised me I'd be able to knit a scarf by the end of the night. This is what I created."

"It's got holes in it," Dazielle said.

"You know, the more I look at it, the more I like it. It's unique. It's just like you," I said.

He grinned at me. "I've gotten the knitting bug. I'm definitely going to try again."

"What did you learn from going undercover?" I said.

"So much. And I was given an incredible recipe for the perfect sponge cake. I'm trying it tonight if you want to come over and taste test with me." Dominic looked at me as he spoke.

"Let's stick to the job in hand," Dazielle said. "Did you get anything useful from the group other than recipes and knitting tips?"

"I did. It didn't take long before I turned the conversation to Elman and Violet. Elman joined the group a few months after his wife. He turned up unexpectedly, and it was clear Violet was surprised to see him. They even argued."

"What was the argument about?" I said.

"They were having it quietly outside, but it was clear to everyone in the group there were problems between them. Eventually, they went back in, and Violet introduced Elman to the group. But apparently, things were tense between them."

"It sounds like Elman was keeping tabs on his wife," I said. "He showed me his knitting when I went to talk to him, and I got the impression he didn't enjoy it that much."

Dazielle sat forward in her seat. "Why do something you don't enjoy?"

"Because he didn't trust Violet." I looked over at Dominic. "Is that the vibe you were picking up from the gossip?"

He nodded. "Apparently, when Elman went to the restroom, they asked if Violet was okay. She made a show of acting like it was fine, but there was tension in their marriage. And on the odd occasion Elman didn't go with her, she revealed things were strained between them and she was glad she could have time alone."

"Elman painted a different story when we spoke to him. He always talks warmly about his wife and claims they were the perfect couple," I said.

"Maybe he's doing that because she's dead," Dazielle said. "You forget the bad side of a person when they're no longer with you and only remember the good times."

"Was my undercover work any good?" Dominic said. "I thought I was being helpful by getting some inside information."

"Not really," Dazielle said. "It's gotten us nowhere."

Dominic's bottom lip jutted out.

I stood and tweaked the scarf around his neck. "You did amazing. And after a few more weeks of knitting, you'll be a professional. Don't give up trying if you're having fun."

His face brightened. "Thanks, Tempest."

Dazielle sighed. "Since our investigation into Grady brought up nothing useful, let's pay Tatiana a visit."

"You should double-check all the information you have on Grady. If his file is out of date, something else could have been missed," I said.

"I'm sure it hasn't," Dazielle said.

I lifted one shoulder. "You're in charge."

This time, her sigh was twice as loud and dramatic. "Tatiana's renting a villa on the posh side of the village."

"I wonder where she got the money to do that," I said.

"We'll ask her." Dazielle led us out of her office. "Dominic, stay here and run through the checks on Grady again. We must make sure nothing has been missed."

"I'll get right on that." He dashed away to his desk.

I resisted the urge to laugh. Dazielle hated anyone pointing out she might not be doing the best job in the world.

We left Angel Force and headed to the wealthy part of the village where the houses were detached and the gardens neat and orderly.

"Do I need to remind you to be less mean to Dominic?" I said.

Dazielle tipped her head back. "I'm trying. But Isda's still on my back."

"You were mean about his scarf."

"So were you."

"And you said his undercover work was pointless."

"Not in so many words." Dazielle's wings fluttered around her. "Isda didn't enjoy our dinner last night. She kept complaining about the music and the other customers."

"She must have loved Tilly's food, though."

"That wasn't the problem. It seems she's sensitive to noise."

"You should have given her noise canceling headphones."

She shot me a caustic look. "I'll try that the next time."

"I really don't know why you think she's so difficult."

"She's always judging me. Isda is particular and doesn't understand how this world works."

"That happens a lot with higher angels. They should spend less time in the clouds and more time on the ground. Has she made any comments to make you think she's unhappy with your work?"

"No, it's just the way her eyes scan over me. And she made a comment about my wing feathers not being white. She said they looked more like a caramel cream." Dazielle spread out her wings. "They don't, do they?"

"Your wings look good to me. Maybe she's jealous of you."

"Of... me?"

"Of course. You run a successful branch of Angel Force, you've got me and Wiggles as your amazing freelancers, you have my family looking after the awesome demon cemetery just down the road, and you've got the best team. You might not think that much of your angels at times, but they're a decent bunch. Although Cassiel can be a grouch."

"Maybe you're right. Isda could be jealous. I have to remember that the next time she's judging me."

We headed to Tatiana's white villa, the front covered in fragrant yellow honeysuckle.

It took several loud knocks and waiting around for a few minutes before she opened the door. "Oh, it's you." She was dressed in a silk green kimono, her feet bare.

"We didn't get you up, did we?" I said.

"No. I was busy in the kitchen. What do you want?"

"We have a few questions about Conan's murder," Dazielle said.

Her lips thinned. "I figured you'd be by, eventually. Have you found the killer yet?"

"We're still following several lines of inquiry," Dazielle said.

"Which means you know nothing." Tatiana opened the door wider. "Come in."

We followed her along a large white hallway dotted with photographs taken in the nearby forest.

Tatiana led us into the kitchen and pulled a plate of cheese and meat out of the fridge and placed it on the counter.

"We're working every angle. We will find Conan's killer," Dazielle said.

Tatiana buttered slices of bread. "What do you want from me?"

"This is a nice place you're renting," I said. "It must cost a lot."

"What if it does?"

"Where did you get the money to pay for a place like this?"

"Maybe I'm a highflying executive. I could be a lawyer charging thousands an hour." She smirked at me. "It's none of your business where I get my money from."

"It is our business if your money comes from the proceeds of crime," Dazielle said.

"I don't know anything about that."

"You're the girlfriend of a career criminal," I said. "You've never seen anything odd? Or maybe accepted cash gifts you knew came from crime?"

"Nope. And I can't help who I fall in love with."

"Perhaps Conan gave you the money to rent this villa," Dazielle said.

"Or Grady?" I said.

Tatiana kept making cheese and meat sandwiches, stacking them on a plate. "I never asked Conan where he got his money from. So long as he looked after me, I couldn't care less."

"Was Grady the same?" I said. "Or is that why you left him for his brother? He didn't pay you enough to stay with him?"

She slammed down the knife. "Grady was always good to me. He never said no to anything I asked for. Don't speak badly about him."

"So you admit you dated both brothers?" I said.

"What if I did?"

"You were involved with two dangerous criminals for a number of years," Dazielle said. "And you never thought to ask them about where their money was coming from? You never had concerns your lifestyle was funded from crimes committed on other people?"

Tatiana shrugged. "They have to do what they have to do. I don't ask, and they never told me about their business. Why are you so interested in Grady, anyway?"

"Who did you date first?" I asked.

Her chin lifted. "Why is that important?"

"Was it Grady?" I said.

"Maybe."

"What changed? Why switch your affection to Conan?"

She gripped the knife. "I got close to Conan when I was dating Grady. I never hid the fact I liked both of them, and they knew what was going on."

"Did you date them at the same time?" I said.

"No. Grady asked Conan to look out for me when he went inside. He didn't want me vulnerable on my own."

"And instead of him doing that, Conan stole you from Grady?"

Tatiana's eyes flashed me a warning. "I make up my own mind about what man to be with. Nobody told me what to do. And I have my needs. Grady was no good to me on the inside."

"You're talking about the money you could no longer get your hands on?" I said.

"Maybe I am, maybe I'm not. Or maybe Grady simply gave good foot rubs, and I missed those. Anyway, Conan was nice to me and made sure I was looked after. Things happened between us."

"What did Grady think about your relationship with his brother?" Dazielle said.

"He wasn't happy at first, but he'd much rather it was Conan than some stranger in my bed. He knew Conan would look after me." Tatiana stacked up a final sandwich and placed a hand on her hip. "So, who do you think killed Conan?"

"We're not certain." Dazielle's gaze shifted around the kitchen.

"You won't find the murder weapon here if that's what you're looking for." Tatiana grabbed a jar of pickles from the cupboard. "I'm sure it was that creepy shaman."

"Did you see Elman do something to make you suspicious?" I said.

"No, but no person is that good, and he must have hated Conan for what happened to his wife. Silly woman, getting in the way of things."

"Violet was simply out for an evening walk," I said. "She didn't know she'd stumble into the middle of a dark magic transaction."

"Then she should have paid more attention. This place is full of magic users. You must come across all kinds around here."

"Not on my watch," Dazielle said.

"You have a good motive for wanting Conan dead," I said.

Tatiana's eyebrows shot up. "Do I really. What would that be?"

"Grady was coming out of jail, and you wanted to start up with him again."

She wiped her hands together. "I was done with Grady. I had no problem with him, but I was happy with Conan. Besides, you're missing something important. I wasn't anywhere near Conan when he was murdered. You're not pinning this on me. Now, if you want to grill me anymore, I'll contact my lawyer. You're not catching me out."

"We're not trying to catch you out," I said.

"If you don't leave right now, I'll file a harassment charge." Tatiana pointed at the door.

"Thank you for your time," Dazielle said. "And don't go anywhere. We could have more questions for you."

"Ask them through my legal team. I'm not interested in hearing from you until you find

Conan's killer." Her arm remain raised until we left the kitchen.

We walked out of the villa, and Tatiana slammed the door behind us.

"Tatiana must know where Grady and Conan keep their money," I said. "Maybe she got greedy and decided to get her hands on all that money. She wanted it for herself. She just needed Conan gone to have a clear path."

"But as she annoyingly pointed out, Tatiana had no opportunity to stab Conan."

We walked along in silence for several minutes.

"Tatiana's staying on her own in that villa, isn't she?" I said.

"I assume so."

"If she's on her own, why was she making all of those sandwiches?"

"She's extra hungry? Or greedy?"

"Or she's hiding someone and needs to keep them well-fed."

"Who?"

I looked back at the villa. "That's what we need to figure out."

Chapter 13

"Hey, Dominic. It's my turn to do a shift on lookout." I raised a hand as I neared him.

"Great. I was almost dozing off."

"Don't let Dazielle hear you say that."

After the earlier visit to Tatiana, I'd spent the rest of the day at the club and had just walked over to relieve Dominic from his surveillance stint. We'd found a nearby site tucked in some trees and were monitoring the villa to see if Tatiana would reveal who her secret sandwich munching friend was.

Dominic stretched his arms over his head and rolled out his shoulders. "It wasn't much fun doing a stakeout on my own. It's better when you're here. You always bring snacks."

I grinned at him as I set down a bag with food in it. "Did you see anything useful?"

"Nothing. No one has visited, and Tatiana's been inside all day. Maybe she really made all those sandwiches for herself."

"There's more to it than that. No one can stress eat that many sandwiches. You should have seen them. There was a mountain of them."

"I reckon Wiggles would give it a good go." Dominic petted Wiggles' head. "He's still sleeping?"

"Yeah, he's still fast asleep." I adjusted the papoose around my waist to give my back a break.

"I'd better get going. Dazielle ordered me to drop into the office and check over some paperwork before I headed home for the night."

"Take a pizza roll. I brought plenty." I pointed to the bag.

"Thanks." He grabbed a roll. "Just what I need."

"I'll see you tomorrow at the office."

"Looking forward to it." Dominic walked away, humming happily as he ate his pizza roll.

I took a few minutes to make myself comfortable and ensure I had a good view of Tatiana's villa before taking out a mushroom and three cheese pizza roll. I held a piece under Wiggles' nose. "If you wake up, you can have all of this."

He didn't stir.

I gently stroked his ears. "What am I going to do with you? You hate being checked over by the vet. I reckon Granny Dottie will have to fix you. Her magical blasts can wake the dead."

He wriggled around in the papoose, but his eyes remained shut.

I leaned back against a tree and finished my pizza roll. Then I ate another and poured myself a coffee from the thermos flask I'd brought with me.

I'd just finished my drink when footsteps approached. I stood and ducked around the tree. It could be a visitor coming to see Tatiana.

"Tempest! Where are you?" It was Aurora.

I poked my head out from behind the tree. "Over here. What are you doing?"

Zandra was with her, and they hurried over.

"Get down. I don't want Tatiana seeing you, or you'll give away my position." I gestured for them to duck. "How did you know I was here?"

"Dominic came into my store just as I was closing." Aurora scuttled over. "I said I wanted to see you, so he told me where you were."

Typical Dominic. He could never keep his mouth shut. "I'm working."

"He said you were doing a stakeout on some criminal's girlfriend," Zandra said. "What's she done?"

"Made too many sandwiches." I tugged Zandra down as she kept peering around.

"Huh? That's a crime?"

"It could be if those sandwiches were meant for a bad guy." I offered around the pizza rolls. "All I know for certain is Tatiana's hiding something, and I intend to find out what it is."

"We have news, too. We found out something exciting today and had to tell you." Aurora grinned at Zandra. "We've been investigating why our magic is misfiring."

"Do you know what's causing all our problems?" I said.

"We don't know the reason, but watch this." Aurora held out her hands, and Zandra clasped them. A red shimmer moved from their toes up their bodies and over their heads. It turned their hair a deep red for a few seconds before vanishing.

I blinked several times. "What was that?"

"I have no idea. We discovered it by accident," Aurora said. "I was stacking the shelves in my store, and Zandra was holding the ladder steady."

"I was actually waiting for her to get down so we could eat the cookies she'd just made," Zandra said.

"Admit it, you were helping. You like helping out in the store."

"I admit to nothing."

"Anyway, I lost my balance as I was coming down. I did a sort of flip-twist in the air, and as I held my hands out, Zandra grabbed them. That's when we experienced the red shimmer," Aurora said.

"What does it do?" I said.

"It makes me feel amazing," Aurora said. "But it's so strange. My magic feels more powerful, but I'm also tempted to misbehave."

My eyebrows shot up. "You want to do dark magic?"

"No, nothing like that. It just makes me feel like being naughty. Maybe go out all night and not brush my teeth when I get home or sleep in my make-up."

Zandra shook her head. "Our sister is so lame."

I chuckled. For Aurora, that was pretty out there. "How about you? Does it make you feel any different?"

Zandra shoved her fingers under her hat and scratched through her hair. "It makes me feel calmer. I don't think I've blown anything up for days. And when I get angry, I find it easier to talk myself out of it. I feel more balanced."

"You don't sound happy about that," I said. "But that's a good thing. Even with the tutoring you've had from Mom and Granny Dottie, your spells can still be explosive."

"I'm used to being explosive." She yanked the hat lower. "And I don't like change. I definitely don't want to become too much of a goody two shoes like Aurora."

Aurora whacked her arm. "You just heard me say I'm no longer so pure. I'm sure it has to do with this red magic. Every time we make a connection, something shifts."

"All I saw was a shift in your hair color, and that didn't last for long," I said. "Are you sure this isn't some parlor magic trick?"

"I'm telling you, this means something. My magic is also more stable. I've had no trouble since I joined with Zandra," Aurora said. "I'm confident in my spell casting again."

"That could be useful." I looked down at Wiggles. "I've gotten exactly nowhere with waking Wiggles using magic."

"That's also why we came to find you. We should combine our magic to help him. I've been so worried about this little guy," Aurora said. "Our powers will work in harmony. My perfection is calming Zandra's chaos."

"And my chaos is making you more like a normal witch with less of a stick up her butt." Zandra gave Aurora a less than gentle shove.

"Don't be mean, or you won't get any more of my cookies," Aurora said.

"What would happen if I joined my magic with yours? Is it safe? Don't forget, I have Frank on board," I said.

"He hasn't been a problem for ages, though. We should try some magic on Wiggles," Aurora said. "This is what he needs. When we all have functioning magic, we'll easily wake him from whatever spell he's under."

"And you're sure your magic is working?" I said. "I don't want Wiggles getting hurt."

"I haven't had a misfiring spell for over twenty-four hours," Aurora said. "And I've done dozens. I've been practicing."

"So have I," Zandra said. "Everything works smoothly. You should join us. Try it out and get this pooch on his paws again."

"My back would love that." I gently unhooked the papoose and placed Wiggles on the ground. "Let's give it a go. But if he acts strangely, we pull back our magic. Got it?"

"Got it," Zandra said.

Aurora held her hands out. "No harm will come to Wiggles. We'll fix him. He'll be a wise-cracking, cookie stealing, fluffy angel in no time."

"How about we use a restore energy spell?" I caught hold of Aurora's hand.

"I can do that," Zandra said, as she gripped Aurora's other hand. "I learned that from your mom a few weeks ago."

"No problem," Aurora said.

I eased down my barriers and allowed my magic to flow out, giving myself time to get a feel for the spell and make sure nothing felt weird. I caught hold of Zandra's free hand, making a connection between us.

My sisters' magic tingled on my fingertips as the spell took hold and flowed over Wiggles. He didn't stir.

"Hmmm, it's not working," Aurora whispered. "Should we try again?"

"Give it a minute," I said. "You two might work fine, but things aren't so—" My spine went ramrod straight as a wave of powerful magic blasted into me. All my barriers lowered, and Frank's demon energy ripped through me just before I blacked out.

My nose felt wet. Something like damp sandpaper was rubbing across it. I shifted my head, but the sensation followed me.

Rasp, rasp, rasp.

I made a gurgling noise in the back of my throat and lifted my hand to my face. It met something hot and furry.

My eyes opened and as my vision cleared, I discovered Wiggles licking my face with his big pink tongue. "You're awake!" I gently pushed him away, so he stopped giving me a tongue bath.

He stepped back and wagged his tail. "Sugar pie."

"Err... it's great to see you too, sweetie."

"Strawberry tart. Sweet lemon pancakes." His nose wrinkled, and he growled as a puzzled look crossed his face.

I sat up slowly. My head felt like an angry unicorn had stomped on me. "I'm not sure how I ended up in the dirt."

"Lemon meringue and vanilla ice cream cone." Wiggles turned and lifted his nose in the air.

My gaze followed the direction his nose pointed, and my eyes widened. Aurora and Zandra were out cold in the dirt.

I tried to stand but fell over and landed on my face, my head pounding and my stomach churning. I groaned as I tried to move. "Wiggles, what happened? We tried to do a spell to wake you up. It obviously worked, but... the magic. It was strong. And Frank came out. I only got the briefest sensation he was arriving, and then everything went black. Did he do this?"

"Sour candy. Burnt Bundt cake." Wiggles growled again and stamped his paws.

"You'll get there, buddy. At least you're awake and talking." I lifted a hand and petted his head, happy to stay on the ground until the world stopped spinning. "We'll figure out why you're talking in cake riddles soon enough."

I was inching across the dirt on my hands and knees to get to my sisters when there was a shout.

My head lifted, and I spotted Rhett racing toward me. "Tempest! What's going on?"

I smacked my lips together. "That's a great question. And I can't answer it. Wiggles is awake, but Zandra and Aurora are unconscious."

He reached my side and knelt beside me. "I saw a huge flash of magic from my workshop. I had a bad feeling you were in trouble. Was that magic flash from you?"

"Maybe. We were doing a restore energy spell on Wiggles. We joined hands, started the spell, and then bam! We were knocked out."

"You've been injured." Rhett took hold of one of my hands.

It was only then I noticed the bright red burn marks on my palms.

His gaze travelled up to my face. "And your hair."

I checked a strand of my hair. It was brilliant purple. "This is too weird."

"Don't move. I'm going to summon Lex to help with Aurora."

"You might like to get Granny Dottie and Grandpa Lucius here, too. They can help with Zandra."

"Give me two minutes." Rhett moved away and spread his arms out. A wave of his warm magic hit me as he sent out messages to Lex and my family, letting them know there was trouble.

Lex appeared in the blink of an eye. He was dressed in running shorts and a too tight white T-shirt. "Rhett. What's going on? I heard your voice shouting in my head that Aurora was in trouble."

"She's over here." Rhett led Lex to Aurora's side but kept looking back at me.

I attempted a cheery wave to let him know I was fine, but I wasn't feeling too bright. Wiggles stayed by my side, leaning against me, which was comforting.

Lex dropped to his knees beside Aurora. "Who did this to her?"

"I think it was me and Aurora," I said. "We were doing a spell. It went wrong. Well, it got Wiggles awake, but we paid the price."

"I'll take her back to the castle," Lex said.

"You should go to the hospital," Rhett said. "We don't know what magic we're dealing with. Aurora could need a healing spell to counteract what happened to her."

"Yes. Of course. I wasn't thinking." Lex picked up Aurora and held her close to his chest. He looked at me. "Tempest, are you okay?"

"I'll be fine. Go take care of my sister. Let me know how she's doing as soon as you can."

"Of course." He blinked out of sight with Aurora in his arms.

A second later, Granny Dottie and Grandpa Lucius materialized in a wave of warm, familiar feeling magic.

Granny Dottie's expression changed from irritation to shock in half a second. "I thought someone was joking with me when I got a telepathic communication from Rhett. What's going on here?"

I was still feeling dizzy and sick, so I waved them over to Zandra. "Rhett will explain."

He took a few minutes to get them up to speed while I rested my eyes and focused on remembering how to breathe.

Grandpa Lucius knelt beside me, and his warm, gentle hand stroked my brow. "You poor girl. What magic have you been using to make you feel like this?"

"Nothing bad. We were doing an average spell. It shouldn't have backfired like this. But..."

"What's going on?" Granny Dottie was sitting beside Zandra in the dirt, her hand resting on her forehead.

It was time to come clean about my magic problem. "I haven't said anything, but there's something wrong with my magic. I think it's broken. It's the same with Aurora and Zandra, but they figured out how to use it again. At least, they thought they had."

"What do you mean, your magic is broken?" Granny Dottie said.

Rhett helped me to sit. "My spells have been going wrong. Even the simple stuff backfires. And when I do get the magic to perform, it doesn't do what it's supposed to do."

Granny Dottie's forehead wrinkled. "You say Aurora and Zandra also had this problem?"

"They were, but Aurora said something happened when they joined hands. They were in her store, and she fell off a ladder. Zandra caught her, and their magic connected. Ever since then, they've been able to do spells. Aurora suggested we join our magic to help Wiggles."

"Chocolate topped waffles," Wiggles said.

I shrugged. "As you can see, Wiggles still isn't himself. But at least he's awake."

"I don't like this," Grandpa Lucius said. "It sounds like someone has been tampering with your powers."

"No one can tamper with a Crypt witch's power," Granny Dottie said.

I looked over at Zandra. "Maybe they found a way. How's Zandra doing?"

"She doesn't seem to be in any discomfort. Her breathing is steady, and her pulse is fine."

"But she won't wake up?"

"It seems not." Granny Dottie ran her hand over Zandra several times. "And she's not responding to my magic."

"Could it be something I did? It happened when I joined the spell." A lump formed in my throat. "Maybe I shouldn't use my power anymore."

"Lucius, keep an eye on Zandra." Granny Dottie moved over to me. She knelt beside me and held her hands over the burns on my palms. They healed instantly. "This isn't your fault. You couldn't have known this would happen."

"They said their magic worked fine. And... I felt Frank. We were doing the restore spell, and it wasn't having an effect on Wiggles. Frank slammed through my barriers, and that's all I remember. What if he hurt Aurora and Zandra?"

"You'd never let him do that." She stroked a hand down my purple hair several times. "Something has gotten a hold of you. My magic isn't touching your hair."

"My hair is the last thing I'm worrying about."

She clutched my shoulders and fixed me with a stern look. "Listen here. You didn't injure your sisters. How was Aurora when Lex took her away?"

"The same as Zandra. He's taken her to the hospital," I said. "We should get Zandra there, too."

"We'll get her looked at," Granny Dottie said. "You should come to the hospital as well."

"I'm feeling better now you're here. Other than the burns on my hands, I don't have any other injuries." And I didn't want them worrying about me when my sisters needed help.

"You should still get checked over," Rhett said.

"I can't leave. I'm on a case," I said. "I'm watching a murder suspect."

"Can't you let the angels handle that?" Granny Dottie said. "You have more important things to worry about."

I took in several deep breaths. "I won't be able to rest if I go to the hospital. I'll stay here. I'm doing nothing other than sitting and watching a house. I can't come to harm doing that."

"I'll stay with you," Rhett said.

"Could you help Granny Dottie and Grandpa Lucius with Zandra? Then check on Aurora for me. I need to know she's okay," I said.

"Are you sure you don't want someone to stay with you?"

"Please, go look after my sisters. I've got Wiggles with me."

"Peanut brownie and ice cream." Wiggles wagged his tail again.

Rhett kissed my cheek. "Of course. Whatever you need, but I'd much rather be looking after you."

"You can do that another time. And thanks for coming so quickly."

"I'll always be here. Whenever you need me." Rhett lifted Zandra off the ground.

"I'll transport us to the hospital," Granny Dottie said. "Look after yourself, Tempest. If you start feeling odd, let me know."

"I will."

She nodded, and they blinked out of sight.

I stayed sitting in the dirt, still feeling like the world was rocking. I petted Wiggles. "How are you doing?"

"Iced bun," he said mournfully.

"I know. This is seriously weird. It's like I'm missing a chunk of memory. What happened after that spell hit us? Where did it come from? None of us cast it. Was it Frank?" I felt him deep inside my mind and was tempted to drag him out and get some answers, but he was just a whisper. It seemed this weird magic had messed with him, too.

"Donut hole," Wiggles said.

"Yeah, I feel the same as you. And if you keep talking in dessert code, we'll have to invent a new way to communicate."

"Apple crumble."

A movement near the villa caught my eye. Tatiana was leaving, and she was carrying two loaded bags.

I repressed a groan. I still felt like a fairy elephant had jigged on me, but I couldn't ignore this. "Wiggles, are you up to following the suspect with me? I need your help."

He nodded. "Warm chocolate chip cookie."

"Then let's go see what Tatiana's got in those bags and who's getting a special delivery."

I needed time to process my weird magic and figure out why Wiggles now talked in cake. And while I was doing that, I'd get to work on hunting a murder suspect.

Chapter 14

I took it slowly and kept my distance as Tatiana walked through the large iron gates of her villa and headed to the edge of the forest. I needed to keep the pace gentle to make sure I didn't tip over and land on my head, as well as make sure we weren't spotted tailing her.

"What's she up to?" I whispered to Wiggles. "There's not much out here, unless someone is hiding in the woods. If they were, Fallon would have found them and chased them off."

"Fairy cake with sugar cream."

"You're making me hungry with all the cake talk." I wasn't feeling quite so stomped on as I kept moving. Whatever spell had slammed into me and my sisters was fading. But it was overtaken by a bone deep worry. Something had gone horribly wrong when we'd joined our magic, and I couldn't figure out what it was.

It was natural to join magic with a family member. It was even expected when we cast powerful spells that required lots of power. Otherwise, the spell caster got weak and became vulnerable. But what we'd done had felt the opposite of natural.

We followed Tatiana for another fifteen minutes. She glanced around now and again as if concerned she was being watched but carried on her journey as if she knew exactly where she was going.

"Hold on. She can't be heading to the old Bouchard place, can she? It's been empty for years," I said.

Wiggles trudged along beside me. "Tangy marshmallow floats."

"Yeah, it's seriously haunted by a bunch of troubled spirits. Only someone desperate or insane would go near that place." I pinched the bridge of my nose as a wave of dizziness hit. "Occasionally, you hear of groups of kids who dare each other to go inside, but if anyone does, they run out screaming and have nightmares for weeks."

"Fluffy meringue with cream."

We kept on Tatiana's tail, and after a few more minutes, it became clear that was exactly where she was headed. She took one more look around, walked through the rusted open gate that led into an overgrown front yard, and headed up the broken wooden porch steps.

I had to hand it to her, she didn't seem scared about going inside. She must have nerves of steel. Or maybe she just wasn't all that smart.

We found a dense patch of shadows and watched the house. It remained dark, and no lights came on. I shuddered. Tatiana was wandering about that place without being able to see. Anything could grab her and whisk her away through a dark portal, never to be seen again, or so the rumors go.

"Maybe she's leaving offerings for the ghosts," I said. "I don't know what kind of witch she is, but I didn't sense any dark power from her."

"Lemon sponge," Wiggles said.

I nodded, though I had no clue what he meant by that.

After another ten minutes of waiting, Tatiana still hadn't reappeared.

"She must be in there with someone. If the place was empty, she'd simply store those bags and leave." I massaged my throbbing forehead. "Maybe she's hiding stolen goods and is planning to sell them when things quieten down."

"Sweet cherry pie."

"Yum. Let's get closer and take a look." It was risky. If Tatiana was looking out a window, she'd see us approaching, but I had to know what she was up to.

I was still feeling shaky, but everything felt like it was working, and Wiggles was operational, so I had backup if Tatiana started throwing out spells to get rid of us.

We made it through the gate without incident and scurried up the path to the front door.

"Wiggles, you go around the back and see what's going on through the windows. I'll stay here and poke about."

He nodded and trotted around the side of the house.

I ducked low and peered through a grimy basement window. I couldn't see much through it, but it looked full of storage boxes and discarded bits of wood. A shadowy, transparent figure hovered in one corner before blinking out of sight.

I crept to the front door and squinted through the glass window. The hallway appeared empty. There was no furniture, not even a carpet on the worn floorboards.

Creeping along on my tiptoes, I headed to the next window and peeked inside. I couldn't see anyone at first, but there were voices coming from somewhere.

With my ear against the glass, I closed my eyes. Yes, there was a male voice. Tatiana was meeting someone.

I tried the window further along, but the curtain was drawn over it so I couldn't see in.

As I was tiptoeing to the next window, there was a crash around the back of the house, and I froze.

The voices inside stopped. Then there was a shuffling noise, and another bang, followed by a low growl. That sounded like Wiggles. He must have knocked into something.

Pressing my back against the house, I attempted an invisibility spell. The magic trickled off my fingers and dripped onto the dirt. The spell refused to take, so I was left exposed for Tatiana and her mystery man to spot me if they came outside.

I was flexing my hands to try again, when the front door was yanked open, and a man looked out.

We stared at each other. It was Grady Nox. The guy who was supposed to be in another part of the country because he needed a permit to travel and had a magic tracker attached to him.

Neither of us moved for several seconds, each waiting to see who'd strike first.

"We've got a problem," Grady muttered over his shoulder, his voice low and full of menace.

I'd have to bluff my way out of this since my magic wasn't cooperating. "I don't want any trouble. I just saw someone go inside and knew it wasn't a smart idea. Everyone who lives around here knows nasty spirits haunt this place. I wanted to make sure she wasn't getting hurt."

"Sure you did." Grady sneered at me. "Maybe you should leave before the ghosts get you."

"Sure. That's a perfect idea. I'll be on my way. I just need to find my dog."

"I thought you were helping some damsel in distress. Now you're looking for a missing dog." Grady stepped out on the porch and glowered at me. He looked similar to Conan, although he had fewer wrinkles and was leaner. He also had tattoos that wove up his neck and down to his fingers.

"Oh, sure. I can do more than one thing at a time. I'm a multitasker."

"You're a troublemaker. Get out of here."

"I'm going. Wiggles, let's move."

It was then my luck ran out. Tatiana emerged and looked around Grady's shoulder. "You! What are you doing out here?"

Grady looked down at Tatiana. "You know her?"

"Of course I do, you fool. This is the witch working with Angel Force. She came by the villa with an angel buddy and questioned me like I was some common criminal. They were asking questions about where Conan had hidden the money and if I knew anything about it. Did I know I was living off criminal earnings? Blah, blah, blah. Like I'd feel bad about that."

"You didn't say anything, babe, did you?" Grady caught hold of her chin in a large hand and tilted her head up.

She knocked his hand away. "I told them to get lost. That witch must have followed me here."

Grady's gaze turned to me, and he flashed his teeth. "Is that so? Turns out you're not telling the truth. Have you been spying on my woman?"

I was done with playing the innocent role. "I thought she was your brother's woman? Or have I got things muddled up?"

He growled at me, and his hands flexed. "You've got a dumb mouth on you. You keep away from me and Tatiana. What we get up to is none of your business."

"It is. Tatiana's a murder suspect, and so are you. How come you're here when your tracker is telling everyone you're at home?"

A low chuckle rumbled in his chest. "I'm not giving away my secrets. And you're not giving away ours. Come inside, and we can have a friendly chat and figure something out."

"Yeah, I'm not going in that nightmare house. I grew up around here, so I know what evil and misery hides in the walls."

"It's not the friendliest of places, but it beats jail," Grady said. "Besides, I kind of like the ghostly company I've been hanging out with. Apparently, they were all murdered in here, is that right?"

"Something like that."

He grinned. "Then get inside and meet my new ghost buddies."

"Nope. If you're friends with them, then we have nothing in common." I inched back. I needed to grab Wiggles and get out of here.

"You can't let her get away," Tatiana hissed. "She knows about you. She'll run to her angel friends and tell them where you are. You'll go back inside."

Grady's top lip curled. "Would you do that, little witch?"

"Most likely. And the name's Tempest Crypt."

"Huh! A Crypt witch no less. The angels must be desperate to work with you."

I shrugged. "We've found a way to work together. And when they find out about you, they'll arrest you and send you back to jail for breaking your probation. Maybe they'll even charge you with murdering your brother. How did you do it?"

Grady thrust out his hands and a stream of gray magic raced toward me.

I had no reliable magic to counteract it, so threw myself to the ground and rolled away. His sharp, hot magic flickered all around me but didn't make contact with my skin.

"I thought you were a powerful Crypt witch," Grady said. "Fight back. Show me what you've got."

"She's tricking you," Tatiana said. "Slam her with something dark. You can't let her talk."

I staggered to my feet, feeling woozy but determined these two weren't taking me down. "If you come quietly and confess to killing Conan, the angels will look favorably on you. We know Conan stole Tatiana from you. It could be seen as a crime of passion. The angels aren't unkind when it comes to matters of the heart."

Grady snorted a laugh. "No, they won't. I know what these angels are like. They'll see me as a criminal. My brother is dead, and they plan to fit me up for the crime. It'll be an easy way out for them, and they can deal with two problems at once."

"It does seem strange you snuck into the village and are hiding here at the same time your brother was murdered," I said. "That'll raise a few questions. And you must have forged a permit and disabled your magic tracker. Why do that if you're only here for the thermal spas and stone circle?"

"They won't ask me any questions, if no one tells them I'm here." Magic sparked on Grady's palms.

"Get her!" Tatiana's voice was high-pitched.

I pointed a finger at her. "I don't like you."

"Ditto. Why can't you leave us alone?"

"Because you're most likely murderers. Were you in on it together?" I focused on Grady. "Will you let your woman go down for a crime you committed?"

"We didn't do anything wrong," he said.

"You shouldn't let her talk to me like that," Tatiana said. "Kill her! We'll bury her behind the house."

I shuffled back several steps, my legs still shaky and my magic shivering inside me as if it didn't know what to do.

Grady's forehead wrinkled. "I didn't think I'd need to commit a murder to sort this mess."

"Is that a confession?" I said. "Do you admit you killed your brother?"

His eyes narrowed. "I wasn't talking about killing him."

I instinctively raised my hands to blast him with magic, but nothing came out.

"There's something wrong with her. Get her before she can fire up a spell," Tatiana shrieked.

Grady appeared to be struggling with the idea of killing me. For that, I was grateful, because it gave me a chance to back to the gate.

"If you loved me, you'd do it," Tatiana said.

He turned to her. "I do still love you. That's why I'm here."

"Then prove it." She pointed at me. "Get rid of our problem."

"Any woman who orders you to prove her love is the wrong woman for you," I said. "If you're constantly having to prove your affection to someone, you'll never win. Their demands will get bigger and bigger until you find yourself standing outside a haunted house about to strike down a witch who's done nothing wrong. It doesn't have to end like this."

Grady rolled his shoulders and rubbed his palms together. "I've always loved this woman. I'll do anything to keep her safe."

A blast of his magic flew toward me. I tripped over a wooden trough and landed on my butt, the spell skimming over my head.

"Keep going. You've almost got her." Tatiana bounced on her toes.

Another spell slammed into the dirt just by my feet. I rolled away but not before some of the spell pulsed across my skin, making my flesh burn.

I scrubbed the spell away with my magic as best I could, but it still tingled like fire ants were nipping at me.

Before I could get back on my feet, Grady was standing over me. Tatiana was clutching his arm, joy in her eyes as she saw me struggle.

Grady raised a lightning bolt over his head. "You should have stayed away. You didn't need to die." He drew back his arm.

A low, menacing snarl filled the air, and a second later, there was a blur of movement. Wiggles slammed into Grady's chest, taking him to the ground.

Grady roared out his anger and plunged the lightning bolt into Wiggles's side.

A shriek of horror flew from my lips as Wiggles was electrified by the magic. His fur stood up on end all over his body, and his eyes glowed redder than I'd ever seen. His stubby legs were stuck out straight as the magic flooded through him.

I leaped to my feet and threw down any barrier I had in place that held Frank back. "You'll pay for that."

As Grady's spell faded, Tatiana picked up an unconscious Wiggles and tossed him to one side. "You're the one who's going to pay for interfering in our business. This is what you get for messing with us."

I opened myself fully to Frank's power. I didn't care what he did to me, but no one hurt my hellhound and got away with it.

His energy was sluggish as it trickled through my veins. It was as if he was waking from a long slumber and had no desire to help.

"What are you waiting for?" I hissed. "Do what you like. You have my full permission to destroy these two."

"Destroy us?" Grady chuckled. "You can barely stand, witch. We've got nothing to fear from you or your useless dog."

I growled at him, and finally Frank's energy slid through my veins. But it was weak. I'd never felt him like this before. I dropped all resistance I had to his power as he slipped into my mind.

"What's up with her?" Tatiana said. "She looks different."

"She's just scared," Grady said.

"Are you going to burst into tears because we hurt your doggy?" Tatiana said.

I snarled as I unleashed Frank's power. His dark demon energy slid through me in unpleasant waves of jagged energy, pulsing slowly out of me.

Neither of them moved as the demon power touched them. Maybe they were too dumb to realize what was about to hit them. I didn't care. They deserved what was coming.

It was Tatiana who moved first. She shook her head and kicked out at the spell slowly covering her. "What's this? Has one of those freaky ghosts gotten out of the house?"

They both tried to move, but they were stuck to the ground.

"This is what you get for messing with me and my hellhound." I spoke through gritted teeth.

"There's something wrong with her," Grady said. "Look at her eyes. And what's happened to her voice?"

"Get me out of here," Tatiana squealed. "I don't like it. There's something wrong with this magic."

"There'll be something wrong with you in a minute. I'll devour every inch of you. There'll be nothing left. You'll both be gone," I said.

"Tempest! Stop!" Dazielle flew from the sky and landed in front of me. Her wings were stretched out wide. "Control Frank."

I could if I wanted to, but I had no desire to stop this. I wanted Grady and Tatiana destroyed. Wiggles had been protecting me, yet they'd plunged that spell inside him and tossed him away like he was trash.

Dazielle grabbed my shoulders and shook me. "Control your demon. Don't make me take you out. You're better than this."

"You have to help us. That witch is crazy. She's done something to us," Tatiana said. "Arrest her."

Dazielle stepped to one side, keeping a close eye on me as she glanced at Wiggles, who hadn't moved. "It's no less than you deserve." Her gaze cut to Grady. "I know you."

"You don't. Mind your business, angel, and do your job."

"Stop the witch." Tatiana was shaking as Frank's power trickled over her. "She's evil. This magic feels so wrong."

"Tempest is a good witch." Dazielle looked at Wiggles again. He was on his side, his fur smoking.

"And from what I can see here, you deserve everything you get."

I nodded. "Let me at them. Fly away and pretend you never found me."

Dazielle turned to me, regret in her eyes. "I can't do that. If you kill these two suspects, you'll go to jail. I understand you're hurting, but Wiggles is in trouble. Focus on that. Get back to yourself, contain Frank, and help Wiggles. He needs you. You won't be able to heal him if I arrest you for murder."

It was the hard nudge I needed. I eased Frank's energy back and stuffed it down, raising the barriers so he couldn't take control. Not that he seemed to want to. He'd been content to cause harm but had no desire to stay. My demon felt as weak as me, and although I should be grateful, I was worried.

As I came back to my senses, the hot energy fueling me faded, and an icy worry flooded my veins. I dashed over to Wiggles and kneeled beside him.

"They did that to Wiggles?" Dazielle was already restraining Grady and Tatiana.

"Yes. Wiggles was protecting me. I followed Tatiana from her villa, and she came here. We were looking around when Grady came out of the house."

"You're going to arrest that witch, too, right?" Tatiana said. "She's using deadly magic. If you hadn't gotten here, she'd have killed us."

"Maybe I should have let her finish what she started," Dazielle said. "You're both coming with me."

"We've done nothing wrong," Tatiana said.

Dazielle pointed a finger at Grady. "This man isn't supposed to be here. And his brother has just been killed. That's not a coincidence."

She shrugged. "It means nothing."

"It means you're both in trouble. You've been helping to hide him. That makes you a criminal," Dazielle said. "Tempest, are you coming with us?"

"You deal with them. I need to get Wiggles healed."

"I'll meet you back at Angel Force." Dazielle shot into the sky, a suspect gripped under each arm.

I gathered Wiggles into my arms and held him against my chest. I tried a transportation spell to get us to Fur Baby Emporium, but it didn't work. Gritting my teeth, I could do nothing but clumsily jog-stagger along until I reached the store. Fur Baby Emporium looked like it had just closed, but I hammered my fist on the door until Abigail stomped over.

Her anger morphed into concern when she saw Wiggles. "What happened to him?"

"He was hit by a lightning bolt spell. I'd heal him, but... I'm having trouble. I need help."

She led us to the examination room at the back of the store. We passed pens full of magical animals waiting for their perfect witch or magic user to show up. Several twittered or squawked when they saw Wiggles.

Abigail took us into a clinical white room and gestured to the table. "Put him down here. I'll see how he's doing."

It was only when I let him go that the exhaustion hit. I'd really messed up out there. I hadn't been able to protect myself, and Wiggles had gotten hurt. My eyes hazed with tears, and I had to look away for a few seconds.

"He'll be okay," Abigail said gently. "He was hit by a powerful spell, but I can feel him regenerating. Remember what he is. This little guy has power."

I looked back, letting out a sigh of relief. "Are you sure? Wiggles has had a tough week. He got a whack of magic that knocked him out. I managed to get him to wake with the help of Aurora and Zandra, but since then, he's been talking in cake riddles. And now this. It's a lot for a hellhound to take."

"Yes, but he is a hellhound brought back by two immensely powerful witches. There's very little that can destroy him." She slowly stroked Wiggles, healing magic pouring into him. "Put your hand on his chest. You'll already feel his breathing is better."

I did as she said and almost started blubbing again. He was breathing, but the expression on his face was so tense and pain-filled. "You'll get him back to normal?"

"That's what I specialize in. Leave him here overnight. I'll stay with Wiggles and make sure he gets all the attention he needs. He won't wake up for a while, and when he does, he'll still feel woozy. Do you know what other spell is affecting him? The one that knocked him out?"

"Not a clue. I was thinking about bringing him here so you could take a look at him if he didn't wake."

"He's here now, and I'll take the very best care of him." Her gaze ran over me. "You look exhausted.

Are you sure you didn't get hit with some of that lightning bolt spell?"

"Thanks to Wiggles, it didn't touch me." I scratched between his ears and then kissed his head. "Be good. Do everything Abigail tells you. I'll be back tomorrow."

"Let yourself out," Abigail said. "I'll stay here and perform more healing spells. I'll send you a message if anything changes."

I took one last long look at Wiggles then walked out of the store and over to Angel Force. As well as being exhausted, I was angry. It was time to get answers from Tatiana and Grady and finally find our killer.

Chapter 15

The interview room contained me, Dominic, Dazielle, and Grady.

Grady sneered at us from across the table, his wrists bound by magical shackles. "A weird witch and two angels watching my every move. I feel so special."

"You shouldn't. You're in serious trouble," Dazielle said. "I've been in touch with your probation officer. She was disappointed to hear you'd lied to her."

"You're breaking my heart," he said.

"She's already filed a report about you breaking the terms of your probation. She's been to your home and dispersed the magic you set up to make it appear you were there. And we're tracking down the source that supplied you with the fake travel permit documents."

He shrugged. "Like I care about any of that."

"You're going back inside because of this," I said, "which means you've got nothing to lose by telling us the truth. Why are you really here?"

Grady's cold stare drifted over me. "I had business to take care of."

"What business?" Dazielle said.

"Business that has nothing to do with you."

I slammed a hand on the table. "You made it my business when you hurt my hellhound."

"He should be dead. I obviously didn't hit him hard enough with that spell."

I growled at him. "Dazielle, Dominic, give me five minutes with this jerk. I'll get all the answers you need."

Dominic walked over from the door he was guarding and touched my arm. "Tempest, maybe you should sit this one out."

Grady chuckled. "Yeah, listen to your angel friend. This is a fight you'll lose. I've already seen how pathetic you are. You can't take me on and win."

"I'll die trying," I said. "Let me have him in a room on my own. It'll be payback for what he did to Wiggles."

Dazielle shuffled in her seat. "I know how much you care for Wiggles, but we can't leave you alone with Grady."

"That's right. And you don't want to get a black mark with these angels," Grady said. "Once your card is marked by them, you don't have a chance of going straight. They always look at you like you're guilty, no matter what you do."

"I've experienced that for myself," I said. "But you can change that if you want to."

"Tempest," Dazielle cautioned. "Perhaps Dominic is right. Leave this to us."

"I can't. This is personal." I looked over at Dominic. "Could you do me a favor?"

"Sure. Anything."

"Wiggles is at Fur Baby Emporium. Abigail is keeping him there overnight. I want to know how he's doing."

Grady snorted a laugh. "Unbelievable."

"I'll go check on him. Don't worry, I'm sure he'll be okay." Dominic looked at Dazielle, seeking her permission to leave.

She nodded. "Fine. Off you go."

He hurried out of the room and closed the door behind him.

"Huh! You've got these angels eating out of your hand," Grady said. "What makes you so special?"

"She's a Crypt witch," Dazielle said. "And Tempest deals with problem magic users, just like you. Maybe I should leave her with you. She can beat sense into that thick head of yours."

"My head may be thick, but I'm still not telling you anything." He leaned back in his seat and stretched out his shackled hands.

"If you won't talk, maybe Tatiana will." I shoved back my chair. "Let's see what the girlfriend has to say. Which brother will she be loyal to? Maybe neither of you. She might tell us everything, so you get charged with her crimes."

"Now, wait a minute," Grady said. "Don't bother Tatiana. She's a good girl."

I shook my head, already at the door. "You had your chance, and you blew it. You'd better hope she's loyal to you, or you're in a world of trouble."

Dazielle hurried out of the room behind me, ignoring Grady's curses and demands that we return. "Do you think he's worried?"

"I would be if I had Tatiana as a girlfriend. Let's see what she has to say about the situation."

We headed into the interview room next door, where Tatiana was waiting for us.

She had a face like thunder, and the expression only grew worse as she glared at me. "You're still here."

"Yep. And I'm thrilled to see you, too." I pulled out a seat and sat in it. "Tatiana was keen on getting Grady to kill me," I said to Dazielle. "She demanded my murder to show he loved her."

"Is that so?" Dazielle settled next to me. "And why is it we find you helping Grady Nox?"

"Maybe I wasn't helping him."

"What was in the bags you took to the house he was hiding in?" I said.

"I don't remember carrying any bags."

"I watched you come out of your villa."

"That was someone else. I don't remember doing that. I have a terrible short-term memory." Tatiana smirked at me. "Can I go now?"

"You're not going anywhere," Dazielle said. "You'll be charged with assisting Grady to break his probation. But we're interested in a more serious crime. Did you and Grady plot Conan's murder together?"

Tatiana stiffened in her seat. "No!"

"Which one of you actually did it?" I said.

Dazielle glanced at me. "The way Grady was talking, it looks like Tatiana is guilty."

Tatiana pressed her lips together.

"You must both be involved," I said. "Did Grady persuade you to kill Conan, or was it the other way around?"

"You don't know what you're talking about."

"We do," Dazielle said. "We've discovered Grady's been in Willow Tree Falls since the day before Conan's murder. He could have gotten into Angel Force and killed Conan to impress you."

She sneered at us. "Only if he was invisible."

We still had that problem to deal with. Whoever killed Conan must have had a secret way into the cells, and we hadn't discovered it. But we'd figure that out after we learned who plunged a blade into Conan's chest.

"I'm certain it was Grady," I said. "You've got him under a spell. You forced him to kill Conan. Do you like having power over men and getting them to do your bidding?"

"Sure. What woman doesn't like guys begging to do whatever she asks? But it's not magic if that's what you're thinking," Tatiana said. "I cared for Conan and Grady, and they loved me. They both have qualities I admired."

"More like big bank balances they were willing to share with you," I said.

"Money always helps. Date a poor guy and tell me money doesn't matter." She shook her head. "They knew how to look after me. When Grady went inside, Conan stepped in and filled the gap."

My nose wrinkled. "How generous of him."

"Grady wanted me happy. And he wanted me looked after. That's all I'm saying."

"You could say one more thing. You could confess to killing Conan. Then Grady would only have lesser crimes to his name. He might even get a reduced sentence for breaking his probation conditions, especially if it can be proven you influenced him into making the trip to Willow Tree Falls." I arched an eyebrow. "You'd be painted as a femme fatale. The jury would eat that up."

"I didn't kill Conan. Neither did Grady."

"Let me set this out in simple terms. One of you confesses, or you're both going down for this murder," Dazielle said.

"You can try to charge us, but you won't get away with it," Tatiana said. "You'll look like idiots, and we'll walk away."

"Neither of you will walk away from this," Dazielle said. "Even if we can't get you for Conan's murder, you're aiding and abetting a known criminal, and he's broken his probation. And I'll make sure the judge who passes your sentence is the meanest, hardest judge you've ever met. He'll throw the book at you."

Tatiana inspected her nails. "Do your worst, angel. I'm not scared of your empty threats."

Dazielle gestured her head at the door, and we both stood and left the room.

"Tatiana won't break," I said. "She doesn't even seem worried. And she couldn't care less about Grady going back to jail."

"I think Grady's the weak link in this investigation," Dazielle said. "And I've got an idea how we can break him. Follow me." She led me back to Grady's interview room.

I grinned. I kind of loved it when Dazielle got sneaky.

"Hey. What's going on?" Grady jerked upright in his seat. "Have you been talking to Tatiana?"

Dazielle remained standing, as did I. "We have. We're planning on charging Tatiana with Conan's murder. We just need to file the paperwork before beginning proceedings."

"You can't." His face went red. "She didn't do it."

"Tatiana has a strong motive. She wanted to rekindle her romance with you, but Conan was standing in the way. And then there's the money." Dazielle looked at me.

I nodded. Tag teaming with Dazielle was fun. "Tatiana wants Conan's assets. She knows where his money is, so he was no use to her anymore."

"But she wouldn't kill him. She loved him," Grady said.

"That's not true. Tatiana wanted you back. She persuaded you to break the terms of your probation so you could deal with her relationship problem," I said. "In return, you'd get back together and could share Conan's wealth between you."

"No! That's a lie. And I don't need my brother's wealth. I've got plenty of my own."

"Now you have more. And Tatiana doesn't have cheap tastes. She's already said she wouldn't date poor. She'll never need to now."

"You've got this all wrong." Grady lowered his head and lifted his shackled hands to scratch his forehead. "Tatiana didn't ask me to come here so I could kill Conan."

Now we were getting somewhere. "But she wanted you here? You're in this together?"

He nodded and raised his head. "I came here to break Conan out of his cell. Tatiana learned when his trial was and contacted me. She had a plan to stop him from going down."

"Tatiana wanted Conan out of jail?" Dazielle said. "She doesn't want to be with you?"

Grady heaved out a sigh. "You won't understand, but I still care for Tatiana. We spent almost ten years together, and she never did me wrong. She was loyal, fierce, and beautiful. We had some great times. When I went to jail, it wasn't fair to expect her to wait for me."

"You had no problem with her getting it on with your brother?" I said.

His expression darkened. "I mean, did I love it? No. But I also didn't want to see her with a random guy who would mistreat her. Conan was the least terrible option."

"Tatiana can clearly handle herself," I said. "If any guy had been mean to her, she'd have kicked him where it hurts. And kept kicking until he didn't get up."

Grady chuckled. "She's always been a firecracker. That's why I still love her. When she came to me asking for help and saying she wanted to get Conan out, I agreed to get involved. He's my only brother, so I wanted him back. I missed our life together."

"Committing crimes and trying to get away with it?" Dazielle said.

"We all have passions," Grady said. "And we worked well together."

"Was it Tatiana who gave the money to Sorath?" I said. "She paid him to cause a distraction so you could break Conan out?"

"I don't know the name of the angel she bribed, but that was part of the plan. A distraction would be caused, we'd sneak in, break open the cell, and get Conan out."

"It would never have worked," Dazielle said. "This place is always full of angels."

"It wouldn't have been if that idiot had set off the right alarm. The fire alarm was supposed to trigger, so the building would have been evacuated." Grady scowled. "Neither of us wanted Conan dead. Tatiana was planning on starting a family with him. I wanted that for both of them. I was going to be an uncle."

I shook my head. This was too weird, but Grady seemed genuine when he talked about Conan and Tatiana being together in this strange little lovefest.

"Was that you running away from Angel Force just after Conan was killed?" I said.

He nodded. "I hung around for as long as I could, but then the wrong alarm went off, and I saw the angels inside flapping around and panicking. I realized it had gone wrong. I hoped to see Tatiana or maybe even Conan. I was waiting with a transportation spell primed to get us out of Willow Tree Falls. Then someone came to the door, and I panicked."

"That was me," I said.

"I didn't stop to see who was coming after me. I just raced into the woods, and I've been hiding out in that house ever since."

"Tatiana found you there?"

"I made contact with her. I kept it discreet, but she knew how to find me." Grady shook his head. "I still love that woman. She's no longer mine, but she gets under your skin. I was happy to have her in my life in any way. She'd planned a future with Conan. She'd never kill him."

"Don't be so sure about that," Dazielle said.

Grady heaved out a sigh. "I don't beg very often, but please, don't charge Tatiana with murder. You've got the wrong person."

My instincts were telling me Grady was being truthful. But where did that leave us?

"We need to speak to Tatiana to confirm all of this," Dazielle said.

"She won't tell you anything. She's loyal."

"Perhaps she'll talk if she thinks we're charging you with Conan's murder." I had a feeling she wouldn't, but there was no harm in planting that seed of doubt.

He looked unconvinced. "Tatiana wouldn't do that. She's a part of the family. I'm not saying any more until her name is cleared and you let her go."

"We can't do that," Dazielle said. "She assisted you in some serious criminal activities."

"I'll say I forced her to do it. She was scared of me."

"No one will believe that. Tatiana's a ball-buster," I said.

"Then I'm keeping my mouth shut. And it'll stay shut until I see her walk out the front door." He leaned back and closed his eyes. "Now, I'm hungry. And I need a break."

We both glowered at him, but Grady kept his eyes closed.

With frustration coursing through my veins, I left the interview room with Dazielle, and she closed the door behind us.

"At least we got somewhere," she said. "Unless Grady is an incredible liar, he's telling the truth."

"I agree. I don't think either of them killed Conan. Tatiana had a future planned with him, and Grady was happy with their weird setup. He was planning on getting Conan out of jail. Why suddenly change his mind and kill him?"

"It's not the only question that needs answering. We still need to figure out how our killer got to that cell."

"Let's give Grady and Tatiana time alone in the cells. They can think about the mess they're in. It might encourage one of them to talk in the morning."

"Agreed." Dazielle patted my shoulder. "And I'm ordering you to go home."

"I do need to leave. I want to see how Wiggles and my sisters are doing."

"Go home, Tempest. Your family is dealing with your sisters, and Dominic will keep an eye on Wiggles. You look terrible. I'm amazed you're even able to stand."

"Thanks. I feel amazing." I felt like I'd been scraped across a grimy firepit and smooshed into the dirt face-first several times.

"Get some sleep. And sort out your ghastly hair."

"My hair? What's wrong with it?" I pulled around a handful of hair. It had blotchy green and red dots on top of the funky purple. "When did that happen?"

"I don't know, but I've never seen you look so ill. Fix your hair, get something to eat, and rest. In the morning, we'll figure out exactly who killed Conan."

I stumbled along the corridor with her, almost grateful to be getting those orders. I was done-in, but it would take more than a single night of sleep to sort out the magical muddle I was in.

Chapter 16

I didn't think I'd sleep last night, but when I got back to my apartment, I stumbled past the bar, muttering apologies to Merrie and the team about not being able to help, and staggered up the stairs. I'd managed to pull off half my clothes before collapsing on the bed.

And I'd slept right through and hadn't woken until after nine in the morning. Despite all that sleep, I was still bone-tired.

I had a quick, hot shower, pulled on clean clothes, and defrosted ready-made croissants from the freezer. I stood at the kitchen counter, dipping them into a pot of honey while I sipped on super strong coffee.

There was a slightly less gross feeling pulsing through me after all that sleep, but I still wasn't feeling brilliant. My hair also looked weird with more blonde bits, and my skin was ghostly white. But I didn't care about the way I looked. My heart missed Wiggles. My stinky little fur baby was usually snuffling around the apartment, begging for food before I got out of bed.

It was too quiet without him, and I owed him big time for saving my life. When he was back to his usual self, he'd be getting an enormous box of whatever cake he desired. He deserved pampering after everything he'd gone through.

My snow globe communicator had no messages about Aurora and Zandra, which I took to be a good sign. They'd be well looked after at the hospital. I'd need to visit them soon, though, to make sure they were on the mend.

I stuffed the last of the croissant in my mouth, left my empty mug in the sink, and walked out of the apartment. I headed out of the club and over to Fur Baby Emporium. It was still early, and the store wasn't open, but after knocking a few times, Abigail appeared.

She waved me in with a weary nod. She had large dark circles under her eyes and stifled a yawn as I entered. "I figured you'd be by early."

"How's he doing?"

Abigail pressed a finger to her lips as her gaze ran over my hair. "Hush! Most of the residents are only just waking up. Some of them can get grumpy if they're disturbed."

I tiptoed past the pens toward the back of the store. "Well? How is Wiggles?"

"He's good. He had an excellent night. I checked in on him regularly, but he had someone with him at all times."

I walked into the examination room and through to the back, where there were half a dozen pens on the floor. Small, angry cats occupied two of them.

Wiggles was in the far pen on the end. Sitting beside it was Rhett.

His head jerked up as we walked in. "Hey. You're here."

I hurried over and knelt by the pen. "I am. But what are you doing here?"

Rhett kissed my cheek. "I knew you'd be worried, so I came by to see how Wiggles was doing. I found Dominic nodding off, so I offered to take the late shift. Then Abigail got an emergency and had to leave for a while, so I said I'd stay."

I hugged him. "You're an amazing boyfriend."

He grinned. "It's no trouble. And I kind of like this little guy. I mean, he's super annoying when he's begging for food, but I know how much you like him. I'd hate for anything bad to happen to him."

I turned my attention to Wiggles. He was tucked under a soft red blanket, his legs twitching occasionally. His eyes were closed, and his breathing seemed even.

"Everything went well overnight," Abigail said from the doorway. "The injuries from the lightning bolt are almost healed."

"That's good. When will he wake up?" I said.

She walked over and crouched beside us. "I'm not certain. I healed his injuries, but there's a strange lingering magic that won't shift. I can't figure out what it is. And it's troubling him."

"You think it's a spell? When he was attacked, I didn't see any other magic grab him. It was just the lightning bolt."

"Something's gotten hold of him," Abigail said. "It's like he's been drugged with some seriously strong sedative. I even tried a magical adrenaline shot on him."

"Did it do any good?"

"He twitched a bit but hasn't opened his eyes. I have a few more things to try today. I thought a night of rest would do him good, though. And he was in safe hands with Rhett looking after him."

"You can guarantee that," I said.

"There's another odd thing," Abigail said. "Wiggles occasionally talks, but I can't understand what he means."

"What's he saying?"

"He's talking about food a lot," Rhett said. "He keeps mumbling about sugar and candy."

"I thought he might be hungry," Abigail said, "but I left a variety of food in his pen and he didn't touch it."

"He was doing that when he was awake," I said. "He was talking, and I could understand the words, but his responses came out in dessert code. I figured it was a side effect of whatever magic was affecting him."

"Maybe he just wants a particular type of cake," Rhett said. "Donuts have been mentioned several times."

There was a knock on the front door, and Abigail left to open it. She returned a moment later with Dominic, who carried a huge tray of cakes.

He smiled when he saw me and nodded at Rhett. "How's the patient?"

"Stable." Rhett stood and stretched out his back. "But still snoozing."

Dominic set down the cakes. "I thought these might tempt Wiggles."

"You're a mind reader," I said. "And thanks for watching over Wiggles last night."

"Any time." Dominic's cheeks flushed, and he glanced at Rhett. "I hoped Wiggles would be awake by now."

"Leave him with me for a bit longer," Abigail said. "I'm determined to figure out what's going on, and I've got the best contacts when it comes to tricky familiars. Don't worry, he's not in pain. As you can see, I've made him comfortable. We'll get to the bottom of this. You'll soon have Wiggles back just as he was." She led us to the main door, and I walked out with Dominic and Rhett.

"You must be tired," I said to Rhett.

"Sure. But I've got work to do. I'll grab a coffee and get going. I'll check in with you later?"

I kissed him. "Absolutely."

We said our goodbyes, and Rhett nodded at Dominic before walking away.

"How did you get on yesterday interviewing Tatiana and Grady?" Dominic said.

"We got somewhere. Grady is more willing to talk than Tatiana, but he's not prepared to give up everything until she's released."

"Dazielle won't be happy about that."

"No, she wants them both in jail. We might have to do a deal with Grady if we're going to get to the bottom of this murder. We need to know how they got in Conan's cell and stabbed him. Without that information, we've got nothing to go on. No murder weapon and no opportunity. We're stuck."

"It's a complicated case, that's for sure." Dominic scratched his head. "Are you heading into Angel Force?"

"Soon. I need to go to the hospital first." A trickle of guilt tickled down my spine. I'd put Wiggles before my sisters. They'd been injured, but he'd been the one I'd seen first. But he was my every day companion, and I was never without him. And my sisters weren't alone. Our family had rallied around and was looking after them. And Lex was devoted to Aurora. He'd make sure she got the best possible medical care.

"I'll see you at work later." Dominic gave me a cheery wave and bounded away.

I headed over to the hospital, checked at the reception desk to find the rooms Aurora and Zandra were in, and then walked along the corridor. I went to Aurora's room first, since it was closest.

Lex was just opening the door as I arrived. He stepped back and smiled at me, but it looked strained. "I'm glad you're here. Aurora needs some new faces to keep her company."

"How's the patient?" I glanced past his shoulder to the bed behind him.

He gestured me into the corridor before easing the door shut. "She's fine. I mean, Aurora's awake, and there don't seem to be any health effects following the spell that knocked her out."

"I'm sensing a but here."

His face crinkled into a rare frown. "She's being difficult."

I laughed. "Aurora is never difficult. She's the sweetest Crypt witch you'll ever meet."

"And that's one of the many reasons I adore her. But… things have changed."

"Maybe she's stressed after what happened. That magic freaked me out, too. I've never felt anything like it."

Lex glanced over his shoulder. "It's more than stress. And I should warn you, she's being mean to everyone. Aurora told me I was a jerk, and she wished she'd never married me."

My jaw dropped. "Are you sure you're in the right room? Aurora would never say that. We all know how much she loves you."

"And I know that too, which is why I ignore her when she says nasty things. But she was complaining about the food she'd been delivered. I told her I'd get her anything she wanted. That's when she turned on me. Aurora snapped and snarled for several minutes before bursting into tears and telling me how sorry she was."

"Lex, don't take it personally. The magic that hit us was intense. I think it had something to do with Frank, because I felt his energy for a few seconds before I blacked out, but maybe it was something else. A dark spell could have zapped us and it messed with Aurora's head."

"Did you see anyone throw a spell your way?"

"No. But that doesn't mean someone didn't sneak up on us."

"Who? Why would they want to harm all of you?"

"I'm not sure. I've got a few enemies, but everyone loves Aurora. Maybe she lucked out and got in the way of something dark that was meant for me." I patted his arm. "This will be temporary. She'll be back to her sweet self before you know it."

"I hope you're right. Aurora's terrifying me at the moment." He shuddered. "What if she doesn't get any better?"

"Then you'll find a way to make things work."

"What are you doing out there, you blundering moron?" Aurora could be heard on the other side of the door.

Lex inched open the door. "I'm getting an herbal tea, my love. Are you sure you don't want anything?"

"Go boil your head, you loser."

He looked at me, his eyes full of tears. "Perhaps you'll have more luck with her."

I hid my surprise as cuss words continued on the other side of the door. "Go get that tea. I'll have a word with my sister and make her calm down."

Once Lex had left, I walked into Aurora's room. The place was a mess. Magazines were dumped on the floor, there were half eaten bowls of food littering the bedside cabinet, and a cosmetics bag had been tipped over and the contents spilled on the bed.

Aurora was rooting through the bag. Her hair was now orange and had three black stripes running through it. "Idiot! He hasn't brought a single thing I need. He's useless."

"Hey, relax. What's going on with you?" I settled on the end of the bed. "Lex told me you were being nasty to him. What's that all about?"

"If I don't tell him exactly what needs to be done, he gets it wrong. He brought me the wrong clothes, the wrong cosmetics, and didn't even get the food

I wanted. And I demanded he grant me wishes, and he said he wouldn't. Lex said I wasn't in the right frame of mind to be trusted with wishes." She shot me a glare. "That's the only reason I married him, so I could get my hands on those wishes. Oh, and all the Jinn loot he's got stashed in that stupid haunted castle he's always bragging about."

"Whoa! We both know that's not true. You couldn't care less if the guy was penniless."

A scowl marred her pretty face. "Yes, I could. You won't find me slumming it in some shack or stuck in a poky apartment above a dodgy club." She arched an eyebrow, as if challenging me. "It's only right he shares with me."

"Lex is always giving you gifts and taking you on amazing vacations. I've barely seen you since you got married because he whisks you off on all-expenses paid trips. You're lucky to have him."

"You take him if you like him so much." Aurora lifted her gaze to meet mine. The anger glinting in her blue eyes shocked me. "I've got an idea. We'll do a partner swap. I bet Rhett is more fun than Lame Lex and all his simpering."

"Aurora, what's wrong with you? The sister I know and love would never say that." I grabbed her hand and held on tight. "Is this because of the magic we did on Wiggles?"

She tried to yank her hand out of my grasp. "There's nothing wrong with me. I needed that blast of magic to bring me to my senses. I'm seen as the sweet, innocent sister. It gets dull. You always get to have all the fun."

"You have plenty of fun. You have a great life. It's the magic. It messed with me, too. Take a look at my hair for starters."

She shrugged. "You do look awful, but you've never had much style."

The door behind me opened, and Zandra shuffled in. Dark circles were clear under her eyes, and she was ghoul pale. Her hair was striped through with black, gray, and pale blonde blotchy patches. She looked like a home dye job gone wrong.

"Hey, I was just coming to see you," I said. "How are you feeling? Are you as grumpy as Aurora?"

"I feel like I've been crushed by a troll and his friends. And my head is pounding. Something is wrong with me. I feel weird. Not myself."

"Apart from the pounding head, what other symptoms do you have?" I stood from the bed. "Should I get the doctor to take another look at you?"

"It's not that." Zandra slumped into a chair. "I keep wanting to be nice to people."

I snorted a laugh. "That's a bad thing?"

"It's not exactly a me thing, is it?"

I looked at Aurora and Zandra. "You both feel different after we did that magic on Wiggles?"

"No. I feel the same as I've always done," Aurora said.

"Not true," Zandra said. "I came in here a couple of hours ago, and you threw a book at my head."

"You were being annoying."

Zandra looked at me and raised her eyebrows. "And my magic doesn't feel right. It's different. It feels mellower."

I looked at Aurora, who was smashing a lipstick lid down with such force it broke. "Do you feel your magic has shifted, too?"

"All I feel is the urge to punch someone if I don't get a hazelnut almond milk latte with dairy free chocolate sprinkles in the next thirty seconds," Aurora said.

I plucked the lipstick away from her. "I reckon something went wrong with that spell we did to wake Wiggles."

"He's awake?" Zandra said. "That's good news."

"Does that mean I have to have that gross little beast back in my store?" Aurora said. "He's such a nuisance and always steals my brownies. I have to mop the floor every time he comes in and spritz perfume everywhere to hide his stench."

"Now I know there's something wrong with you. You adore Wiggles. You're always the first to kiss his head and give him a treat," I said. "And your familiars love him."

"They pretend to like him. They secretly mock him when he's not around. Is it his fault I'm in such a bad mood?"

"So you admit you're in a bad mood?" I said.

"Only because I'm surrounded by idiots." Aurora shoved the cosmetics bag off the bed. "Where's that fool, Lex?"

"He's escaping from his terrifying wife," I said. "And he'd be wise to stay away until you sort yourself out."

"I'm not the one who needs to get sorted. You're a mess. You need a self-tan, a haircut, and some new clothes. When was the last time you slept? You look—"

"Enough!" I raised my hand, cutting off my sister's insults. "Stop being awful to everyone."

"Aurora sounds like me on a bad day," Zandra said.

"I'm nothing like you," Aurora said. "And why are you even here? We're only half-related."

"We're not going back to that," I said. "You're friends now. You've been getting along great."

"I've been tolerating her." Aurora's top lip curled. "There's a difference."

Zandra shrugged. "You like me. You just need to quit being such a jerk."

Aurora's expression shifted several times before her eyes widened. She thrust her hand over her mouth, and tears filled her eyes.

"Err... I didn't mean it," Zandra said. "You're not really a jerk."

Tears trickled down Aurora's cheeks, and she lowered her hand. "I am being horrible to everyone. I can hear myself saying these terrible things, but I can't stop. You're all so annoying and hideous. Oh! Sorry! I didn't mean that. But I hate you all. What's wrong with me?"

I shook my head. "We've been affected by this magic. We joined our power, and it felt like I lost control of Frank. He burst through my barriers. Ever since then, I've barely felt him. I figured he must have messed with us, but he hasn't been in control of me for ages. He can't have been hiding all this time, can he?"

"You think your shady demon has something to do with how weird we feel?" Zandra said.

"I hate Frank. He's the worst," Aurora said. "If I ever see him, I'm going to punch him on the nose."

"Think back to when we did that magic spell to wake Wiggles," I said. "What did you both feel?"

"I felt hot," Zandra said. "And I got the feeling something was trying to take me over."

"I got angry," Aurora said. "I wanted to hurt everyone. I still feel like that. I'm trying to be sorry about it, but I'm really not. Everyone, apart from me, is ridiculous. They should bow at my feet and beg me to allow them to live."

The door opened again, and Mom and Dad came in.

"We found your room empty." Dad walked over and hugged Zandra. "I was worried about you. You should be resting."

"I'm doing better," she said. "It's Aurora you need to worry about."

"Oh, wind your neck in," Aurora said. "You always were Dad's favorite."

"Hey, now. We're trying to be nice to each other," I said.

"You're a fine one to talk. You're sarcastic with everyone."

"Maybe I am, but you're not. That's what makes us work so well together." I tugged Mom to one side as Aurora bickered with Dad and Zandra. "Has she been like this since she woke up?"

Mom's expression was full of worry as she nodded. "I thought it would fade, but the bad mood won't break. She must be feeling terrible to be so snappy."

"She's not the only one struggling." I gestured to Aurora and Zandra who were arguing over a cookie. "I think we did this to each other when we cast a joined spell."

"That's not possible. Whenever Crypt witches join their magic, it only strengthens. You're more powerful when you're together."

"You've never heard of a time when a spell has backfired?" I said. "When we linked our magic, it was like a bomb went off in my head."

"I heard about what happened from Zandra." She shook her head. "It's never happened before. Not in my living memory."

"Maybe we've set a trend."

Mom hugged me. "How's Wiggles? Is he better?"

"Not really. He's with Abigail. She said there's strange magic attached to him. I don't know what it is, but it could be what's affecting us, too."

"You can't do that. I won't let you." Aurora's sharp voice drew my attention to her bed.

"What's going on?" I said.

"Dad says they're thinking about postponing the cemetery party because we're ill."

"It was just a thought," Dad said. "We want you all there. It wouldn't be right if you can't make it."

"We're having that party, and I'll be there," Aurora said. "You can't stop me. If the doctor tries, I'll discharge myself and go anyway."

"Is this true?" I said to Mom. "You're really thinking about postponing?"

"We won't be able to enjoy ourselves if you're all sick," she said.

"It's too late to cancel. The party is in two days."

"We'll be fine," Zandra said. "Everyone else shouldn't miss the party because of us."

"You're an important part of the celebration," Mom said. "You're the next generation of Crypt witches. You'll be the ones managing the cemetery when we're gone."

"Not me. I'm not spending my life skulking about some damp cemetery," Aurora said. "Zandra and Tempest can deal with the demons."

"We'll all deal with the demons when it's our turn," I said. "But this is an important anniversary. You can't cancel."

"And you're my important daughters," Dad said. "There won't be any celebration if you're not there."

"Then we'll make sure we are there," I said. "We just have to figure out what's going on with our magic and repair it."

"You two should stay home," Aurora said. "I'll have a better time if you're not there, cramping my style with your weird hair and terrible taste in clothes."

"Quit being a jerk," I said at the same time as Zandra.

Aurora huffed out a breath but wisely didn't say any more.

Granny Dottie strode into the room. "You're all in here! What am I missing out on?"

"Aurora being mean," I muttered.

"Has she still got a bee in her bonnet?" Granny Dottie walked to the bed and pressed a hand against Aurora's cheek. "You are running hotter than usual."

Aurora glared at her. "That's no concern of yours. Tell Mom and Dad to stop being nasty about this party. I've got a dress to wear especially for it. They can't cancel because of my two ugly sisters."

"I'm sure your sparkles will impress the demons in the prison," I said.

Granny Dottie clapped her hands together, sending a shower of magic sparks around the room. "No more sniping. I've been thinking about what Zandra and Aurora told me about your magic. I want to hear your version, Tempest."

"Um, there's nothing much to tell. We joined our magic, tried a spell to help Wiggles, but it blasted back at us. Something misfired."

"The magic blasted back? Are you sure? What exactly happened?"

"It was like a strong electric shock," I said. "And I couldn't control Frank. After that, it's a blank. I woke up when Wiggles licked my face."

"This is the first time it's happened?" Granny Dottie said.

I nodded then paused. "We did get a weird shock a while back. It was when we were all touching. Do you both remember?"

Zandra nodded. "Yeah, it was just like an electric shock. Sparks of magic flew out of us."

"Do it now," Granny Dottie said.

"Do what now?" I said.

"Connect your magic."

"I don't want to touch either of them," Aurora said. "They don't look clean."

I scowled at her but held my hands out to them both. "We might as well see if anything strange happens while everyone's here to watch over us."

Zandra caught hold of my hand. I got no weird tingle from being connected to her.

I wiggled my fingers at Aurora. "Stop being difficult. Join the circle."

After some dramatic sighing, she grabbed our hands.

A flare of magic shot out from each of us and sparkled around the room.

Granny Dottie threw herself in between us, breaking the connection as she knocked me away.

I staggered back and hit the wall. "What was that?"

"It was odd, that's what it was." Granny Dottie focused on the fading magic. "You three have a connection. Your magic is trying to do something, but it's blocked."

"What did we just feel?" Zandra flexed her fingers repeatedly.

"The effects of the spell's power trying to take hold." Granny Dottie followed a trace of the magic around the room, sniffing the air and poking her tongue out.

"What kind of spell are we talking about?" I said.

Granny Dottie pursed her lips. "I'm not sure, but it's powerful. My advice is don't make contact with each other. Let me look into this and see what I can find out."

A nurse strode into the room, and her eyes narrowed. "You're only supposed to have two visitors at a time."

"I can have as many as I like," Aurora said.

"The nurse is right. You need to rest," Mom said.

"She does. And so do you." The nurse pointed at Zandra. "Back to your room. No complaints. You need another healing spell."

"We'll take you back to your bed." Dad caught hold of Zandra's arm and gently led her out of the room, along with my mom.

"You need a healing spell too," the nurse said to Aurora. "And the rest of your visitors must leave."

"You said I could have two visitors. Can't you count?" Aurora said. "You're changing the rules. I should report you for incompetence and wearing terrible shoes."

"Listen to the experts." I glanced at the nurse. "Although I wouldn't mind staying if I could."

She shook her head. "After this healing spell, Aurora will need to sleep. She needs quiet to do that."

"How many years have you been a nurse?" Aurora said. "Do you even know what you're doing?"

"We'll both leave." Granny Dottie tried to kiss Aurora's cheek, but she pulled away. "Stubborn girl. Don't worry. We'll get things right with you."

I left the room with Granny Dottie, still hearing Aurora complaining to the nurse. "Do you really think there's something weird going on with our magic?"

"I do. And I'll get to the bottom of it." She cupped my cheek in her hand. "Take care of yourself. Something powerful has linked the three of you. Try not to use any magic until I've found the source, and we can neutralize it."

"Can you do that?"

Her expression soured. "Don't doubt me, girl. I can do anything when I set my mind to it."

I smiled as she hugged me. "Of course you can."

"Remember, no magic."

"I hear you. Since using magic is off the table, I'll make myself useful and interview some murder suspects."

"Are you still working on the murder that happened in Angel Force? Zandra was filling me in on it." Granny Dottie caught hold of my elbow as we walked to the hospital exit.

"I am. And I'm about ready to see if our remaining suspects will reveal how they did it, and why."

Chapter 17

I left Granny Dottie to puzzle out what was going on with my weird magic and headed to Angel Force. I'd just walked through the door when I was almost run down by a panicking Dazielle. Her wings beat around her, and her eyes were wide as she grabbed my shoulders and shook me.

"Easy. I'm feeling fragile. What's going on?"

She shook me again. "It's Isda. She told me the case must be solved today."

"Then she'll be disappointed. There's no guarantee we can get this resolved without a confession, or murder weapon, or any clues."

Dazielle squeaked and squeezed me. "We must. If Isda reports back to the other higher angels that I failed on this case, my career is over. She might demote me or send me to some remote office with only one or two angels to look after, and I'll have to deal with neighbor arguments over boundaries and misbehaving imps."

"That doesn't sound so bad. You always say this job is stressful and you need a vacation. A rural backwater job sounds perfect for you."

She shook me again so hard my teeth rattled. "It would be hideous. I love my life here. I even love you being an idiot and irritating me all the time."

"Awww. You love me?"

Her hand gripped my throat. "Of course not. But you must solve this case, or I'm finished."

"And what's the incentive for me to do that?"

Dazielle's hand tightened. "You get to live."

"That's hardly fair. But I'm not in the mood for dying today, so I'll help."

She lowered her hand and gave me another jiggle as if she wasn't sure she believed me.

"Although, if you shake me again, I'll puke all over your pristine white shoes."

Dazielle dropped her hold and scuttled back, her gaze running over me. "You don't look quite so ill, but I can tell you're not yourself. And your hair is something else."

I rubbed my neck. "Thanks for noticing."

"I... I didn't mean to hurt you."

"Sure you didn't."

Her gaze slid to the floor. "I'm under a lot of stress."

"So you keep saying."

"Are you up to working today? We really have to find out who killed Conan. And I do need your help."

"Apology accepted."

"I didn't... Oh, never mind. Will you live through the day, or should I hand in my notice now and accept defeat?"

"Don't quit just yet. I'm feeling better than yesterday. Let's go to the office and see what we can figure out about this murder."

I grabbed another strong coffee, and we headed into Dazielle's office.

She slammed the door and paced the room. "I've already spoken to Grady and Tatiana this morning. Neither of them are changing their stories or revealing how they planned to break out Conan."

"I was thinking they could be bluffing about the whole thing. The escape story is an attempt to hide their killer intentions." I sipped my coffee. "Although I was sure Grady would crack if we left him for long enough."

"We made a mistake about him. I should have grilled them both without a break. Maybe one of them would have gotten tired and let something slip. Instead, we gave them the easy route out."

"Have you ever noticed, when you're having a problem, it's always our fault, and whenever things go well, you take the credit?" A grin crossed my face.

She flapped a hand at me. "Not now! I'm doing my best."

I shrugged. "Just saying. The higher angels might like to look at that in your next appraisal."

"There won't be an appraisal if we don't fix this problem." She glared at me. "And I give you credit where it's due."

"If you say so."

Dazielle huffed out a breath and continued to pace. "Grady's had time to think about his story. He knows we've got nothing on him or Tatiana. And we can't keep him here forever."

"Technically, we could. He's supposed to be at home. The evidence shows he hasn't left. If he went missing—"

"We aren't killing a suspect."

"Who said anything about killing? But if Grady was left in a cell on his own for a very long time, he might talk."

Her gaze cut to me, and she shook her head. "No. I'm not breaking the law. Besides, that won't solve the case today. It could take months to force a confession."

"Grady has a point about us having nothing on him. I don't want to side with the bad guy, but we still can't figure out how the murder was committed."

"He was outside Angel Force just after the murder."

"Yes, but he was still outside. He wasn't close enough to stab Conan. Grady might not be our guy."

Dazielle froze to the spot, and her eyes widened. "Isda's arrived. I can't deal with her again. What if she's got bad news for me?"

"Then you'll handle it." I looked over my shoulder as Isda glided around the main office, greeting the other angels. "I could always tell her she's being unrealistic by giving us such a tight deadline. Until we get all the pieces in place, we can't charge anyone with Conan's murder. If she forces us into a corner and we make assumptions, the wrong person could go down for this crime. That means the real killer gets away with it."

"I told Isda that, but she simply smiled and shook her head. She said we must work harder and smarter."

"That sounds like a new tagline for the modern Angel Force. Working harder and smarter and making even more mistakes."

"That's not helpful." Dazielle grabbed my arm, making me spill my coffee. "We'll creep out of here. She's distracted talking to Cassiel. We can get out before she sees us."

"Which will achieve nothing." I wiped hot coffee off my hand.

"It'll buy us time."

"I have no problems with hiding from an angel. I've done it plenty of times. But are you sure about this?"

"Yes! We must escape while we can."

"If we lay everything out for Isda, what we've investigated, who the remaining suspects are, and what the problems are, she must understand."

"She doesn't. And I can't risk her turning unpleasant. We leave now, or it's over for us."

"Again with the us when there's a problem. I don't work for Angel Force. Isda can't fire me."

"No, but they can do a lot worse than that if they turn against you."

"You make it sound like she's going to do something drastic."

"You never know with a higher angel." Dazielle kept peeking at Isda. "I heard a rumor there was a higher angel who could disintegrate someone with the power of her thoughts."

My eyes widened. "I'm sold. Let's get out of here."

Dazielle waited a second then snuck open the door. She kept hold of me as we crept out of the office while Isda's back was turned. Once we were at the front door, we raced away.

"Do you think she saw us?" Dazielle looked over her shoulder.

"Nope. We got away with it. How about we celebrate by going to Patti's? Her coffee is nicer than yours."

"I could do with a pick me up," Dazielle said. "This case is exhausting me."

"And since you made me run away from a higher angel, you're buying. And I want a large mug."

"I accept those terms."

We headed into Patti's café, and Dazielle collected our drinks. When she returned to the table, she surprised me with apricot breakfast pastries, liberally sprinkled with sugar and pale pink icing. I'd already had a croissant, but I never said no to a delicious breakfast pastry.

"So, what have we got to focus on in this case?" I said. "The victim was a dark magic pedaling warlock. He got stabbed by what we thought was a knitting needle, but we can't find it."

"We found one in the washroom, hidden by Elman," Dazielle said.

"But it had no prints on it, other than his, or any blood. And Elman admitted he lost his nerve and couldn't go through with killing Conan."

Dazielle sighed. "And we still have the dilemma about Conan being alone in a locked cell."

"As far as we can figure out, no one got in to stab him."

"I said you should have stayed with Conan after we locked that cell," Dazielle said.

I almost choked on my sugary pastry. "Your memory is wrong. I suggested staying there, but you told me there was nothing to worry about. You said the cell was secure and Conan was safely locked up."

Her forehead wrinkled. "Maybe I said something like that. But I didn't see there being any problem."

"Hindsight is an awesome beast. So we have a murdered warlock, and the suspects are a peace loving shaman or his mean girlfriend who has the most complicated love life I've ever come across."

"Tatiana seems to have had strong feelings for Grady and Conan." Dazielle wrinkled her nose. "Why does love have to be so complicated?"

"Beats me. Tatiana is deceitful, though. She hid the plan to break Conan out of his cell with Grady as her willing assistant, and that she was hiding Grady in the village. Could she be hiding something else?"

"Even if she is, all that information blows apart any motive about her planning a new life with Grady. She didn't want Conan dead. She wanted a family and a future with him," Dazielle said.

"Which means she doesn't have any motive," I said. "And Tatiana was nowhere near the cells when Conan was killed."

Dazielle ate a piece of pastry. "For a while, I really thought Elman was the killer. He seems like such a peaceful man, but losing the love of his life could have broken him."

"I wondered about Elman, too. And he concealed his plan to kill Conan until we found the knitting needle. But he couldn't go through with it. He genuinely lives a life of peace," I said.

"And again, he had no way to get to Conan. He has the perfect motive but no opportunity." Dazielle stuffed half her pastry in her mouth, and sugar sprinkles dropped onto her shirt.

"We shouldn't forget Sorath," I said.

"We should. He's a foolish angel for getting in debt and making himself vulnerable to bribery, but he's not a killer," Dazielle said.

"I'm not saying he is, but he was given a bribe to set off the alarm. That was supposed to give Grady and Tatiana a chance to break Conan out of his cell."

"You're not telling me anything new."

"What if, just like Sorath, one of your angels received a similar bribe? But they were bribed to actually stab Conan."

She shook her head but didn't say anything for a minute. "I'll admit some of my angels aren't perfect."

"Hold up now. You've never admitted that before. This is a big moment. I need a few seconds to process it." I couldn't stop the wicked smile appearing on my face. "Angels aren't perfect. I should get that put on a T-shirt."

"Tempest, stop being an idiot."

"I'm not. And I think it's great you're finally admitting angels aren't infallible. They mess up, they fall in love with the wrong people, they miss clues, they—"

"Fine. Angels aren't perfect. But my angels are reliable, and I trust them. They always do their jobs to the best of their abilities. I'm certain, if any of them were contacted and offered a bribe to murder someone in our custody, they'd say something." Dazielle dabbed at the sugar on her bust. "And I'm happy to say Sorath isn't a part of my team. I'll have you know, there are certain angels who have a very relaxed approach to management. They don't even do quarterly appraisals in some offices."

"The world is about to end. Where would we be without our quarterly appraisals?"

She narrowed her eyes at me. "Sorath's a good angel who made a mistake. He'll have to pay for that. It'll change his life forever."

"Sorath could become a bouncer. I'm always looking for reliable people to work the door at Cloven Hoof."

Dazielle simply rolled her eyes.

"He'll have to do something. Maybe he could marry for money. Sorath's a cute angel. He might catch a wealthy widow's eye."

"I don't care what he does. He can't keep working for us."

Puddles Lavern, my landlady, paused by our table. She held a bag bulging with pink bundles of wool. "Are you talking about that charming angel, Sorath?"

"Hey, Puddles. We might be," I said.

Her round cheeks flushed, and she blinked rapidly. "I heard he was back in Willow Tree Falls, but I haven't had a chance to see him. I want to invite him over for dinner. Is he staying long?"

"You know Sorath?" I said.

"Do I know Sorath!" Puddles giggled like a teenager. "He's incredible. I've never met such a talented knitter. For months, he traveled to our little knitting group. He said we were the best group he's ever been involved with and couldn't stand to miss a single meeting."

"I didn't know Sorath was involved with your group," I said. "I also didn't know he knitted."

"Oh, yes." She adjusted the pale pink sweater she had on. "And he made me this. It's my favorite cardigan. He's such a cutie pie. I've missed him not being around. I'm thrilled to hear he's back."

"Sorath was a regular at your group?" I said.

"He was, but I haven't seen him for a couple of months. I don't know why he stopped coming, but he was so friendly. Sorath always had a kind word and a twinkle in his eye for me. I was thrilled when he gave me this cardigan, but my boyfriend got jealous. He said he didn't like men giving me clothing." Puddles smoothed her hands over the fabric. "It's not as if he got me a set of lingerie to try on in front of him." She giggled again.

"Sorath's likely to have free time on his hands from now on. He's got a big career change planned," I said. "Maybe you'll see him back in the group."

"I hope so. We've all missed him. Although Elman wasn't a fan."

I glanced at Dazielle, who was still brushing sugar off her shirt. "Sorath and Elman know each other?"

"Yes! Don't say I told you, but I have a feeling that's why Elman started coming to our group. His lovely wife was friendly with Sorath. They always sat together and would talk for ages."

"Did they now? What did they talk about?" I leaned forward in my seat.

"All sorts of things. I used to get jealous because Sorath paid Violet so much attention. And I did wonder... Perhaps Elman got a little jealous, too. He was never interested in knitting until Sorath got involved. I think Elman came to our group because Violet was flirting with that charming angel." Puddles stroked a hand over her cardigan again. "Who could blame her? He's such a sweetheart. Anyway, I can't stop. I see my friend." She bustled away, clutching her bag of knitting.

I stared after her as the puzzle pieces fit together. "Dazielle, did you get all of that?"

"Yes. Sorath likes knitting, and he was a flirt."

"Sorath, Elman, and Violet were in the same knitting group. Sorath didn't mention that. Neither did Elman. And Sorath traveled here just to go to the group. Why? It can't be that special? A knitting group is just a knitting group, isn't it?"

"I know nothing about knitting. Maybe they do something special with their wool or have unusual patterns. Why should I care?"

I stared at my pastry and the sugar sprinkles on the table. "Knitting, Wiggles's obsession with sugar, and Sorath joining our local knitting group."

"Tempest, you're not making sense. Perhaps you shouldn't have worked today." Dazielle finished her pastry. "Should I take you to the hospital if you're relapsing?"

"No." I pushed back my seat. "Get everyone involved in this murder at Angel Force. I know who killed Conan and how they did it."

Chapter 18

Dazielle flew off ahead of me to gather everyone involved in the investigation. I was on foot but slowed as I got to Fur Baby Emporium. I pushed open the door and hurried inside.

Abigail emerged from behind the counter. "I was about to get in touch. Wiggles is awake."

"How is he? Have you got him talking?"

She tilted her head from side to side. "Kind of. He's saying words, but none of them make sense."

"He's still talking about desserts, isn't he?"

"Yes! Why is he doing that?"

"I know exactly why. Is he okay to leave?"

"He is. There's nothing more I can do for him. Follow me." Abigail led me through the examination room and into the back of the store.

Wiggles was standing up on his hind legs in his pen. His tail wagged when he saw me. "Butter cream cups."

"Yes. I'm here to get you out. And I think I know why you're talking in cake all the time." I knelt in front of his pen. "I'm just not sure how to stop it."

"Ice cream cone?" Wiggles jammed his nose through the bars.

"It's all to do with Conan's murder. I'm going to Angel Force to reveal who the killer is and how they did it. Do you want to come?"

"Devil's food cake."

"Is that a yes?" Abigail said.

"We'll have to assume it is."

She opened the pen, and Wiggles jumped out.

I gave him a quick pet. "We need to move. Can I pay you later?" I said to Abigail.

"It's already written out. I sent the bill to Cloven Hoof." She shooed me to the door. "Go catch your killer."

I hurried out of the store, Wiggles trotting along beside me. "I've got the crime solved, but I'm not certain how we're going to get you talking normally again."

"Cherry pie and vanilla ice cream."

A grin crossed my face. It was so good to have Wiggles back by my side. "I'm gaining weight just listening to you talk. Let's get this murder solved once and for all, then we can focus on you."

I headed into Angel Force and through to the main office. I was impressed to see Dazielle had gotten all her angels gathered, along with Tatiana, Grady, Elman, and Sorath. Isda stood to one side, a serene expression on her face.

Dazielle's hands were clasped in front of her, her wings quivering slightly. She inclined her head at Isda and glared at me.

"Thanks for coming here, everyone." I looked around the room and spotted Oriel, the super introverted angel who looked after the evidence room. I walked over to her. "Do you keep a log of everyone who goes in and out of the evidence room?"

She nodded. "Of course. It's a secure room. I'm always there to make sure I know who goes in and out."

"Perfect. Go grab that log and get back here. It will have an important clue as to who our killer is."

Oriel hurried away and returned a moment later, clutching a red logbook. She glanced at Dazielle, who nodded. Oriel handed me the book.

I flicked through it and frowned. The name I was expecting to see wasn't in there, but I'd come back to that. I was certain I was right about this.

"Tempest! You said you know who killed Conan," Dazielle said. "We're all waiting to hear. Especially Isda. She has a report to file."

I set down the logbook. "I know who did it. I was just doing some fact checking."

"So..." Dazielle waved at me to get a move on.

"When Conan was murdered, we looked at Elman as the obvious suspect. His wife had been murdered by Conan, and he had every right to feel angry and want revenge," I said.

"I don't disagree with any of that, but I couldn't have done it," Elman said.

"But you thought about it. And you brought a weapon with you to kill the victim."

"Elman killed Conan?" Tatiana lurched forward in her seat.

"No. Despite having a murder weapon and a strong motive for wanting Conan dead, he didn't do it," I said. "At the last minute, Elman changed his mind. He hid his weapon in the washroom."

Elman lowered his head. "I had a moment of weakness. I had dark thoughts about Conan, and I admit to those, but I could never kill another person."

"So although Elman was our prime suspect, we ruled him out." I turned to Tatiana. "Then we have Conan's girlfriend. A woman with a tangled criminal past and a complicated love life. Tatiana freely admits to loving Conan and his brother, Grady."

"There's nothing wrong with that. I never cheated on either of them. They always knew what was going on," Tatiana said.

"And I believe they both loved you," I said. "Grady still does. So much so, you convinced him to help you break Conan out of his cell when he was brought here to stand trial for Violet's murder."

She shrugged. "You've got no proof."

"It's sitting beside you." I nodded at Grady, who kept glancing at Tatiana and had already tried to hold her hand more than once. "We know Grady disabled his tracker and forged travel documents so he could come here without being arrested. He did that to help you and his brother."

"We stick together. There's nothing wrong with that." Tatiana's glare was intense.

Grady nodded. "I'd do anything to help my family. I don't care about any tracker or probation rules. I did what was right. Conan deserved happiness with Tatiana."

"He didn't deserve happiness." Bitterness traced through Elman's voice. "He killed my wife."

"I'm confused. Did Grady and Tatiana change their minds?" Isda said. "They decided they wanted Conan dead?"

"No, they didn't. They had it planned out, but they weren't working alone. To pull off their scheming, they needed someone on the inside." I looked at Sorath. "They needed help from an angel."

There were several gasps from around the room. Isda's wings fluttered, and Dazielle didn't look happy.

"That's the only way this murder could have happened," I said.

Sorath shifted in his seat. "I've already admitted to what I did to assist Conan's escape."

"What did he do?" Elman said.

"Sorath got in debt. He received a bribe in return for agreeing to set off the alarm in Angel Force once Conan was inside his cell," I said.

"And I deeply regret doing that," Sorath said. "I thought Tatiana and Grady were breaking Conan out, not setting the scene so he could be killed."

"That's exactly what we were doing." Tatiana's eyes narrowed as she glared at me. "Fine, we were planning to break out Conan, but Sorath was an idiot and set off the wrong alarm. We wanted the building empty, or at least only a couple of angels left behind who would be easy to take down. We didn't expect everyone to rush to the cells. It ruined our plan."

"I didn't realize there'd be more than one alarm option," Sorath said. "I hit the nearest alarm and hoped for the best."

"You messed everything up." Tatiana jabbed a finger at him. "You got Conan murdered."

"But how?" Elman said. "Conan was in a cell. Part of the reason I changed my mind was because there was no way I could get to him. There were too many angels around. I didn't realize the place would be so busy."

"Of course. And your pure heart also stopped you," I said.

His lips pursed, but then he nodded.

I remained focused on Sorath. "You met Conan before bringing him here to stand trial, didn't you?"

"Yes. At his pre-trial hearing."

"Was that when he first spoke to you about helping him break out?"

Sorath swallowed so loudly everyone must have heard. "He might have."

"He did. And that's when you formed your plan."

"What plan is this?" Isda said.

"Sorath knew Conan murdered a good woman. Everyone who knew Violet Oakley spoke kindly about her. Even her husband, despite their marriage difficulties," I said.

"There were no difficulties in our marriage. We had a wonderful relationship," Elman said.

"Only according to you. According to other people, it wasn't so blissful," I said. "Your wife spent a lot of time with friends and on her hobbies, rather than with you."

"Why is the state of Elman's marriage important?" Isda said.

"It's very important. When Conan suggested a deal with Sorath, he realized this was the perfect opportunity to get justice," I said.

"Sorath avenged Violet's murder?" Isda said.

I nodded. "He did. But for his own reasons. Sorath and Violet were having an affair."

Elman turned his head slowly and scowled at Sorath. "Is this true?"

Sorath's cheeks paled. "No, it isn't. Tempest has this all wrong."

"You joined our local knit and natter group because Violet went there," I said. "I'm not sure how you first met, but it was the perfect cover for you to meet without arousing much suspicion. You'd go to the meetings to see Violet. The relationship grew more serious, and Elman became suspicious. That's when he joined the knitting group. He wanted to keep an eye on his unhappy wife and find out if she was being unfaithful."

"I... I joined the group because it's important for couples to do things together," Elman said.

"It's also important for couples not to cheat on each other," I said. "And when you joined the group, Sorath and Violet had to find somewhere else to meet, or their affair would have been obvious to you. Sorath stopped going to the group, and they started having clandestine evening meetings out of the village."

Elman slumped back in his seat. "They continued to see each other?"

"They did. And it was on one of those evening meet ups that Violet had the bad luck of stumbling into Conan's shady business dealings. She didn't know a dark magic trade was going down. She simply planned to meet her lover that night." I looked at Sorath. "And you saw it all, didn't you? You were waiting for her when Conan cast the dark curse. There was nothing you could do, and she died in agony."

Sorath looked away but didn't say anything.

"You were eaten up with anger and the desire for revenge," I said. "And when Conan offered you that bribe, you saw an opportunity to get to him. So you went along with the plan to help break him out. You transported Conan here and made sure you were the one to put him in the cell. While you were in there, you slipped him fake blood."

There were several murmurs, and even Isda looked startled.

"Then all you needed to do was get everyone away from the cell and set off the alarm. That was Conan's cue to break the blood packet. When we rushed to the cells to see why the alarm had been triggered, it looked like Conan was dead." I pointed at the alarm buttons on the wall. "And you've been in plenty of Angel Force buildings, so you wouldn't have made a mistake over which button to hit. You knew what you were doing."

"And Sorath went into the cell first to check if Conan was alive," Dazielle said. "I didn't double-check Conan's body for several minutes."

I nodded. "He did. And while Sorath was checking on Conan, who was playing dead, we rushed off to find the killer. Which left Sorath and Conan alone."

"I'm still at a loss as to how Conan was killed," Isda said. "Sorath had a knife on him?"

"He used the exact same weapon Elman planned to use. A long, thin metal knitting needle would slide up an arm sleeve or inside a sock and be hidden. There was no magic attached to the weapon, so it didn't trigger any alerts on the wards," I said. "Conan must have had the shock of his life, when he thought he was about to escape, and Sorath plunged the knitting needle into his heart. Then all Sorath needed to do was remove the fake blood packet before anyone else came back. Everyone assumed the killer had escaped the building, but the whole time, he'd been with us."

Sorath remained silent.

"What about the murder weapon?" Isda said. "Where is it?"

I opened the logbook. "This is where things get tricky. Oriel, you said everyone must be logged in and out when they go into the evidence room."

Her gaze was on Sorath. "That's right. That's… that's what I'm supposed to do."

"Do you ever make an exception?"

She ducked her head. "I'm sorry to say I did on one occasion. Sorath is charming. He said it was our secret, and he just wanted a quick look. He'd heard how impressive my evidence room was and wanted to get tips from the best. I was flattered. And he was in there less than a minute."

"So you didn't log him into the evidence room?" I said.

Her wings drooped. "I didn't. Now I'm hearing all of this, I regret it."

I glanced at Isda. "What's the one place we'd never look when searching for a murder weapon?"

She appeared perplexed and shook her head. "I don't know. The building was thoroughly searched."

"But one room wasn't. The only room in Angel Force with twenty-four-hour security, a login system, and secured boxes of evidence. The evidence room wasn't searched, was it?" I looked at Dazielle.

She shook her head. "As you said, there was no reason to look in there. It wasn't accessible to anyone."

"Yet Sorath sweet-talked himself in among all the chaos. That's where you'll find the murder weapon. Oriel, take someone with you and have a look around. Look for any boxes that have been disturbed. You're looking for a long metal knitting needle."

She grabbed a colleague, and they raced away.

Sorath stood from his seat. "This isn't right."

"When the knitting needle is found, we'll discover your fingerprints and Conan's blood on it. And I expect we'll find something else, as well." I stroked Wiggles. "My hellhound licked Conan's stab wound."

Cassiel made a sound of disgust in the back of her throat. "And almost ruined my autopsy."

"He was licking it for a good reason," I said. "Fake blood is usually made up of something sweet. Wiggles thought he'd found a yummy treat and was having a taste. When he licked it, he passed out. Did you use stasis magic on Conan, so he appeared dead when we showed up at the cell?" I asked Sorath.

He simply glowered at me.

"We can test for traces of that magic," Cassiel said. "It might still be there."

"It will be," I said. "Wiggles always hunts out sweet treats. His nose led him to the wound on Conan's chest. He had a taste and got a hit of the stasis magic. It knocked him out, and when he came to, the only thing he could talk about was desserts. This whole time, Wiggles has been trying to tell me that, when he licked the victim's wound, he tasted sugar, not blood."

"Iced bun, strawberry flan, treacle tart." Wiggles jumped up and down.

"Exactly. The magic affected Wiggles, but he was still trying to tell me about Conan's murder." I looked at Dazielle, and she was no longer scowling. Hope glinted in her eyes. "Put it all together, Elman's unhappy marriage, Sorath settling down and no longer being a flirt with everyone, the bribery money, the gossip we heard from the knitting group, and Wiggles being affected by the stasis magic, and Sorath is our killer."

"This won't hold up in court," Sorath said.

"It will with this." Oriel rushed in. She clutched a clear evidence bag. Inside was a bloody knitting needle.

I grinned at her. "That'll do it. Cassiel, could you do the honors?"

For once, she didn't protest, simply grabbed the evidence bag and headed to her examination room.

"You can confess now or wait until the results come back off that knitting needle," I said to Sorath. "But you murdered Conan."

Everyone looked at Sorath to see what he had to say for himself.

He scowled and rubbed the back of his neck. "Conan was a terrible person. He killed the love of my life. Violet was such a kind, sweet woman. Getting rid of Conan did the world a favor."

Dazielle let out a loud sigh. "Sorath, you're under arrest for the murder of Conan Nox."

He didn't argue as he was shackled and led away by two angels.

Dazielle shot me a grateful look before turning to Isda.

I knelt and petted Wiggles. "Sorry I didn't pay more attention to you and your cake talk. I might have figured this out sooner if I had. Now all we need to do is work out how to get this lingering magic off you so you can talk about something other than treats."

He licked my hand. "Chocolate peanut butter cups."

Chapter 19

Following Sorath's arrest for Conan's murder, I'd left the angels to tidy up the loose ends. I'd heard from Dazielle a couple of hours ago that Conan's blood and Sorath's fingerprints were on the knitting needle. The evidence against Sorath was damning. He wasn't getting away with this murder.

"You should take a break from those books," Merrie said. "You've been reading for hours."

"That's because I need to find a solution to my magic problem. I need to fix this. It's not just affecting me but also my sisters."

"Your magic is still being naughty?"

"Sugar cookies." Wiggles wandered out of the kitchen, chewing on something he most likely shouldn't.

"Yes. Nothing I've done has gotten Wiggles talking normally. And I don't feel strong enough to perform any spells. Not even the simple ones. How will I get my hellhound talking normally again if I can't break whatever's holding him?"

Merrie set down the crate of drinks she held. "Is there anything useful in those books?"

"I've found dozens of possibilities, but I keep returning to the power of three. Something happened when I connected with Aurora and Zandra. I think we linked to each other, but I don't know why or for what reason."

"That's serious stuff." Merrie walked over. "You don't want to play around with that."

"Do you know much about the power of three?"

"Sure. I mean, we all learned the basics in witch school, but my mom's side of the family went rogue years ago because they messed up their connection."

"They did? You never talk about her."

Merrie glanced around, but the bar was empty. "Because she's the black sheep of the family. She had two sisters who got into some dark stuff, and she joined them. They weren't so bad when they were doing it on their own, but they formed a trifecta of power. They linked their powers and became impossible to control."

"What happened to them?"

"They died when a demon took control of them." Her eyes widened. "Not that I'm saying that'll happen to you and your sisters if you have a link. None of you are into the dark stuff."

"I walk a gray line."

"Only sometimes and only to handle the nasty demons you deal with."

"I don't want that darkness messing with Aurora's white magic." I rubbed my forehead. "And it is. You should have heard her at the hospital. She was awful to everyone."

"There's an upside to forming a trifecta of power, though. If you get it right, the power of three is incredible. You'll all be super powerful," Merrie said.

"It's that easy?"

"Nope. Just like my family, it can go horribly wrong. It broke my heart to see my mom and aunties get messed up because they chose the wrong path and concentrated on dark powers." Merrie shook her head. "But imagine what you could do if you all had pure white magic and linked it together?"

"My magic has never been pure. I'm not sure it would work. Maybe I'm the one messing with the connection."

"There's no going back now. If you've started a connection with your sisters, the magic needs to be sealed."

"We didn't do it intentionally. We just touched, but it was like something whacked us with a stun gun."

Merrie grabbed a book and flicked through it. "Zandra is new to the family, though."

"She's been here a while now, but it took time for everyone to get used to her. Aurora wasn't a fan to begin with."

"She is now?"

"They get along great most of the time."

"Maybe Zandra was your missing piece. You needed her before anything could happen. The magic is giving you all a kick up the butt and showing you what you can achieve when you connect your powers. Don't think of that zap as a bad thing."

"But all it's done is mess up our powers. Aurora has turned mean, and Zandra is quieter. She was never the quiet one in the group."

"And how are you feeling?" Merrie said.

"Not myself. And not enjoying the fact my magic's not working, or when it does, it goes wrong."

"It must be working okay," Merrie said. "You wouldn't be able to control Frank if you'd lost your power."

"That's another weird thing. I've barely felt him for months. I know he's there, but he's weak, too."

The club door slammed open, and Zandra rushed in. "I need your help."

"What is it? Shouldn't you be at the hospital?"

"Aurora's gone into the demon prison."

I dropped the book I was holding. "She was taken? Did a demon abduct her from the hospital?"

"No. She left the hospital and walked straight there." Zandra beckoned for me to follow her. "I only realized something was wrong when I went to her room and found it empty. I asked around, and no one had seen her for an hour. I did a location spell, and it showed she'd gone to the prison."

"She's in the demon prison or just the cemetery?" I was already hurrying out of the club with Zandra. Wiggles was at my heel.

"Aurora's inside. She opened the prison and walked in. And the demons are getting out."

"Does the rest of the family know?"

"I told them first. Then I came to get you. They're fighting the demons and trying to stop them from getting out of the cemetery and wrecking the village."

"What's Aurora playing at? Did she say anything odd to you before she left?" We were running toward the cemetery. I could see plumes of magic sparking in the air as my family fought the demons.

"She was still being mean to everyone. It only got worse when you left. Aurora punched a nurse."

"Something's wrong with her," I said. "But she won't survive inside the prison. The demons will eat her alive."

"She will with the anger burning inside her," Zandra said. "Aurora could probably take down the whole lot of them."

We reached the large black iron gates that led into the cemetery. Strong binding magic kept them closed.

I peered through the gates just in time to see Granny Dottie slam a spell into a huge demon and send it sprawling onto its back.

"Granny Dottie," I yelled. "Let us in."

She glanced at the gates and flicked her wrist. The binding magic lowered and allowed Zandra and me through. It rose again the second we were inside.

The air simmered with hot, dark magic as my family fought the escapees.

My mom and dad were by the entrance to the demon prison, blasting anything that tried to get out. Grandpa Lucius stood back to back with Uncle Kenny as they fought off half a dozen angry looking demons with horns and killer claws.

Auntie Queenie was in one corner, chasing a herd of furry demons with long arms.

I raced to the entrance of the prison with Zandra and Wiggles. "Is Aurora out yet?"

My mom turned, keeping magic blazing on her fingers. "She won't come out. I haven't seen her. I keep calling for her, but she's ignoring me." Tears streaked down her cheeks.

"Tempest! I need to talk to you," Granny Dottie yelled.

I turned and looked at her and then back at the dark entrance leading into the demon prison.

"It's important. Get over here."

"Zandra, you help Mom and Dad." I raced over to Granny Dottie, dodging a demon, knowing my magic would be no good against it.

"I found out something that could help you and your sisters." Granny Dottie blasted another demon onto its butt. "Your power has gone wrong because you've only partly joined."

I stared at her for a second. "You mean the power of three?"

"Yes! I wondered if you'd accidentally forged a link with Zandra and Aurora, so I have been doing my research."

"I've been looking at that all day, too. And I was talking to Merrie about it." I ducked as a demon flew over my head, its claws tangling in my hair for a second.

"You girls need to finish the connection, or your power will keep malfunctioning."

"How do we finish making a connection?"

"I need to know how the process began to tell you that." Granny Dottie shot a spell into a demon's chest, and it staggered away.

My frantic gaze went around the battles in the cemetery. If we didn't stop this soon, the village would be destroyed. "I don't know how we did it. We weren't trying to form a link. It just happened."

"Well, you have one. And you need to get back together and finish what you started. This chaos is due to your wonky connection."

"Is that why Aurora has gone inside the demon prison?"

Granny Dottie tapped a finger against my chest. "Her magic is as messed up as yours. She's confused and no longer feels in control. You have to help her."

I looked at the entrance to the prison. "I'll get her."

Granny Dottie thrust a wand into my hand. "Use this. It's charged with my magic. It won't last forever, but it should clear a path on your way down."

I turned and raced back to the opening. I grabbed Zandra's arm. "We need to get our sister out. Are you with me?"

Zandra's face paled, but she nodded. "Of course. She's an annoying idiot, but she's our annoying idiot. Those demons don't get to keep her."

"We'll keep the entrance open for you," my dad said.

Mom squeezed my arm. "Give them hell. And if any of them have hurt Aurora, make them pay."

"Of course." I kissed her cheek, made sure Wiggles was by my side, and entered a gloomy tunnel that stank of sulfur and fire.

Zandra was clutching my elbow as we hurried along the stony passageway. "I've never been inside a demon prison before. Are there cages to keep the demons in?"

"Only the really nasty ones get cages. They can roam around but not go far. The cemetery boundary is as far as they get before our magic repels them." I tilted my head as I listened for any hissing or growling coming our way. "You'll find all kinds of demons in here. Some have been here since it began. They're likely to be insane and angry."

"How are we supposed to fight them with our magic malfunctioning?"

I handed her the wand. "Use this. You focus on keeping the demons away from us, and I'll look for Aurora."

"Jam tart and custard." Wiggles thumped my calf with his head.

"Of course. You need to help too," I said.

"Will Wiggles be okay down here?" Zandra said. "Isn't he too small to fight off a demon?"

"He'll be fine. Demons kind of like him. We can use that to our advantage."

"Lemon drizzle cake," Wiggles said.

"Don't hold back on the lemon drizzle cake attacks," I said to him. "Bite to kill."

We hurried along the passageway as it sloped down to the first open room. I heard the snarling and roaring of demons before I saw them. A high-pitched female laugh cut through the grumbles and roars.

"That must be Aurora," Zandra whispered. "What's she finding funny down here?"

"No idea, but if she's laughing, she's still alive." I slowed as we neared the entrance, not feeling prepared for battling a horde of demons. "Did Granny Dottie tell you about the power of three?"

Her nose wrinkled. "She gave me a book to read, but I'm not into reading. She said it would help me figure out what's going on with us."

"I think we started something we have to finish. That's what's affecting Aurora."

"She's gone dark because we did something to her?"

"She's gone dark, you've gone quiet, and I got messed up. We need to make this power of three thing stop. Or complete it. Although I don't know what it wants from us."

Zandra flinched as a huge shadow flickered across the entrance. "Why aren't the demons attacking?"

I stopped by the open doorway, and my heart plummeted. "Because of her."

Aurora stood in the middle of the stone cavern, surrounded by over fifty demons. They were staring at her as if they couldn't believe she was there. Magic sparked around her in long, dark jagged spears that shot out and occasionally slammed into a demon. Every time a spark hit a demon, it disintegrated.

"Wow! So that's where all our power has gone," Zandra said. "Aurora took it and added a dark twist."

"Not by choice. I don't know how we did it, but we've made her way too strong. She can't control all that power on her own."

"And now we're the weak ones. This sucks," Zandra said.

"Sweet potato pie!" Wiggles launched at a demon that lumbered our way and sank his teeth into its throat.

The demon exploded in a gooey, green mess.

Wiggles dropped to the ground and shook out his fur, sending green globules of goo everywhere.

Zandra scowled at the mess on the ground. "Gross. I forgot demons often explode when you kill them."

"This fight will get messy. And we've been noticed." Three more demons headed our way. "Zandra, use the wand to blast them."

I risked testing my magic. It was weak and scattered, but if I had to, I'd take on a demon.

"Look, everyone. We have guests." Aurora's voice rang out around the cavern.

"What's she doing?" Zandra hissed.

"Giving us a whole heap of trouble," I said. "Keep your back against the wall. You don't want anything sneaking up on you."

I'd just lifted my hands to blast a demon who was looking at me with murder in his eyes when a pain so sharp it stole my breath ripped through my chest. I felt like I was about to puke, and I gagged as I bent over double. A hot wave of power shot through me, lifting my hair as it flooded out of me.

"Tempest! What's wrong?" Zandra's voice sounded far away as the pain savaged me.

"Keep the demons away." I dropped to my knees as black dots danced across my vision. If I passed out in a room full of hateful demons, I was dead.

Several warm, sticky globules of demon goo landed on me as Zandra and Wiggles fought to keep me safe.

"You shouldn't be here. It's dangerous for both of you," Aurora said.

"And you," I gasped out. "Why did you come here?"

"I thought I'd have some fun."

"We need to leave," Zandra yelled. "Stop being an idiot and move your butt. Zap those demons and let's go."

"You go. Before I set my new demon army on you." Aurora's singsong voice had a hint of insanity in it.

I staggered to my feet and pressed my back against the wall. My gaze traveled up, and my jaw dropped open. Standing in front of me was the demon I'd carried around since I was a child.

Frank was free. He was a muscular demon, with gray, warty skin, fangs, and glowing red eyes. It had been so long since I'd seen him in the flesh that I'd almost forgotten what he looked like. But that memory of him, standing over Aurora's bed and about to take her life, was burned into my brain.

Amusement shifted across his face as he watched my shock. "My witch companion. We finally meet face to face again." His voice was no longer a deep rumble in my head but was growling all around me.

I sucked in a breath to steady my racing heart. "How did you do that?"

"I'm surrounded by my own kind. We're more powerful when we're together. And I needed to be free. You have damaged me, and I no longer had control over you. That was unacceptable."

"You could always get out of me if you wanted to?"

"No. Although I came close more than once." His gaze cut to Aurora, and he growled. "Especially when something so tempting was in my path. And you grew sloppy and let me get near the delicious white witch too often."

"You're not having Aurora." I lifted a hand, but the magic failed me.

A blast of red magic slammed into Frank's chest. He roared and knocked it away, sending it back toward Zandra. "Foolish child. You can't hurt me."

Zandra dodged the spell by dropping to the ground and rolling away. She flipped to her feet and tried another blast of magic.

Frank was ready for her. He batted aside the magic like it was an annoying fly, thrust out his fists, and spun gray swirls of energy into Zandra.

She smashed against the rough stone wall and dropped to the dirt with a groan.

"Leave her alone," I yelled. "Leave both my sisters alone. You're not having either of them. Zandra, are you okay?"

She lifted a hand but remained in the dirt.

An evil grin crossed Frank's face. "I will have a Crypt witch. You can guarantee that."

Aurora's laugh filtered across the cavern, drawing his attention back to her.

I grabbed a rock and slung it at Frank. "Keep your demon claws away from Aurora. She's not for you."

His glare slid back to me. "Are you offering to take her place?"

"No! You get no one."

He spread his large hands in front of him. "We've spent many years together. I know all about you, Tempest Crypt. I know what you love, what you hate, what you fear the most. Perhaps an eternity spent together wouldn't be so bad. You have a dark side I could feed."

"None of that's true." I swiped my hands down my arms, trying to scrub those awful words off me.

"And I've never met a witch so fearless of demons before."

"Then you've had little to do with my mom, Granny Dottie, and Auntie Queenie. They're not afraid of you."

A growl slid from his lips. "They should fear me. I've compromised your abilities since you were young. And Aurora has been near to death several times because of me. I can destroy the Crypt witches if I choose to."

"We were always able to see you off," I said.

"But now I'm here and free, and I'm surrounded by my brethren. I'm unstoppable."

"You're also an arrogant jerk." I raised my chin. "And since you're inside our demon prison, you're not free."

"You can't stop me from leaving. Or are you going to fight me with your magic?" His grin turned feral. "From what I've seen, there's not much left. Is something the matter, my beautiful Crypt witch?"

I showed him my teeth, which were nowhere near as impressive as his fangs. "It's nothing I can't deal with."

"I'm tempted to ask you to test that, but I don't want to humiliate you in front of your family. What's left of them." He glanced at Zandra, who was still on the ground. "So, I'll make you a deal."

"No more deals. We've done too many trade-offs over the years. I'm finished with you."

Frank lifted a clawed finger in the air. "Give yourself to me. Allow me to consume you entirely, and I'll never bother Aurora again."

My heart pounded, and my knees shook. To save Aurora, I had to give myself to Frank... forever?

His eyes glowed red as he rubbed his hands together. "What will it be, Tempest Crypt? What will you sacrifice for your sister?"

Chapter 20

"Don't do it. He'll trick you. You can't trust a demon." Zandra's words were full of pain.

I stared at Frank as I processed what he'd just offered. "You'd really leave Aurora alone? And you'd never bother any of the Crypt witches again?"

His gaze ran over Aurora several times before turning back to me. "You're not my first choice of witch, but you'll do."

"Why are you so interested in us, anyway? All these years, you've hounded the family. What's your problem?" I kept my hands behind my back as I tested my magic, but it still wasn't sticking.

"Because you hound my kind. I sense the thousands of demons in this prison. You trap them for pleasure. We demand vengeance."

"They all deserve to be here," I said. "As do you."

"I have been in my own prison of sorts, trapped inside you," Frank said. "But I've enjoyed some of our time together, and once I've taken everything you are, I'll have your memories and even some of your witch abilities. Having you will make me more powerful."

"Stay away from him." Zandra dragged herself to her feet. "We can take him. It's just one lousy demon."

"I'm not debating this," Frank said. "I take Tempest, or I destroy Aurora."

Aurora appeared oblivious to Frank's threats on her life as she danced around the demons, the dark sparks occasionally shooting out of her and destroying one.

I should set Aurora's newfound power on Frank. But the magic she exuded tasted of darkness and danger. If she used too much of it, she'd lose control. I'd lose my white witch sister and have a new dark enemy to battle.

"Take me," I said.

Wiggles leaped in front of me and snarled. "Yogurt covered raisins!"

"My favorite hellhound. You may join us, too. You'll even get fragments of your witch keeper from time to time while her powers settle into this form." Frank tried to touch Wiggles and almost got bitten. "Your place isn't among the witches in this tired little village. Your home is down here with those who have true power. With the demons who inspire terror and have people shaking in their beds at night, hoping they don't catch our eye and we take what we want from them."

Wiggles' hackles rose. "Cold gray rice pudding."

"Tempest, you don't have to do this." Zandra staggered over to me. "The three of us can handle Frank."

"It's not the three of us, though," I whispered. "Aurora's messing around with the other demons, you're injured, and my magic is malfunctioning. We can't even take on a basic demon, let alone Frank."

"We can. Aurora, get over here," Zandra yelled.

"Get lost. I'm having so much fun. Come meet my new minions. They're entertaining." Aurora's hand shot out, and a spark of jagged black magic slammed into a demon, making him explode. "Although I hated him."

"That's the power we need for this fight," Zandra said to me.

I shook my head. "We can't let Aurora keep using that magic. The darkness will destroy her. I don't even know where it's coming from."

"My special white witch does seem sullied by her experience down here," Frank said. "Still, we all come with baggage. Perhaps it would be more entertaining if I take Aurora and exploit the darkness she's enjoying feeding on."

"Aurora will never be yours," I said.

"If I wanted her, she would come to me."

"Make a grab for her if you really think you can take our sister," Zandra said. "Although you should stay away from that magic she keeps using to blow up your buddies. Otherwise, you'll end up a pile of goo on the walls."

Frank scowled as a demon exploded in a gooey mess and splattered across his face. He scraped a hand across his chin and flicked the slime away. "Aurora, come to me. I've spent too many years waiting for you."

Her head snapped up, and she stared at him. "Frank? Is that you?"

He exposed his fangs in the demon version of a smile. "You recognize me. It's been too long, my sweet white witch."

"Don't you dare go near him," I said. "He's taking me."

"What does he want with you?" Aurora sauntered over, not seeming to have a care in the world that the demon who'd wanted her dead since she was a kid was right in front of her.

"Don't let her get too close to Frank." I shoved Zandra at Aurora.

She grabbed Aurora's arm and kept her from getting any closer.

"You'll miss me when I'm gone," Frank said to me. "You won't feel whole. You must have lost count of the times you used my power to help you. Without me, you won't last a month. Then there'll be nothing left of you but a few dreary memories."

"I've always been able to control you," I said.

A deep, growling laugh slid from his lips. "Because I let you. You know how powerful I am. You're able to sense it."

Frank was hitting my weak spots. I'd always doubted my ability to control him and wondered what would happen when I finally lost the battle. Was he right, and all this time he'd been playing with me?

"Don't listen to him," Zandra said. "You did a great job of... Ouch!"

Aurora whacked Zandra hard on the arm. "Let go of me, you weirdo."

Frank chuckled. "I always knew there was more to Aurora than her pretty face. She has a real fight in her."

"No! Focus on me." I snapped my fingers at Frank. "I'm the witch you want. And I won't fight you."

"I'm disappointed to hear that. I wanted one last battle with Tempest Crypt before she was destroyed."

"Plain stale scone." Wiggles growled. "Lumpy custard and sour grapes."

"Get out of my way, mutt." Frank slammed magic into Wiggles and sent him rolling away.

Wiggles yelped but was already scrambling to his feet. He coiled like a spring and lunged onto Frank's head, his teeth sinking into the demon's cheek.

I used the distraction to reach Aurora and Zandra, keeping half an eye on Wiggles to make sure Frank didn't hurt him.

"What's the matter with both of you?" Aurora shoved Zandra away and snarled at me.

"I should ask you that, since you came into the demon prison on your own," I said.

"I'm having fun."

Zandra grabbed my arm. "You can't trust Frank with this deal. Once he gets you, he'll turn on us."

I let out a sigh. "I know, but I had to distract him from Aurora. And you're right. We can only beat Frank together. I don't know what will happen when we join our magic, but we have to use that power to get rid of him."

Frank whirled around and growled. He plucked Wiggles off his face and dropped him. "You're mine, Tempest. Come to me. We made a deal."

"Wiggles, are you good?" I grabbed Zandra's free hand.

He was already up and snapping at Frank's ankles. "Blancmange on kippers."

"Tempest! I own you," Frank roared.

"No, you don't. We didn't shake on the deal. We were still negotiating."

His claws flexed. "Then I'll take you all."

I grabbed Aurora's hand. "We're stronger together. We can do this. We can destroy Frank."

She pursed her lips and then nodded. "Let's kill this pigheaded demon."

The powerful jolt of magic I'd felt the last time we joined rocketed through me. Heat flared up my arm to the top of my head. But it felt different this time. I had no demon inside me to challenge the power. It felt freeing to have raw, primal witch energy pouring through me and connecting me to my amazing sisters.

Another roar from Frank echoed around the cavern, but it sounded muted as if he was a long way away.

A bubble of protective yellow magic encased us, and it couldn't have come a second too soon as demons hurled themselves in our direction, trying to get us with their claws and teeth. They bounced off the magic time and again in their desperate attempts to destroy us.

Frank was circling the bubble, trying to get through and devour us.

"What's happening?" Zandra said through clenched teeth.

"We're happening," I said. "When we accidentally joined our magic, we became more powerful. It's been happening by accident for months every time we touched. We've created a trifecta of witch magic."

Zandra shook her head. "A trifle of what?"

"You should have read the book Granny Dottie gave you."

"I feel strange." Aurora swayed on her feet but remained standing. "What are we doing here? Is this the demon prison?"

I took in a steadying breath as magic pulsed through me in powerful waves. "Has the mean Aurora gone?"

She blinked at me several times. "I'm not sure. I'm feeling conflicting things. I sort of want to punch you and then hug you."

I laughed. "We'll all feel different from now on, but we can't stay here. We need to see if this joined magic can destroy these demons and get us out in one piece."

"I don't feel in control of this magic," Zandra said. "What if it goes wrong when we use it?"

I lifted one shoulder. "We duck?"

"What do you want us to do?" Aurora said. "Yuck! Is this demon goo on my dress?"

"It is. You've been blowing up demons ever since you got down here," I said.

"It's in your hair, too," Zandra said. "It looks like a troll sneezed on you."

Her nose wrinkled. "Demon goo is the worst."

I spotted Wiggles bolting through a demon's bandy legs. I opened a hole in the protection bubble just big enough for him to squeeze through. He wriggled through and stood in the middle of us.

"Did you get in a few good bites?" I said.

"Rhubarb crumble."

"Great. Let's channel this magic out. We have more demons to destroy," I said.

"I don't know how to do that." Zandra's hand shook. "What spell should we use?"

"Don't think about it. Just feel. Focus on destroying the demons and protecting us," I said. "Channel the magic out rather than inward. I don't know how big this blast will be, but there might not be any prison left by the time we've finished."

"Are you sure about this?" Aurora's eyes were wide as she stared at the demons rampaging around us.

"Not really. But it's either this or get consumed by Frank."

She poked out her tongue. "Let's do it. I'm sick of Frank messing with our lives. It's time he went for good."

I tightened my grip on both their hands. "Are you ready?"

"No," they said at the same time.

"Focus on protection magic and make sure none of the demons get too close." The magic was still flowing through me in hot waves, but it felt erratic, like it was about to bubble over at any second.

There was no gentle way of doing this, so I let it flood out of me. It poured through the protective bubble around us and smashed into the surrounding demons in a powerful wave. The bubble vanished, and one by one, demons exploded. There was nothing we could do but stand there and get covered in gross demon goo.

Even Aurora stopped covering her head and simply stood there, taking her demon goo shower with a quiet resignation.

It took about five minutes before the last of the demons in the cavern vanished.

I swiped green goo off my face and flung it to the ground. "How's everyone feeling?"

"Like all the showers in the world will never get me smelling sweet again," Aurora said.

"Did we really just do that?" Zandra said. "Our magic blew up all those demons? There must have been over a hundred. They kept coming out of the walls."

I grinned. "We did. Our magic, us working together, destroyed them."

"Um, soggy gray pastry." Wiggles jabbed his paw in the air. "Sour cherries."

We all turned, and my stomach sank. Frank was still alive.

Chapter 21

"How is he not dead?" Aurora dropped my hand and marched over to Frank.

I grabbed her before she got too close. "Careful! He might be wounded, but that doesn't make him safe."

Footsteps descending into the demon prison had me tensing. A second later, Granny Dottie appeared. She was with Isda.

Granny Dottie looked around, a huge grin spreading across her face as she saw the devastation. "My girls. I never doubted you for a second. I knew you could take on those demons and whip their butts. Good work."

"How's it looking outside?" I kept an eye on Frank, but he wasn't moving.

"It's all quiet in the cemetery. We got most of the demons into secure areas to make sure they couldn't get you while you searched for Aurora. We kept away as many as we could," Granny Dottie said. "And no one got hurt."

I glanced at Isda, who stood among the goo and demon remains with an expression of calm on her face. "Did you help with the demons?"

"No, I brought her here," Granny Dottie said. "I've been working on a theory, and it involves the angels, or more specifically, the mark they gave you."

I rubbed my sticky forehead. "I always forget it's there."

Isda drifted over, the demon goo not seeming to touch her soft white glittering gown as she moved. "We were always surprised how little you used the higher angel mark after it was gifted to you. We discussed it in several committee meetings."

"Well, I never really knew what it was for. I mean, I knew it connected me to the higher angels and you could transport me wherever you wanted by using it."

"It's so much more than that," Isda said. "Perhaps we assumed too much when we gifted it to you. We forgot you're only a witch. All other supernaturals have such limits to their power."

I tried not to be insulted. "A user guide would have been handy, but it's never really bothered me. What's the higher angel mark got to do with this?" I gestured to the demon carnage.

Granny Dottie was striding around, inspecting what was left of the prisoners. "That mark made you unique. Mixing witch and angel magic meant you had powers none of us have ever seen before. And add in a hint of demon, and you had a heady brew of magic in your hands."

"What kind of powers? And why wasn't I told about them?" I checked on Frank again, but he still wasn't stirring.

"Again, that was an oversight on our part," Isda said. "And in truth, we weren't sure how the two kinds of magic mixing would work. But we had theories. You were our guinea pig witch."

"Care to share those theories?" I said.

"You've worked it out for yourself," Granny Dottie said. "Combine your power, your higher angel mark, Frank's energy, and link with your sisters, and you become a triple threat. And as you've just experienced, it means you can destroy any demon you come across."

I looked at Frank, and hope made my heart stutter. "Does that mean I can finally get rid of Frank for good?"

Isda pursed her lips, and her gaze ran over Frank. "No. This demon is as much a part of you as your beating heart."

"That's an unpleasantly worrying concept," I said. "I should be able to destroy him like we did the others. If Aurora and Zandra join with me and we focus our power on him, he won't survive."

"If you destroy Frank, then you'll die too," Isda said. "You've been connected for so long that you can never be completely uncoupled."

"You make it sound like we were in a relationship," I said.

She stepped over a lump of dead demon and touched Frank with the toe of her white ballet pump. "His true name is Zokis."

Frank, or rather, Zokis, growled but remained on his back.

"Now I know who he really is, I'll have even more power over him. I can finish him." I looked at Granny Dottie. "Frank has to die. Aurora must remain safe."

"Not if keeping me safe kills you," Aurora said. "You're not sacrificing yourself."

"It seems the old Aurora really is back," Zandra said. "The other version would have happily let you die so she could be safe."

Aurora shoved her. "Don't be so hateful. I didn't do anything mean to either of you."

"I'll be happy to fill you in on what a vile toad you've been," Zandra said.

I remained focused on Zokis. "What should we do about him? If I can't destroy him, do we leave him down here?"

"You can't do that either," Granny Dottie said. "Isda is right. You'll always have this demon in your life."

My shoulders slumped, but I didn't feel as defeated as I thought I would. Having a demon living inside me was something I was used to. "I can live with that. Although swallowing him the first time wasn't fun. Is there an easier way to get him back inside me?"

Isda nodded. "There's a simple way to make this demon easy to handle. You share him with your sisters."

I sucked in a breath as my stomach clenched. "I'm not doing that. They'll never have any peace if they have to deal with Frank. I mean Zokis."

"You must. The three of you unwittingly started a process of linking your power. By doing that, you opened the door to Frank influencing Zandra and Aurora. That can't be changed," Isda said.

"What does that mean?" Aurora said.

"I think it means Zokis is the reason you've been acting like a giant pain in my behind," Zandra said.

"And most likely why you stopped being so erratic," I said to Zandra. "Frank, sorry, Zokis, was messing with our magic."

"Correct. And you're all permanently linked," Isda said. "Your separate magic recognized the power you all carried. It also identified how incredibly strong you could be when you were joined. Magic always desires to be stronger."

"You're blaming this on our Crypt witch magic?" I said.

"No. Magic comes from all around us," Isda said. "It's in the sun, the stars, the moon, and the air. You also draw your power from the ancient stone circle in this incredible village. You've all been feeding off the same energies for a long time. That energy wants to be even more powerful. It can do that through your connection."

I took a few seconds to digest what Isda had said. "I'm still not sure about sharing Frank. He can be hard to control. There have been times when I've struggled."

"You won't any more. Frank's power will be divided. You'll each take a part of him," Isda said.

"That doesn't sound so bad," Zandra said. "I'm sure I've tangled with worse demons than Frank when Tempest dragged me on her demon hunting missions."

"You really haven't," I said. "He's mean, greedy, and sly. And he'll give you a really bad sweet tooth."

"If we each take a portion of Zokis, he'll only be a third of the strength he was when Tempest had him?" Aurora said.

Isda nodded.

"Will I keep being mean to people?"

She nodded again. "You'll all change. It'll take time to adjust, but it's well within your abilities."

"Don't do it," I said. "This is what Zokis wants. He wants to be a part of you. What if you absorb some of his power and it takes you over?"

Granny Dottie swiped demon goo off my arm as she tutted. "You've always underestimated your younger sister. Aurora is as powerful as you, and she can control Frank's energy. When you girls complete the power of three ceremony and meld your magic together, you'll barely notice you have a piece of demon inside you. And if he ever becomes a threat, you'll beat him down."

"We'll always have some demon in us?" I didn't want my sisters to suffer the way I'd done with Frank.

"You will. And it's not something you can negotiate," Isda said. "You must be linked. Complete the magic joining you. I assure you, he won't be strong. The battle is over. You won."

I stared at my sisters. It wasn't fair to do this to them. Aurora was so pure, and Zandra had her control issues. What if giving them a piece of Zokis made things worse for them?

More footsteps descended into the prison, and Auntie Queenie, Uncle Kenny, Grandpa Lucius, and my mom and dad appeared. They hurried over and joined us.

"I was just explaining things to the girls," Granny Dottie said.

Mom looked at us, worry on her face. "I know this sounds strange, but this is for the best. For all of you."

Dad stepped forward, pride and concern shining in his eyes. "My three girls are the most powerful Crypt witches in existence. You can handle one annoying demon between you. But if ever you need backup, we're here to support you."

Aurora caught hold of my hand. "We should do this."

"We don't have a choice," Zandra said. "Take a piece of that disgusting scumbag demon, or Tempest dies."

"I never meant for this to happen," I said. "I could have stopped it if I'd known about our connection."

"You can't stop the primal power of our magic," Granny Dottie said. "It's what makes us so strong against the demons. It's why we were chosen all those years ago to be the guardians of the cemetery. Magic knows best. It wouldn't guide you along this path unless it was the right thing to do."

"We've got to trust the magic," Aurora said. "And trust Granny Dottie."

Zandra nodded. "Yeah. She's ancient. She must know more than we do."

Granny Dottie swiped at her, but she was smiling as she stepped back.

Our family formed a protective circle around us and joined hands as they all closed their eyes.

"It looks like we're doing this," I said to Aurora and Zandra.

Wiggles ran over to Zokis. He caught hold of his ankle and dragged him closer.

"Whoa! That little hellhound has some muscle," Zandra said.

"Yeah, he's always pulling surprises on me," I said.

It took Wiggles a couple of minutes, but Zokis was finally dragged into the circle and laid out in front of us. A comforting wave of protective magic covered us as our family poured positivity and strength around us.

Any trepidation I had about doing this faded, and determination took over. My family loved me, and they always looked out for me, no matter how often I messed up. It was a favor I intended to return for the rest of my life. And I was certain they'd do the same for me.

I held out my hand to Zandra. "I guess it's time to be formally joined."

"It feels like we're getting married," Aurora said. "I'm not sure what Lex will think about that. Oh! Lex. I was a horror to him. Do you think he'll forgive me?"

"Of course he will," I said. "Despite you being a pig, he's still head over heels in love with you."

"I don't know about that. I saw him looking through the lonely hearts ads in a paper in the hospital waiting room," Zandra said.

Aurora whacked her arm. "Don't even joke about that. I have so much making up to do with my poor husband."

"Let's get this over with, and then we can fix things on the outside." I looked at Granny Dottie.

"Is there anything we need to do? Say a blessing or do a spell?"

She flipped open one eye. "Let the magic do the work. Keep your barriers low and accept everything. Frank's energy will feel strange when it goes into you. At least for Aurora and Zandra. Tempest, this will be a walk in the park for you."

I wasn't so sure about that.

"What does demon energy feel like?" Aurora said.

"You might want to invest in super strong antiperspirant and get used to a sweating top lip," I said. "But you've already got the sweet tooth covered. Everything else, we'll figure out along the way."

We stood around Zokis and joined hands again.

A wave of black energy poured out of Zokis' chest the second we completed our circle. It hovered in front of our faces before covering us in a cold wave.

My hands remained warm and my grip solid on my sisters' hands as our magic joined. I didn't resist. I just let it happen.

The witch and demon energy battled for a few seconds, each trying to get control. Then there was a ripping noise, and the black wave vanished.

I was left with a warm, welcoming glow all over me. I thought I heard a tiny voice in my head. It was like a mouse squeak and was easy to ignore. If this was the new Frank, I was more than happy to accept it.

"Is it done?" Aurora said.

I nodded. "I think so. How do you feel?"

"Less angry. But hungry." She dropped her hold on our hands. "How about the two of you?"

"I feel good," Zandra said. "Great. I've had no energy since I got my last zap of magic, but I can work with this. Although I can hear something in my head. Is that Zokis talking?"

I looked at his motionless body. He was gone from that shell and now lived inside all three of us. "I think it is. We all have a little darkness in us now."

"And it feels amazing," Aurora said. "I never thought I'd say that about demon energy, but I feel freer."

The comforting warmth of protective magic faded as Granny Dottie stepped away from the circle. "You girls might have a few growing pains, but this should work well. You've combined your witch powers and have a little extra spice on top should you ever need it."

I held out my hands and magic sparkled on my palms. My powers were back, and this time, I didn't need any barriers in place to stop Zokis from sneaking through and messing things up. My witch mojo was back. And I couldn't be happier.

As Mom and Dad hugged Aurora and Zandra and checked up on them, I kneeled next to Wiggles. "Let's see if we can't get you talking again." I ran my hands over him several times, feeling a sticky residual of stasis magic embedded throughout him. I raked my fingers through his fur, scraping away the magic bit by bit.

It took several goes, but Wiggles finally shook himself, and amber sparks shot out of him. He looked up at me and wagged his tail.

"Well, are you still talking cake?"

He wrinkled his nose. "Triple chocolate brownies."

My eyes widened. "It didn't work? Is there still a problem with my magic?"

His tongue poked out. "Got you. It worked fine. But I do have a craving for triple chocolate brownies."

"You know I don't like you eating chocolate." I lifted him up and squeezed him against my chest, despite us both being covered in demon goo.

He licked my cheek. "And I don't know how many times I need to tell you, but I'm a hellhound. I'm immune to the dark powers of chocolate."

I laughed as I stood and lifted his front paws over my shoulder. "Maybe just this once we can split a box of brownies."

Granny Dottie hurried over and hugged me and Wiggles tight. "Good job, my girl. You finally tamed your demon."

I stepped back and looked around. The demon prison was a mess, and it would take time to clear up, but standing there, surrounded by the love of my family, I knew we could achieve anything.

Granny Dottie tugged a strand of my hair, and I was happy to see it had returned to its usual black color, with just a few strands of blonde running through it. "Now, don't we have a party to get sorted?"

Chapter 22

The ground throbbed with the music coming out of the cemetery as I drew near the large black gates that had been thrown open to welcome everyone inside. I rubbed my hands up and down my bare arms as people headed into the cemetery in their best party outfits.

"I said you should have brought a jacket," Wiggles said. "I never feel the cold because of my amazing fur coat, but you must be chilly with all that skin on display."

I grinned at him. Wiggles had been talking almost nonstop since I'd removed the stasis magic from him, and you'd hear no complaints from me about that. My awesome hellhound was back exactly as he should be.

"I'm not cold. It's this party. It's a big deal. And it feels even more important after everything that happened between me, Zandra, and Aurora. We're different. Don't you sense it?"

"I see some changes. Aurora might not be so sweet anymore, but Zandra is more settled. And you..."

"What about me?"

"You're relaxed."

"When was I not relaxed?"

"You did your best, but I didn't blame you for being tense about carrying around that idiot demon all the time."

"That idiot demon is still inside me."

"Sure. But he's now a pipsqueak. He can't do anything to hurt you or the others. You finally defeated him."

I stopped outside the entrance to the cemetery. "And it was all thanks to my family. You included. We did it together." I'd spent a long time thinking I had to work alone and keep my distance from the people I loved for fear of hurting them. All along, I'd needed them to make things right. And it only took having to plunge headfirst into a huge demon prison to figure that out.

"Hey, I stopped by the club, but you'd already gone."

I turned to see Rhett walking toward me. He was dressed head to toe in black and looked deliciously yummy in his new black leather jacket. "I didn't know you were going to pick me up."

"I thought you might like the company." He kissed my cheek.

"She's got some already," Wiggles said.

Rhett petted his head. "I'm still not forgiven for leaving without saying goodbye?"

"You need to provide plenty more cookies before I'm fully on board with your return or the fact you're dating Tempest again."

"Then consider it done." Rhett tucked an arm around my waist. "Because I'm here to stay. Shall we?"

We were about to walk through the gates when there was a low rumble of bike engines behind us. Rhett's old gang drove up, led by their new leader, Roman Hawkins.

"How's the new guy working out?" I said.

"Roman's had a few teething problems, but he's solid. And the gang will be on their best behavior tonight. I stopped by to see them and let them know they weren't to cause any trouble."

"If they do, I'll set my sisters on them." I'd told Rhett all about what had happened in the demon prison.

"I have no doubt they could take down the gang." We walked side-by-side into the cemetery.

The place had been transformed. Lights sparkled in the trees, and each headstone shimmered with pale white glittering magic. There was a huge temporary dance floor at one end and a long buffet table laden with food and drink. The place was buzzing with excited chatter and laughter, and the moon had only just risen. It wouldn't be long before the entire village was here to celebrate our success over the demons.

"I told you not to wear the purple dress." Aurora stomped into view, Zandra beside her.

"I'll wear what I like. I wasn't going to wear that white glittery thing you chose for me. I'd look like a Christmas fairy on sugar icing crack."

"That thing was designer. And you look like something out of a Gothic horror novel," Aurora said. She turned, looked at me, and groaned. "Unbelievable! You're wearing black, again."

I looked down at my dress. "What's wrong with black?"

Aurora thrust her hands out and blasted me and Zandra with magic.

I staggered back as a spell swirled around me, and my dress transformed into a sparkling red fitted number that stopped at the knee. Zandra was in glittering white and not looking happy about it as she tugged at the revealing neckline.

Aurora grinned and clapped her hands together. "Perfect. I no longer have boring drudges as sisters."

"Is that your new demon talking or you?" I ran my hands over the beautiful fabric of the dress. Maybe I could make an exception and wear red just for one night.

"It's me! And get used to it. This magic is incredible. I plan on using it all the time." Sparkles appeared on Aurora's fingertips.

"If you blast me with another spell, I'm going to hex you and turn your hair white," Zandra said.

Aurora flicked magic at her. "I'd like to see you try. I'm more powerful than you."

"Quit bickering. We're as powerful as each other. Although Aurora, you need to stop hitting us with spells when we're not expecting them. They tingle," I said.

"I can't help it. I've got so much energy, and it needs to come out."

"You three should form a demon hunting crew," Rhett said. "If you worked together, Tempest wouldn't have to leave the village so often. You could take it in turns to go slaying."

"I love that idea. I'll be in charge of the group," Aurora said.

"In your dreams," Zandra muttered. "Now, get out of my way. I want to try some buffalo wings before Wiggles destroys the buffet table."

"Too late," I said. Wiggles had already made a beeline for the food the second we'd walked in.

My sisters hurried away, squabbling about food, clothes, and their hair. It was just as it should be.

"I'll go get us some drinks." Rhett walked off in the direction of the buffet table.

I picked Dominic out from a crowd of angels lingering around a large mausoleum. He was dressed in a dazzling white suit with a neat white bowtie, his hair slicked off his face. All the angels looked striking in their white outfits.

"Are you enjoying the party?" I said as I walked over to him.

A grin lit his face. "I am now. Shall we have a dance?"

I looked around and spotted the witch who would help me tackle Dominic's crush. "Actually, I've got someone I'd like you to meet."

His eyebrows rose. "Who is it?"

"This way." I walked him through the crowd. "Elspeth Roseberg was my best friend when we were in school together."

Elspeth turned at the sound of my voice and grinned. "There you are. I was about to come drag you out of that club if you didn't show up soon." She threw her arms around me. "It's been too long."

"Tell me about it. I haven't seen you for three years."

"More like four." Her gaze cut to Dominic, and an appreciative look crossed her face. "Who's the gorgeous guy?"

I smiled. Dominic was just Elspeth's type. She'd always had a thing for super clean-cut guys with brilliant blue eyes. "This is Dominic. He works for Angel Force. He's one of their best detectives."

A blush crossed his cheeks. "I wouldn't say that. Tempest is much better than me at catching criminals."

Elspeth tossed her silky dark hair over one shoulder, and her green eyes glittered with delight. "Hasn't he got delicious manners? Please tell me you're single."

Dominic spluttered a few words. "Um... I mean, I am. I..." His panicked gaze went to me.

"Then what are you waiting for? Or does a girl have to ask a guy onto the dance floor in these modern times?"

"No! Of course. Would you like to dance?"

Elspeth grabbed his hand. "I thought you'd never ask." She winked at me and then dragged Dominic to the dance floor.

I chuckled as she sashayed around him. While he stared at her curves and tried not to blush too much. I'd done some groundwork with Elspeth before she arrived, so she knew what to expect when meeting Dominic. I'd told her what a great guy he was and how they'd be perfect together. And I really thought they would. Elspeth was smart, funny, and had looks that always made a guy stop and stare if they were into curvy brunettes. Even if it wasn't a happily ever after for them, Dominic and Elspeth would have fun together.

Rhett returned with our drinks just as the music was turned down. Granny Dottie stepped into the middle of the dance floor, and the crowd of revelers parted. She had enormous peacock style feathers in her hair and wore a shimmering green dress that showed plenty of cleavage.

The rest of my family gathered around behind her, and I walked over with Rhett beside me.

"I won't take long. I can see everyone's having a great time." A spell enhanced Granny Dottie's voice, so everyone could easily hear her. "Tonight is a special celebration, not only for all the Crypt witches, but for the whole village. Willow Tree Falls is a unique place. It houses not only powerful magic but dangerous demons. And the Crypt witches have been protecting the world from these dangers for many years."

There were murmurs of agreement from among the crowd and several raised glasses.

"We've lost incredible witches along the way, all dedicated to ensuring this village, its inhabitants, and everyone else remain safe from the darkness beneath our feet." She stamped one silver booted foot, and a shower of magical sparks flooded across the ground.

The crowd stamped their feet in a show of support.

"We plan to be around for another thousand years to ensure that protection continues." Granny Dottie looked at me and nodded. "And we recently witnessed the joining of three powerful Crypt witches who'll continue our hard work."

"It sounds like Dottie is thinking about retiring," Rhett whispered.

"She wouldn't know what to do with herself if she did. Granny Dottie has plenty of good demon fighting years in her. She'll be whacking them over the head alongside me for decades."

Granny Dottie continued. "Our strength comes from our family unit. We support each other, nurture our powers, and encourage others. And of course, we also get to have fun when capturing those pesky demons."

Chuckles and laughter rang out through the crowd.

"Tonight is about remembering those who've been lost in the battle against the demons and celebrating our successes, too." Granny Dottie raised her cocktail glass. "Please take a moment to visit our memorial board and pay your respects to the fallen."

"Long live the Crypt witches," someone called out from the crowd.

"May they always be happy to smack down demons," someone else yelled.

There were several loud cheers, then everyone was celebrating us by downing their drinks and cheering some more.

Granny Dottie laughed and shook her head as she waved her hands in the air. "Very well. I've said enough. Everyone have a wonderful evening. Get drunk, make out with someone you think is gorgeous, and I hope you all wake with hangovers and smiles in the morning."

The crowd broke up, and I turned as someone tugged on my elbow. Isda stood beside me. "I'm glad you could stick around for the celebration."

Her sparkling gaze flickered around the cemetery. "This is all so stimulating, but I'm here to talk to you. Have you got a moment?"

I glanced at Rhett. "Sure. What's up?"

Rhett squeezed my waist before letting me go. "I'll leave you to it." He walked away to speak to some friends.

Isda led me to a quieter spot in the cemetery. "There's something I need to do." She pressed a finger to my forehead.

There was a momentary burning sensation, which was replaced by a cool numbness. "Did you just take my angel mark?"

She nodded as she stepped back. "You don't need it anymore. You've proven to the higher angels you have all the support you need."

"Uh... thanks?"

"You were given that mark because we identified you for great things. And you've achieved exactly what we hoped for. You've helped unite the witches and angels in a way we've not seen for a long time."

"You might want to talk to Dazielle about that. She doesn't always think we're united."

"Dazielle may grumble from time to time, but she's fond of you."

I laughed. "Are you sure about that?"

"Just as I'm sure you're fond of her. You're good friends, and you've been a valuable ally to the higher angels. Now you have your sisters supporting you with any future challenges, you won't need our help."

I wasn't certain the higher angels had been that helpful, and I'd been figuring things out with Dazielle long before they stuck their mark on me, but I decided not to mention that. "Any time you need a helping hand to deal with a tricky demon, you know where Dazielle is."

Isda smiled. "You'll always be around to help us. You're that kind of witch. You hate to see others suffer, and you're always putting their needs before your own."

I rubbed the back of my neck. "I'm not sure that's true."

"It is. The work you do in Willow Tree Falls and the help you offer the angels make you special."

"Well, thanks." I looked around, not sure how to respond to all this praise. "Do you want a drink? I can introduce you to some people."

When Isda didn't reply, I looked back. She'd vanished.

I shook my head. Higher angels were weird, but I kind of liked hanging out with them now and again. And I was sure, when they had a problem they needed my help with, they'd be back.

Leaning against a shining white headstone, I took a few minutes to enjoy watching my awesome friends and family hang out together. I lived in an incredible place. I had people who loved me, a great boyfriend, and a thriving business. I could even count some angels as friends.

Rhett walked over and joined me. "Everything okay with the angels?"

I touched my forehead. "It's all good. Isda was saying goodbye and tidying up a loose end."

His gaze lifted to my forehead. "No more mark?"

"Nope. I'm officially all witch again. Well, with a small amount of demon, but I can handle him."

"That sounds perfect to me." Rhett wrapped an arm around my shoulders. "And I'm sure this place will continue to keep you busy. There'll be plenty more adventures for you."

"Adventures! Are you two talking about marriage?" Aurora dashed over, a pink cocktail in one hand and a brownie in the other.

"Hey! Stop listening into private conversations," I said.

"It wasn't private. You weren't even whispering." Aurora bounced on her toes. "Are you really getting married? Will you have children before me and Lex?" She looked around. "Lex, get over here. Tempest and Rhett have big news."

"Shush! If you spread rumors like that, it'll get out of hand," I said. "We were talking about going on more demon hunting adventures, not settling down with a ring on my finger and half a dozen witch babies to deal with."

Lex arrived with a fresh cocktail for Aurora. "What's the news?"

"Tempest and Rhett are—"

I clapped a hand over Aurora's mouth. "Enjoying the party. That's all Aurora wanted to say."

Lex smiled as he caught hold of his feisty wife. "Same here. It's an amazing evening. I'm so glad everything is back to normal."

I slid a glare at Aurora as I removed my hand. "Well, almost normal." It seemed my baby sister had a new spicy side. It was something I'd have to get used to.

"You should at least talk about marriage," Aurora hiss-whispered. "You two have been together for ages. It's the logical next step."

"What about kids for you and Lex?" I said, deciding it was time for some serious deflection. "And you two are already married. Isn't that the logical next step for you?"

"Don't think we aren't trying." Aurora nudged Lex with an elbow.

His cheeks flushed as he grinned. "How about we go get something else to eat?"

"I already have a brownie." Aurora pursed her lips. "Although I did want to try that pecan tart Patti brought with her."

"Then let's go enjoy some of that." Lex led Aurora away, throwing us a silent sorry as they left.

I laughed and shook my head. "Lex will have to get used to dealing with a fiery Aurora from now on."

"He seems to be handling things just fine," Rhett said. He was quiet for several seconds. "I wouldn't mind talking about that other option."

I tilted my head. "What do you mean?"

"The marriage and kids option. It sounds great to me."

I turned and faced him. "That's one adventure I really am scared of. Are you sure you're ready?"

"How can you ever know for sure? But I think so. And we don't have to rush anything, but we have been together a long time."

"With a few hiccups along the way."

"Which all relationships have. And we survived our hiccups." He held me close. "My business is flourishing, your demon is tamed, and you have the support of Aurora and Zandra when you go demon hunting. Plus, you've got your family here to help if ever you need a babysitter. The timing seems right."

"Wow! That almost sounded like a proposal."

"I could get down on one knee." The intensity in his eyes made my heart stutter.

A quick glance around made me realize this place was way too hectic and public for something so intimate. "Another time."

"It's something you're open to, though?"

The thought of settling down, getting married, and doing normal stuff had always scared me. It wasn't that I didn't want it, but because I'd never felt in control of my power. Things were different now. I had more support, I was no longer afraid of hurting my family, and the demon that had plagued my life was subdued.

"Tempest? You've gone quiet," Rhett said. "Is that a good sign?"

"Yeah, it's a good quiet," I said. "Everything feels quieter. It's finally peaceful in my head. And now I have room for other things. Including marriage and children."

Rhett grinned and kissed me. "Then that's an adventure we will go on together." He was leaning down for another kiss when there was a yelp, and something smashed on the ground.

"Tempest Crypt!" Dazielle yelled. "Your fat hellhound is stamping across the food table and grabbing all the sausage rolls. If you don't get him off there, I'll zap him in the butt."

I laughed as I untangled myself from Rhett's arms and raced over to rescue Wiggles from Dazielle's wrath. Some things never changed. And I was glad of it.

About Author

K.E. O'Connor (Karen) is a cozy mystery author living in the beautiful British countryside. She loves all things mystery, animals, and cake. When she's not writing about mysteries, murder, and treats, she volunteers at a local animal sanctuary, reads a ton of books, binge-watches mystery series, and dreams about living somewhere warmer.

To stay in touch with the fun mysteries:

Newsletter:
www.subscribepage.com/cozymysteries

Website:
www.keoconnor.com

Facebook:
www.facebook.com/keoconnorauthor

Also By

Luck of the Witch
Hell of a Witch
Revenge of the Witch
Curse of the Witch
Son of a Witch
Framing of the Witch
Trickery of the Witch
Wishes of the Witch
Harmony of the Witch
Remedy of the Witch
Gift of the Witch
Toil of the Witch
Jinxing of the Witch
Craving of the Witch
Union of the Witch
Chaos of the Witch
Sleighing of the Witch

If you enjoyed

Chaos of the Witch

turn the page to read an extract from the next Crypt
Witch Mystery

SLEIGHING OF THE WITCH

*To learn more about the series,
scan your country-specific QR
code.*

Chapter 1

I brushed a snowflake off my eyelashes and peered along yet another gloomy, icy alleyway. "Wiggles! Get your furry butt home before my toes turn to popsicles."

I checked the time and frowned. My club, Cloven Hoof, would open in less than three hours, and I needed to get back to make sure everything was running smoothly. We had another night of Christmas parties, and tonight, it was the elves. They always got overexcited whenever the tinsel got strung and the trees went up, and they were hard to keep control of when they'd had a few too many peppermint flame drops.

"Wiggles, I'm done looking for you. It's freezing." I stared into the ominous yellow sky. Any second, a ton more snow would tip down on me. It was the only reason I was out in the frozen gloom, looking for Wiggles. Usually, I let my furry little hellhound do his own thing, but with a huge blizzard forecast, I wanted him home, snuggled under the duvet or snoring on the couch.

My heel slid from underneath me, and I wheeled my arms to keep my balance and avoid landing in the snow. I staggered to the side, hit another hidden patch of ice, and crashed down with a thud on my right hip. I lay there for a few seconds, grumbling to myself. Snow was only beautiful when you experienced it from somewhere warm, preferably with an open fire blazing and a plate of gingerbread iced cookies on your lap.

"Mind if I join you?" Rhett Blackthorn strolled over, a grin on his handsome warlock face.

I shuffled around in the snow. There was no way to make this look dignified. "It's cold. You wouldn't like it down here."

He held out a hand and hoisted me up before kissing my cheek and brushing snow off my back. "I would if I was with you. What are you doing? Making snow angels?"

"No time for angels. I'm trying to find Wiggles. What about you? It's not the evening for a walk around Willow Tree Falls."

"Saving my girlfriend from being snowed in, by the looks of things." Rhett chuckled. "What's Wiggles gotten himself into this time?"

"I've no idea, but he's been missing for most of the day. Usually, when the weather is like this, he retreats to my bed and barely moves, other than for food. He's up to something, but I don't know what it could be."

"He's not in trouble, is he?"

"When isn't Wiggles in trouble?" I looked around, blinking as the snow fell faster. "I'm not sure he knows how bad things are about to get. He gets distracted when he picks up a new, exciting scent, and I don't want him getting stuck."

"He's a tough little guy. He can handle himself. If things get too cold, he'll just light a fire."

"That's what I'm worried about. His fires can get out of hand. I don't want him burning down the Christmas tree in the center of the village to keep his frozen paws warm."

"We can look for him together if you like. How about we take a detour and go for a drink first, though? We can ask in the bar if anyone has seen him."

"I wish I could, but I've got a busy night at the club. And I'll need to change before starting work. Snow-bedraggled witch will put off the paying customers."

"Since when do you care about what your customers think about your outfits?"

"True, but it's the elves, and you know what designer snobs they are. And they're bringing in a huge party tonight. I need them to stay late and spend large, so I can afford all your Christmas treats."

Rhett kissed my forehead. "I only need you as my Christmas treat. How about an early dinner before you start? You need to eat."

My stomach grumbled in agreement. "I could go for food. And where there's food, there could also be Wiggles."

"Everywhere has their festive menus up. I even saw a pizza being promoted that had cranberries on it." He wrinkled his nose.

"I'm more a classic cheese and meat fan, but pizza sounds good. We could get takeout, so we can eat and look for Wiggles at the same time."

Rhett's phone buzzed in his pocket, and he pulled it out. His forehead crinkled as he read the message.

"Everything good?" I asked.

He turned away. "All good."

"Is someone after you?"

"No one important. Sorry, I'll have to raincheck the pizza. I need to go." Rhett's mouth twisted to the side as he typed back a reply to whoever contacted him.

"Are you sure there's no problem?"

He looked at the phone again, then tucked it away. "Nothing I can't handle. Work stuff."

"I can help if you like."

"You know how to sculpt a piece of scrap metal into a work of art?" His smile was lopsided.

"Err... I'll try anything once. Although not Christmas pizza."

"You've already got enough on. You have a missing hellhound to find and will soon have a club full of demanding elves to look after."

My eyes narrowed. Why wasn't he telling me the truth? Rhett hadn't answered my question about what he was doing out on a freezing night like this, and now he wasn't telling me who needed his attention. Should I be concerned?

He grinned. "Relax. It's just work. Everyone's so demanding, wanting last-minute Christmas commissions."

"Someone wants a piece of your artwork? That's so urgent you have to abandon pizza and hellhound hunting?"

"No, it's not. But it is to them. And I just told them they'll have to wait. I've been booked solid for months, and there's no way I can squeeze in any last-minute jobs, no matter how much money they're offering."

"Exactly how much are we talking?" I arched an eyebrow. "You could always pull an all-nighter."

He chuckled as he slung an arm around my shoulders, and we walked along together. "I have been." His phone buzzed again.

"Someone wants you bad."

"Yeah, I'd better go. I'll catch up with you another time. I need to deal with this." Rhett pulled out his phone and made a call as he walked away.

As I watched him go, a trickle of worry ran through me. Rhett enjoyed working as a full-time artist, but I wondered if he missed his old life. When he'd been head of the local biker gang in Willow Tree Falls, he had everyone's respect, plus a healthy dose of their fear. The gang wasn't to be messed with. Now, his life was different. Did he miss the old days? Was he sliding back into those old days? It must be a temptation.

I headed to the next alleyway, the snow falling so fast it filled in my footsteps in a few minutes.

"Got you." I spotted a pile of half-destroyed trash bags and a trail of prints around them. Someone had thoroughly investigated the trash and rooted around to find abandoned treats. It was typical Wiggles style.

"I knew I'd catch up with you," I muttered. The prints were fresh, so Wiggles was close by.

After nudging the trash bags out of the way, I followed the prints. There was a scuffling up ahead, and I squinted through the chilly gloom. "Hey, get out here. I want you back at the apartment. If you get stuck in the blizzard, I'm not coming to rescue you."

Wiggles didn't emerge, but the scuffling continued. Sometimes, when he got obsessed with something particularly disgusting in the trash, nothing would distract him.

I made my way carefully past a large dumpster and found more fresh prints. These weren't distorted by the snow, and as I bent to inspect them, they didn't look much like Wiggles's paw prints. They were too small. Was I following the wrong trash bandit?

A hissing noise came a second before something hot and heavy slammed into my back. I staggered into the wall, just avoiding smooshing my face into it by shoving out my hands at the last second.

I whirled around and discovered a glinting-eyed raccoon wearing a bright red Christmas hat with a fluffy bobble on the top. It hissed at me again as we made eye contact.

"You made this mess?" I pointed at the damaged trash bags.

The raccoon hissed its response.

I groaned. I'd been following the wrong prints and tracking a greedy raccoon and not a greedy Wiggles.

The raccoon rushed me, its teeth bared and aimed at my leg. I shrieked and scrambled back, hitting a huge bank of snow and toppling backward into it.

The raccoon bounced onto me, knocking the breath from my lungs. Then it sped away, leaving behind its small red hat.

I lay on my back, staring at the wintery sky. This was the last time I landed in the snow tonight. I was so done with snow.

A huge pile of the white stuff from the building's roof slid off and landed on me with a wet thud.

"You have got to be kidding me." I swiped snow off my face and lay there, a freezing, icy, wet mess of failure. Wiggles had so much making up to do to me if I ever found him.

I should get up. My clothes were soaking and my teeth chattering. Instead, I made a snow angel, moving my arms and legs back and forth. It was my destiny to be covered head to toe in snow this evening.

"Hold it right there," a familiar voice rumbled along the alleyway.

I lifted my head to discover Dazielle, the Head of Angel Force, striding toward me wearing her usual grumpy expression, her enormous wings outstretched in a threat display.

"Hey! What are you doing out on a night like this?" I stayed in the snow, gently swishing my arms about.

"Someone called in a report about a tramp lurking in the alleyway. They said they looked dangerous. I should have known it would be you."

"It sure is. I'm tramping it up in style tonight." I wrinkled my nose. "Wait! That sounded wrong."

"Why are you in the snow?" Dazielle stopped beside me and fluttered her wings back into place.

"I'm auditioning for a role as one of you. Do you like my snow angel?" I flapped my arms and legs again.

Dazielle hauled me out of the snow by the front of my coat so fast my teeth rattled. "Stop messing around. Don't you have a Christmas party to go to or something equally noisy to deal with?"

"Several. The club has been full to bursting every night for the last three weeks. People can't get enough of my Christmas parties."

Dazielle's pale blue eyes narrowed. "I know. We've had six noise complaints about Cloven Hoof. You're making extra work for my overstretched team."

I raised a hand. "I know how late I can stay open. And I always ask the last revelers to keep it down when they leave. But you know what they're like when they get full of Christmas spirit."

"It's not the Christmas spirit that's the trouble. It's those super strong lemon drops you serve."

"Cinnamon-infused lemon drops," I said. "We're also trialing Christmas pudding flavor this year. You should come along and have a taste test. I'll even give you a discount, since I'm feeling festive, if a little frozen."

Dazielle arched an eyebrow. "That sounded like a bribe. Do you expect me to ignore these noise complaints?"

"It could be a bribe, so the angels don't spoil the fun. Or maybe it's a drink between two friends."

I grinned up at her. "I hope you're getting me something great for Christmas, old pal."

"You're not even on my Christmas card list."

"Awwww. I guess your radiant smile is gift enough."

That comment earned me a wonderful scowl from my favorite grumpy angel. "You still haven't answered my question. Why are you lurking in this alley? People are worried you're up to no good."

"They don't need to be. I'm looking for Wiggles. I haven't seen him all day. Has he dropped by to see any of the angels today?"

"Definitely not. He received another ban after he snuck in and ate the entire Christmas buffet last week."

I roared out a laugh. "Was that on Tuesday?"

"It was. Why?"

"He rolled in that evening with a huge smile on his face. His stomach was so round he could barely get up the stairs, but he wouldn't say where he'd gotten the food. Wiggles just said friends gave him treats."

"Friends! We're not friends. He left fur all over the remains of the cake, and don't get me started about what he did to the raspberry pavlova. We had to get takeout for our party. It was a disaster. You need to keep better control of him."

"As Wiggles is always telling you, he's a free roaming hellhound, and I have little say over what he does." I looked along the alleyway. "Which right now, isn't a great thing, since I can't find him."

Dazielle waved her wings around to dislodge some snow that had settled on her feathers. "You need to get indoors, or you'll freeze."

"I will. As soon as I've found Wiggles."

"Tempest, he's a hellhound. You always say he runs hot. Something as insignificant as a blizzard won't stop him."

"I guess. I just don't like to think of him out here in the cold."

"He's probably snuggled up with a giant sausage he stole off someone's plate. You should go where the food is. That's where you'll find Wiggles. And even if he gets stuck out here, he's hardy." Dazielle fluffed out her feathers. "I'll ask my angels to keep an eye out for him, if that's any help."

"Admit it, you like him really," I said.

"I'd like him better if he wasn't a food thief. He ate three pounds of mini savory pies from our buffet. Everyone was so disappointed. Even Dominic, and he loves everyone."

I felt bad about Wiggles ruining the angels' Christmas fun. "How about you all drop by the club? I'll buy a round of drinks and a burger for everyone to make up for it. Call it my Christmas gift to Angel Force."

Dazielle's eyebrows shot up. "That's generous. I suppose it means you want an extension to your licensing hours, or you're late with your liqueur license renewal."

I folded my arms over my rapidly freezing coat. "You always think I want something out of this friendship, but I'm not a Christmas Grinch. And I enjoy a party as much as the next person. I'm sure your angels would, too."

She pursed her lips as if trying to figure out what I was up to. "Maybe we'll take you up on that. I'll mention it at the next staff meeting."

"Don't have too many meetings about it, or you won't get to the club until next Christmas after three rounds of voting and a formal report has been written."

Dazielle shooed me out of the alleyway. "Get home. And no more skulking around and scaring people."

I shot her a salute before hurrying to the club, keeping a lookout for Wiggles as I walked.

Someone stepped out of the shadows close to the club door, and I jumped back.

Granny Dottie grinned at me and waved a sprig of holly in the air. "Tempest! Just the witch I need. I have a job for you."

Sleighing of the Witch is available in paperback and e-book.